I0747882

SILENT HEARTS

A HEARTFELT SMALL TOWN NOVEL

ANITA RENAGHAN

KITCHEN ENTERTAINMENT

Copyright ©2022 by Anita Renaghan
anitarenaghan.com
Kitchen Entertainment
All rights reserved
ISBN-13: 978-17335671-5-2

No part of this book may be reproduced in any form or by any electronic or mechanical means, including information storage and retrieval systems, without written permission from the author, except for the use of brief quotations in a book review.

This book is a work of fiction. The characters, incidents and dialogue are drawn from the author's imagination and are not to be construed as real. Any resemblance to actual events or persons, living or dead, is fictionalized or coincidental.

For Saint and Ashley. For Denise and Gracie. For Anne and Cody. And for all parents who have lost a child. May your child rest in peace, and may you find a way to live in peace, and to find hope in the possibility of life after death.

ACKNOWLEDGMENTS

Thank you to my family and friends who support me and help in editing my work, especially Mom, DD Call, and Pam Gould.

This is especially bittersweet for me to acknowledge this time, because this is the last book that Mom will have first eyes on as she has passed on to her eternal rest. Mom has encouraged me my entire life, and I would not still be writing without her encouragement and gentle nudges asking when she will get to read my next book. We both love the characters, and I will continue writing with Mom's gentle voice in my head as I edit my future works.

CHAPTER 1

*L*iz Campbell imagined herself floating above the earth with a rope around her waist that was keeping her from floating away into space forever. She wasn't wearing an astronaut suit, just floating on her own in the black expanse. She imagined the intense cold of outer space freezing her and the lack of air suffocating her, and she welcomed her end. She listened for her heartbeat but remembered that outer space was a vacuum, and it was completely silent. She welcomed silence.

Liz Campbell was not in space though. She was in hell. She heard her mother's footsteps coming down the hall, and she pulled the blanket over her head.

"You have to wake up now, honey. You have to get out of this bed and get on with your life."

Liz had no life though. It had ended the minute her son had died.

"I know you can do it, Elizabeth. Today is your day."

No matter how many times her mom said this, there was no reason to get out of bed. Liz had used up all her sick days and was on leave from the school. She couldn't face going to work at the grade school and seeing students right now. Liz taught first grade and her son was in fourth grade. He was ten years old, and they would all remind her of him. She couldn't be around children anymore.

"You have to get up, honey."

Liz heard the pull of the curtain and white sunlight filled the room, so she slipped a pillow over the blanket that was already on her face. She didn't know why her mom had to torture her like this. There was no future without Sean.

Liz had contemplated suicide, but for some inexplicable reason, she hadn't carried it out. She just lay in bed day after day, thinking of herself floating in space. It was quiet up in space, and there was no one there to ask her about Sean. Her parents weren't there either with their grieving eyes and half-smiles on their lips trying to prod their own daughter forward in life.

The thought of Sean summoned the tears and the suffocating weight on her chest. Sean was dead, and it was her fault. She should have been paying closer attention, and with the screech of tires, both of their lives had ended, Sean buried within the week, and Liz a zombie still above ground.

"Go away," Liz groaned. There had been a mouse in the house once. She remembered it now. She wished she was a mouse, and she could crawl inside the walls so her mom couldn't find her.

Liz felt the bed move, and her mom put her hand on the blanket to touch her shoulder.

"I love you, honey, as you love Sean. I'm your mother, and I can't watch you do this." A long sigh. "I can't imagine..." Liz heard a sniffle and the bed moved again as her mother stood. "We buried Sean three months ago, Elizabeth. You have to get up."

Liz wished that she had her own apartment again. After the Great Recession in 2008 when she lost her job at the bank, Liz and Darren had struggled. They'd married young, and it was a tough couple of years, and then they had Sean and even though they struggled financially, things were good for a little while longer. After the divorce, Liz found herself a stressed single mom, and she had to move her and Sean in with her parents.

Having her parents around for Sean had helped. She'd finished her certification and became a first-grade teacher. Liz had meant to find an apartment for her and Sean so many times. The memory and the regret strangled her. Without Sean, there was nothing left to live for.

She pulled the blanket tighter over her head and suffocated in her warm breath. She was above the house and the town, and above planet earth. She was looking down, holding on to a thread that was connected to the planet, and that was all that was keeping her from floating away into the open arms of the nothingness. Liz slipped all her fingers off the thread but one thumb and forefinger, and she floated there, barely hanging on, letting her fingers slip closer and closer to the end of the thread. The thought of letting go sometimes scared Liz. She knew she wasn't really in space, but it somehow seemed tangible in her mind.

The thread and the earth disappeared as her mom's footsteps returned. Liz knew that her mom was standing in the doorway waiting to see any movement, but there was no way that today could be any different than yesterday.

"Please, honey. You have to do something."

She'd heard this speech from her mom for two months already, but something was different today. Liz was really hearing her mom's words for the first time, and she felt the self-loathing and sadness retreat behind her growing anger. In this moment, Liz hated her mother for asking her to go on without Sean. She gripped tight to the thread in her mind and threw the covers off and stood. The fast movement startled her mother.

"I'm sorry to have burdened you," Liz spat sarcastically as she put on the jeans and sweatshirt that lay on the floor.

"That's not what I mean."

"Well, what do you mean?" Liz pulled on socks and tried not to notice her mother's tears.

"You have to move past this tragedy."

"Are you saying you could get over it so easily if you lost me?"

"That's not what I'm saying, and you know it."

Her mom followed her to the back door and watched as Liz pulled on her low boots and a coat.

"I'm up, Mom. I'm up and out, so don't worry about me." Liz snatched her father's key ring from the table. Her own car had been repossessed last month.

"Elizabeth!" she heard as she slammed the door. Tears blocked her view, but she made it to her dad's 1998 Saturn station wagon and backed out of the driveway. She went slowly through the neighborhood, stopping in the spot where Sean was killed. Stopping in the spot where her life had ended.

She absent-mindedly moved the sign of the cross over her head and chest. She didn't know why she did it aside from that it had been engrained in her since childhood. She hadn't attended church or really prayed in years, but now Liz held on to the thought of God if only because she wanted to believe that her son was in heaven.

She pulled out of the neighborhood and out of the city, not paying any attention to where she was going. She drove away from the place of such devastation and sadness. She drove for hours but it followed her, and she knew there was no outrunning it. When the car was almost out of gas, she pulled into a station to fill up. That's when she noticed that she had her dad's coat on. It was a green military jacket that he used around the house. She didn't have her wallet, and she'd left her cell phone turned off in the nightstand. She had thrown it in the drawer a month ago.

She couldn't handle the calls of concern, and the texts and messages of everyone checking in on her. If they tried to get in touch with her and she didn't respond, someone would inevitably stop by and that was worse. Her mother had come to lying to those who looked in on her, saying Elizabeth was fine, and she was out for the rest of the day. They would chat with Liz's mom as Liz lay in the room down the hall wishing that death would take her, and since her car wasn't parked in the driveway anymore, no one was the wiser.

Liz found twenty dollars in the coat pocket, and she felt under the floor mat for more cash. Her dad always left money under the floor mat for emergencies, and she was glad to find three crisp fifty-dollar bills. She hoped it was enough to take her to another life.

She filled up the tank and drove out of New York state. The momentary anger that her mom had stirred up in her was gone, replaced by the solitary blanket of depression she had been living under. Liz didn't have many memories since Sean had died. She was in shock the week of his funeral and could barely remember anything since. It was as though she had blacked out three months ago and woke up one day to an entirely different reality.

She turned the wheel at an exit and let the car wander. It didn't matter where she was or when it was or even that she existed at all. In fact, that was the problem right now, that she existed.

Liz drove for three days, sometimes on the interstate, sometimes on dirt roads. There was no real direction to follow. When she left the suburbs of New York City, the fierce winds of spring pushed against the side of the car. She drove south to where she thought the sun might shine on her soul, but halfway through Georgia, she decided that she wasn't good enough for the sun or its happiness, so she turned right and headed west. What was west didn't matter, only that there was more road in front of her to run away on.

Liz wondered if distance from her tragedy might save her heart, but as the miles flew by, the pain only grew louder, and she was forced to cry it out. It was three months since her son had died. The calendar had turned over, but the tears still flowed effortlessly. She remembered Sean's sweet smile, but sometimes even that had eluded her. The memory of the accident tortured her again as Liz tried to figure out how this had happened.

She had wished many things in her life and seldom had anyone been listening. But when Liz had said out loud that she wished she had never met her ex-husband, the devil was listening, and with his mighty hand, he took the only person that tied she and Darren to their past. The words left her mouth with the screeching of tires, and in the same instant she had wished her ex away, her son was gone. In the haze of fog that had become her life, Liz wasn't certain that it had really happened simultaneously, but she knew she'd said it, and it had come true.

She was sobbing again somewhere east of Cincinnati. She didn't remember entering Ohio, and she distracted herself from her memories long enough to realize that she had never been this far from home before. There was no such thing as home though, not anymore. She had destroyed it with her words, summoning a drunk driver upon her child in the middle of a sunny, Saturday afternoon.

Her eyes were bloodshot and open only enough to keep the yellow line on her left. She found herself backtracking once, following a New York license plate north for a couple of hours. She sped up with the plate and slowed down with it and took its off ramps until she awoke outside of Cleveland and turned left again. She'd been on the road for two or three days, but it was somehow only seconds since the screech of tires, and years since she watched his tiny casket folded under the earth.

Thoughts of her son played like a television show in her mind, and she remembered every moment of his life as if he was right here in the car. And then she thought of his birthdays and Christmas' yet to come and how empty every day of her life would be. She thought of crossing the yellow line and delivering herself into her own salvation, but she didn't. Still, she couldn't recognize the part of herself that was hanging on to this empty life. It was as though time was feeding off her pain and forcing her to continue breathing, her heart pumping blood and simultaneously rotting in hell.

It was night again, and she was sitting outside of a truck stop in Indiana listening to herself breathe. She didn't know how many other cars had come and gone since she had been sitting here waiting for her death. This car, her dad's Saturn, reminded her of someone else's life. It was the life of woman who dropped her child off at school and worried about the bills on the way to work and lived the same days every week, days that were good enough for a struggling single mother and her son.

Now it was three in the morning somewhere south of Chicago as Liz wove her way north and west, turning the wheel whenever instinct told her to. She was afraid to stop driving, but she wasn't outrunning any of her memories. The orange glow in the sky above Chicago lured her in like a moth to a flame. She didn't want to be near anyone, yet the anonymity of city life seemed appealing. Then the image of Sean in a crowd standing alone and crying caused her to take the next exit and pulled her car west again. She had never lost him in a crowd, but she remembered how he had told her once that he had been scared on the streets of New York surrounded by all the strangers. Liz needed to be somewhere that Sean would feel safe to haunt her. Maybe that place was her parents' house, but she couldn't go back.

She was on the tollway and out of money, so she took the first exit and traveled for a while on dark two-lane roads. It was past four in the morning when her gas gauge read empty, and she felt the slow jolts of an empty fuel tank choking the engine. She coasted into a gas station a couple blocks off Route 64 and stopped her car at the edge of the property. The silence whispered for her to rest, and the exhaustion of driving for days allowed her body to slip into a coma-like sleep.

~

LIZ WOKE a couple hours later and looked out the window. She saw another car in the station getting gas, and she cleared her throat and rubbed her face. She stepped from the car and stretched, looking around. This was a very small town. She went to the door of the station, but it was still locked. Two more cars pulled in and filled up at the pumps. The drivers watched Liz as she stood in front of the station, and she wondered just how small this town was. She noticed a man sitting on a bench at the edge of the lot. She walked over to him and looked up and down the street.

"Your car didn't sound so good," the man said. Liz knew that she had pulled in before sunrise, and she wondered if he had been sitting on this bench in the cold for hours.

"I'm out of gas."

He nodded his head and then pulled a paper bag from inside his long, wool coat. "Thirsty?" he drawled.

Liz realized he was a drunk on a bench and her car might have woken him up as she sputtered into the station. He looked too clean and well-dressed for her to surmise that at first, but she could see him clearly now with his hand extended toward her as he offered her a swig from his bottle of booze, and the silly half-smile of too much alcohol on his face.

"No, thank you." She noticed a payphone behind the bench and then thought of her mom who must be worried sick. Liz had empathy for that state, and she felt guilty for leaving like she had. Picking up the receiver, she found a small amount of change in her pocket, but she knew it wouldn't be anywhere near enough to call home.

The drunk stood and looked at her. He was very tall and leaned over a bit, most likely due to the drink. He reached into his other coat pocket and pulled out a plastic bag that was stuffed with quarters.

"Need to borrow some money for the payphone? They're not as cheap as they used to be now that everyone has one of those fancy cell phones."

"Do you have one of those fancy cell phones?" she asked, hoping she could borrow it to make the call.

"Would I have a bag of coins in my pocket if I did?" he chuckled.

"You got me there. Can I borrow some change?"

"Sure." He stuffed the paper wrapped bottle in his coat pocket and then approached the payphone. "Where are you calling?" he asked.

Liz hesitated. "New York City."

He smiled and held out his hand to her, and Liz looked at it before she accepted his hand in greeting. "I'm Ted Barlow," he offered. His hand was calloused but surprisingly warm.

"Hi," she said, but didn't offer her name.

He started pulling coins from the bag and lined them up neatly on the top of the payphone, six short stacks in all.

"That's five dollars and forty cents," he told her. "That will get you five minutes." He took his seat on the bench again and looked across the street. She wished he would walk away and give her some privacy, but he was a stranger who she would probably never see again, so she surmised that it didn't matter.

Liz dialed her parent's home number and was surprised to find that the drunk was right about the amount of money it would cost. She started the slow effort of depositing twenty-three coins into the slot and waited. After two short rings, her mom picked up. "Hello?"

"Mom," she croaked. She didn't know what else to say, but she didn't need to say anything.

Her mom started in a string of questions, "Frank! It's Elizabeth. Pick up the phone in the front room!" her mom yelled. "Where are you, honey? Are you okay? We've been worried sick. How could you leave for three days without calling? And you didn't even take your cell phone."

"I didn't know what I was doing when I left, Mom."

"Come home, honey. Where are you?"

Liz looked around, but she didn't see anything that could tell her exactly where she was. She covered the receiver with her hand. "Hey, you," she said to the drunk.

"We just met. I'm Ted Barlow," he said, craning his head around.

"Where am I?" she asked.

"Sycamore, Illinois," he told her, and she felt a bit surprised that she was in Illinois. Liz had a vague memory of heading toward Chicago. She decided immediately not to share that information with her mother.

"I'm okay, Mom," she answered. This was followed by a moment of silence. Liz could hear sniffling, and she knew that her mom was crying. "Listen, Mom. I don't know what I'm doing, but I had to leave. I had to get away from that place."

When there was silence again, she could hear a muffled, "Frank! Pick up the phone!"

"Mom," Liz whispered, and then her own tears started. She was alone and had no money and was four states away from her parents, but she couldn't go back. She knew her mom loved her, but the pressure of the expectation that she could do anything but mourn her son right now was exhausting. It was as though her family and friends were waiting for her to wake up one day and forget about her beloved Sean and just go on with life. It was an impossible place to be.

Her mom was talking and trying to convince Liz to come home, but she was curious about the place she had ended up. She looked around the gas station trying to notice something about the town she was in. It was a rinky-dink town made up of small brick buildings, and from where she stood, she could see nothing over two stories high. It didn't matter though. This was a place that people lived. People like this Ted guy who seemed to be a homeless drunk and yet had lent her the money for the phone call.

The phone chirped and gave her the one-minute warning.

"Listen, Mom. I don't have any more money..."

"Oh my God, Elizabeth. Tell me where you are, and I'll send you some money so you can come home."

"I meant change for the payphone, Mom." Ted stood and walked over with a bag of coins, but she waved him off.

"Frank, Elizabeth needs some money! Pick up the phone!"

But her dad didn't pick up the phone. She could almost hear him sigh four states away. He'd been the one person who had let her mourn the way she needed to. She knew that he was worried about her, but he never pressured her to move on, and she was sure he wasn't picking up the phone in an effort to keep his opinion to himself.

"I'm going to get something to eat, Mom. I'll call you back soon." Liz could still hear her mom begging her to come home when she dropped the receiver into its cradle. She wiped the tears from her cheeks and moved back toward the refuge of her car.

"Thanks, I owe you," she told Ted.

"You owe me five dollars and forty cents," he replied.

She was less than ten steps away when the payphone started to ring. Liz grunted and didn't look back. She should have borrowed enough money to block the number, but she was sure that her technology-challenged mother wouldn't be able to find her. And anyway, she'd be gone as soon as she could put some gas in her car.

Liz pulled on the door to the station, but it was still locked. She could see a clock on the wall inside and knew that someone should have been here by now. She grunted in frustration and then noticed two more drivers stare at her as they filled up with gas. Liz slipped into the back seat of her car to wait. She didn't see Ted Barlow rise from the bench and pick up the payphone receiver.

In the car, Liz felt safe from the prying eyes of the townspeople who pretended not to stare at her. She had thought of crying again but decided not to.

Decided not to cry? Liz marveled. She had lost herself for months in shock and misery and was now conscious of what she felt and how she would feel it. Anger rose like a lightning strike during her months of mourning, even causing her to smash one of her mom's plates in a fit of rage. It wasn't like her, but nothing anymore was like the Liz she'd been. As she waited for the gas station to open, Liz traded in her emptiness for anger. She felt its energy tingle on her skull, and she seethed over the injustice of having to go on without Sean. Although it came on in a fit, she decided that the resurgence of anger was a sure sign that she had decided to live.

Decided not to cry, and now decided to live? she wondered. She had thought many times of taking her life, of running a sharp blade the length of her pale arm from wrist to elbow or hanging herself everywhere. There were many bridges around New York City, all for the taking. She could have jumped. She hadn't, though, and as she studied the idea of death in her mind, she didn't know what compelled her to live. Her anger was snuffed out, and Liz slumped over and hid her face and cried uncontrollably. When she was certain that she was drowning, the desperation willed her back to sleep.

In her sleep, she could hear herself exhaling deeply as though the life within her was going to escape. It startled her awake. The inside of the car had been warmed by the sun, and she snuggled

herself deeper into the upholstery. For a long minute, she medi-
tated as she listened to the air enter and exit her body, her
trachea whistling like a small wind tunnel. The repetition was
mesmerizing, and in this half-sleep, Liz was nothing but a dream.

The peace came and went as her mind began to wake itself to
memory and reminded her that she was still of this earth. Her
recollection brought back her nightmare. It was difficult to open
her eyes as her tears had dissolved and dried into an invisible
crust. She knew that another day would only bring more pain,
but the subconscious hope that had kept her alive this long
caused her hands to rub her eyes clean so that she could look out
at the world.

She sat up too quickly and wished that she hadn't. The sun
made her squint. The world was out there. It was the same world
that had welcomed her in and then took her son out.

Liz remembered that she was at a gas station somewhere in
Illinois. She looked toward the payphone and saw the back of the
head of the drunk who was still on the bench. Cars came and
went as she watched, trying not to wonder what to do. Thinking
meant that she was contemplating moving on with herself,
getting on with her life and all the stupid simple things that
wasted everyone's time but were necessary in this version of
existence, like filling up on gas. Liz decided to search the car for
more money, but she knew that she had none. If she had money,
she would still be driving aimlessly away from everything that
she knew.

Her credit cards, along with her dreams of what marriage
should have been, had been wiped out with bankruptcy. She
found amusement in a situation where most would find cause for
panic, and she almost smiled. Running out of money or gas had
played such a prevalent role in her life as a single parent, and it
was not unfathomable, but now it seemed ridiculous. All the
material things in the world were utterly ridiculous.

She sat in the car for a long time and shirked off the rest of the world and their goings on. She would have none of them. The cars driving by on the road behind her, all the fools filling up their gas tanks, checking their tire pressure, or talking on the telephone. The human experience seemed all too pointless up until her body remembered food. Liz tightened her stomach and tried to make it forget but that didn't last. She fought the pangs and told herself that the body's needs were useless, but the animal inside the human growled. The more she tried to ignore it, the hungrier she got, and she had to eat.

With all the gas station traffic, Liz was sure that it was mid-morning. She walked to the front door again and pulled, but the store wasn't open yet. This made her more aware than ever of her hunger. An old, scratched sticker glued to the front door said that store hours started at seven o'clock in the morning. Liz looked in the window. No one was inside, yet a few more cars came and pumped gas before moving on. She walked back to her car and waited a while longer, and then she felt the anger again.

At first, the anger seemed as pointless as the hunger, but it eventually smothered any other thought. She began to seethe with every minute that the store was still closed. The world was fighting her at every turn, Liz was certain. It wasn't about the hunger and the need for food; disgust had distracted her from that. It was about how the world was supposed to go around, and the sun was supposed to rise and set, and the child was supposed to outlive the parent.

Liz tried the door again and then banged on the glass. She walked over to the single garage door and looked in, but it was dark inside and she didn't see any cars in the shop. She went back to the store and yelled insanely and then caught herself and talked more slowly and reasonably, as if she were throwing her voice into a canyon, certain that the returning echo would open the door.

A few patrons stopping for gas watched as the mad woman yelled at the building, but none approached. They had credit cards to pay with. Little plastic attendants that allowed for more convenience and less and less human interaction. She didn't care what anyone might think. She just wanted this door unlocked when the sign said that it would be open. She wanted black to be black and white to be white without the gray areas of the world to confuse her.

CHAPTER 2

*J*osh Davis pulled his pickup truck around the corner and waved to Ted who pointed over his shoulder and nodded moving Josh's gaze toward the Saturn station wagon that was parked on the side of his lot. He noticed one person filling up at the pumps, but he didn't bother to wave. There were few people left in town who Josh would bother acknowledging.

He parked his truck behind the station and saw Billy waiting at the door, his round body and round face accentuating his round glasses.

"Hi, Billy," Josh said as he unlocked the back door to the store.

Billy shoved his notepad in front of Josh. *You're late.*

Josh chuckled at the reprimand from the young man. Billy pushed his notepad toward Josh again, but Josh ignored the paragraph of writing. He held the door open for Billy and then turned the lights on in the back room. Josh dropped his keys on the small desk in the corner.

"Straighten this place up," he said to Billy. But there wasn't much to straighten up, and Billy followed Josh to the front. Billy unlocked the front door and then went to the corner behind the register and perched his bulk on an old stool, dropping his back-pack on the floor. Josh flipped the overhead fluorescent lights on and moved behind the register, unlocking it with the small key that he kept on a nail under the counter. Billy kicked Josh lightly in the back of the knee, and when Josh turned to protest, Billy pointed out the window.

Ted Barlow was standing at the window looking inside. When he had Josh's attention, he pointed at the Saturn station wagon. Josh shrugged, but Ted just pointed again, and Josh threw his hands up in exasperation.

"Well, this should be interesting."

Billy held up his notepad when Josh walked around the counter.

"Not now, Billy."

Billy dropped his bulk off the stool and followed Josh outside, but he waited back by the front door while Josh walked to the side of the lot to look at the car. Ted had retreated to his bench, but Josh could see him watching.

There was a girl asleep in the driver's seat. Josh looked closer. She had the window rolled halfway down and the sun was on the bottom half of her face. He could see a little pink on the skin of her chin and her neck, and he wondered how long she had been sleeping there. Josh moved to block the sun, and her eyes opened. He was stunned, as though he'd been caught doing something he shouldn't. She was young, maybe thirty. Her mid-length hair was light brown, and her fair skin was drawn to her cheek bones. Josh wondered if she'd had anything to eat recently.

They looked at each other for a minute, and Josh felt caught off guard. He didn't like to talk to people, but this girl was very pretty. He needed to say something.

"Gas and go," he said through the window as he pointed to a sign that said the same. "It's a gas and go." Her eyes were light brown in the sunshine, and Josh wished he could think of anything else to say. She was more than pretty, even with the pink that the sun had left on her chin. It was cute, and Josh tried to grin, but he was pretty sure his face was contorted in a grimace. Josh wasn't good at small talk with anyone, and especially not with pretty girls.

She stared at him, so he looked away to study the tall trees that edged the lot. When he couldn't take the pressure of her stare anymore, he walked back to the store, shooing Billy inside. Josh tried to ignore Ted who was still watching from the sidewalk. Josh felt self-conscious. He didn't want her to go, but he had just invited her to leave.

It wasn't long before the woman came into the store. She was awake now; Josh could see that. Her brown eyes were round, almost bulged when she looked at him. She was short to Josh, but average height for a woman. Josh admired her figure beneath the oversized green coat she was wearing. She looked at Billy with her wide eyes as though she was daring him to speak.

Billy pushed his notebook in front of Josh. *She looks mad.*

"Can I help you?" Josh asked. He never said that to the customers, but Josh felt a strange pull to help this woman. She looked lost in a way, but she was also the prettiest girl he'd noticed in a long time.

"Your sign says that you open at seven o'clock A.M. That's seven in the morning." She drew out the word 'morning' for effect. "It is now afternoon," she said angrily. She stared at him and let the words weigh on his conscience.

Josh didn't answer. He was tongue-tied which seemed to infuriate her. He tried to smile but he was pretty sure he looked ridiculous.

She took a step closer and paused, looking straight into his eyes. "Yes, you can help me. I need gas. Only, I needed it this morning when you were supposed to be open, but there was no one here."

She was a city girl, Josh thought. Her accent was from out

east, but he didn't know enough about accents to place her exactly.

"Ted was here, out front." Josh pointed out the window to the bench by the payphone, and she followed his gaze. They could see the back of Ted's head over the row of bushes.

"That guy is on a bench on the sidewalk. He's not here." She pointed at the counter.

"He's keeping an eye on things," Josh replied innocently. He shrugged and hoped that she could understand that things here were not the same as in the fast-paced place she had come from.

But she didn't understand. "This is ridiculous! I want to speak to the owner."

"Okay, go ahead," Josh offered. He wanted to talk to her. She seemed lost in a way. But he could see that she was not in the mood for conversation. Her face flushed red, and she was winding up to yell at him.

She pointed over his head to the clock on the wall. "Do you know what that is?"

He turned around slowly and then nodded. "That's a clock."

"Yes! And it's two o'clock in the afternoon, and you were supposed to be here hours ago!"

Billy huddled into the corner on his stool and scribbled in his notebook again, but he didn't show it to Josh.

Josh shrugged. "Well, I don't know that I was *supposed* to do anything. I mean, two is just a number really."

He smiled, and she bit her lip. He was trying to be polite, but for a second Josh was worried that she might slap his face.

"It's two o'clock!" she demanded.

He leaned forward and said conspiratorially, "How do you know?"

She rubbed her eyes as though trying to contain the rest of her outrage. She put her hands on her hips, and Josh tried to smile again but he felt awkward. He looked down at his shirt to make sure it was clean and then wondered why he even cared. She was very beautiful.

"I think that there should be some compensation for my time since I've been waiting here for hours. You should give me what I need for free. I'm sure that in a town like this, a man's reputation stands for a lot, and believe me, mister, I'm willing to spread the word if you don't make amends." She still had her hands on her hips, and this time Josh withheld the smile.

Billy cleared his throat and made another note on his notepad.

Josh was bewildered. He had no intention of giving away the store to a ranting customer, no matter how cute she was. He'd spent enough time with Ted Barlow to know that she wasn't drunk. Drugs maybe? Josh looked closer into her brown eyes, but they weren't bloodshot.

She didn't budge, so Josh turned from the counter and looked up at the clock behind him. He hadn't cared about clock time for over thirty years, but he bit his tongue and nodded his head to himself. Billy grunted and turned his notepad toward Josh.

You are forty-three years old. She's too young for you. She's closer to my age.

Josh grit his teeth and Billy pulled his book back to his chest afraid that Josh might snatch it away. Josh reached up to the clock above him and twirled the minute hand counterclockwise seven times until the hour read seven o'clock. He faced the brown-eyed doe again and blinked. "Can I help you?"

LIZ GROUND her teeth and looked at the short, round boy sitting in the corner. He watched every move she made behind his black, round-rimmed glasses, and she wondered what was wrong with him. It would have typically given her the creeps, and in New York City she would have barked something like, "What are you looking at?" But here she just stared back. He seemed harmless with his small notebook and pencil. He looked at Liz and at his notebook and back at Liz and then wrote something down on the paper. Liz wondered if he was sketching her image.

She looked back at the other man behind the counter. He had straight dirty-blond hair and calm, green eyes. Even though she had snapped at him, his eyes weren't defensive. *They were innocent,* she thought. She felt seen when he looked at her, a deep calm settled her nerves. She closed her eyes and tried to start again.

Liz came from a city where people lived on arguments. She had raised her voice to rant at this clerk as was the custom in New York City, and she couldn't believe that her words were met with sheer silence. Back home, she would have received a slew of insults by now. The silence was strange. The boy in the corner looked at Liz again and then down at his paper, scribbling away. Perhaps he was writing down a rebuke that would never be heard.

She stared at the green-eyed clerk ready to bicker because an argument was the only thing that would give her a fighting chance. To return to the world of pettiness was her only way to escape her reality. But he wasn't going to give her an argument. He'd stunned her by calmly turning the hands of the clock back.

She almost laughed, thinking it a joke until she realized that this man was quite sincere in his actions. She looked where her watch would normally be on her wrist, but it wasn't there, and its absence made her second guess herself.

"Can I help you?" he questioned again. She had no smart remarks left. Liz was dumbfounded at what had just occurred. The clock read seven o'clock in the morning, and she could not dispute it. Liz needed proof. She could take him outside and argue about the sun's place high in the sky, but what was the point?

Her forehead tightened in a question, and she wondered how

the clerk would respond this time. "I need some gas and something to eat," she conceded.

"Well, gas is two-forty-one a gallon, and for food, I have potato chips and candy." He seemed uncomfortable under her gaze, so he rattled on, "There's a diner a block over if you want to eat a meal and not just junk food."

She looked out the window at her car, trying to recollect her situation.

"How much do you want to put in?"

She stood still as if she hadn't heard his answer. She looked back at the clock and wondered if she was even awake at this moment. Maybe she was dreaming.

"I don't have any money," she heard herself confessing.

His lips flattened, and he looked at her matter-of-factly. "Well, that's too bad, because we exchange gas for money at this station." It wasn't sarcasm that she heard. He sounded sorry for her, but Liz didn't mind. She was sorry for herself. His words and actions were all too ridiculous. She was sure that she was dead and then knew that she was not. But this was hell, wasn't it?

She pulled a small amount of change from her pocket and put it on the counter and took a pack of cookies and left the store. She watched the door close behind her just to see that it would in this part of the universe. Her car was the only place left for her, so she resumed her position behind the wheel and waited, eating two small cookies, stuffing the rest of the package in her coat pocket.

Liz waited for what felt like an eternity, and the man eventually left the safety of the store and approached her car. She didn't roll the window down but sat looking straight ahead. Any movement at this point seemed wasted. Liz thought that if she sat still long enough, the world would cease to notice her, and she would simply melt away into the vinyl.

She breathed in slow motion. She had always loved slow motion in movies, the way it made the actors look like gods and the world around them like a dream. It was magic. She was outside of herself and beyond the gas station attendant who had begun to walk around her car. He must have been studying the original, chipped, brown paint because there was nothing else to see.

In her mind, Liz was over by the gas pumps looking back at herself, taking a picture and memorizing it. The image was a painter's wand begging its canvas to come to life, but she was no Norman Rockwell.

The attendant was back, standing still outside her window. "I could buy your car."

"What?" she asked as she rolled her window down.

"I could buy your car, then you'd have money."

She eyeballed him, baffled. She waited for the punch line. It never came. He stuck his hands in the back pockets of his worn jeans. "You know, for gas and food and things." He seemed sincere in his conclusions, but his reasoning was that of a little boy.

"I need gas for my car, for this car." She waited while he slowly nodded, but he was merely being agreeable, not really under-standing her point. "If I sell you this car for money, then I won't need gas." She explained this slowly to give him time to keep up, and he nodded again, and a smile crept up his thin face.

"Then I'll buy it from you, and your problems will be solved. You won't need gas, and you won't need money for gas. Pop the hood so I can take a look."

Her stomach was catching fire as it had inside the store when he had been so pompous as to turn the clock back. This wasn't righteousness controlling his actions though; it was a sort of naiveté that she had not encountered in the city that she had lived in her entire life. And it wasn't dimwittedness either like she had previously thought. His intentional movements showed a self-assurance that Liz hadn't known before. It was as if this man held a secret about everything around him. He was odd and gentle, crazy, and yet more sane than anyone else.

She didn't feel like arguing, but she had a point to prove, an alternate way of thinking to introduce to his simple mind. "If I sell you my car, I won't have any way to get to where I'm going."

"You've got somewhere to be?" He answered quickly, and for a moment Liz was going to laugh. Everyone had somewhere they had to be. But the only place she had been for ten years was in the daily tornado of motherhood. It was all she knew. Her life was the tumultuous days of loving her child and hating the insane pace of single parenting; the will to be free of all burdens mixed with the simple need to care for her child. He was right. She didn't have anywhere to be, not anymore.

She was unaware of the tears streaming down her face. They had made a home there, and like parasites on a shark's skin, these tears were both necessary and revolting. The man fidgeted for a moment before pulling the dirty rag from his back pocket. He methodically wiped his hands as he stared at the ground. He stole a few glances at her and that made Liz aware of her state, so before giving it another moment's thought, she pulled the hood release lever.

The attendant nodded and glanced at her and then looked back at the ground. "I'll take a look then." He moved around the front of the car and suddenly he was gone beneath the brown metal square of the raised hood.

Liz was trying to think straight, trying to figure out how to get gas and to move on, how to keep driving. But there was no way to outrun her past, and this stranger had already reminded her that she had nowhere to be.

"Start her up," he told her as his subconscious habit took hold and he wiped his hands with the rag again.

She turned the key once without thought, and then he bent over the engine that tried to shudder to life. He stood up and gave her the kill sign with a finger across his neck. He was smiling.

"You don't have any gas. Good thing we're at the 'Gas and Go'."

She stared up at him in silence, forgetting about her tears and not recognizing his joke.

He looked around the lot slowly as if he was trying to make his next sentence out of the words printed on the gas pumps. He wanted to bring some gas to her, but he couldn't seem to walk away. He waved toward Ted Barlow, and Liz watched the tall man from the bench lumber toward her car. Ted leaned one arm on the roof of the car, and then the attendant walked away.

"Josh waved me over. Do you have my money?" he asked. His words were less slurred now.

"No. I don't have any money."

The small, round man stepped out of the store and watched Liz in her car. He pushed his round glasses up his nose and then scribbled something in his notebook.

"What are you looking at?" she yelled across the gas station lot.

The man looked around as though he was making sure that she was talking to him, and then he made a note in his notepad.

"That's Billy Noodles. Don't mind him. He's got a screw loose, but he doesn't mean any harm. He just likes to write stuff down."

"Billy Noodles?" she said to herself. Liz was beginning to think that everyone in this town had a screw loose based on the three men she had met so far.

The attendant, Josh, returned with a red, metal container full of gas.

Liz tried to ignore them all. She zoned in and out of reality as she remembered moments from the past months that she had spent in destitution. Three weeks ago, she had gotten on a commuter train at five in the morning. It had swept south taking her and hundreds of others from her parent's borough into New York City. Everyone in the world got on and off that train except

Liz. She just sat there through the evening rush hour and into the night waiting for someone or something to tell her what was next. The announcer had told her that it was the end of the line fourteen times that day, but it never really was because the train came alive again a few minutes later and headed back up the track. It had been the first day in over two months that Liz hadn't cried.

Now, as she sat in her dad's car in a gas station parking lot in the middle of nowhere, she knew that if she could have moved herself from that train seat three weeks earlier, she would have flown off a bridge or stepped into traffic or washed down enough capsules with enough booze to find the end of her own line. She'd sat there all day waiting to decide, and by some providence she hadn't been able to move an inch.

It was dark when the train pulled into the yard. A tall, thin, black woman approached with two security guards. The black woman sat down in front of Liz and waited for some recognition, but Liz didn't respond.

"This is the end of the line, honey. It's time to go. You don't belong here." The woman turned to leave so the security guards could escort the invalid from the train. Then she turned back around to share one last thought. "Sometimes it's best to move on, honey. You know? Don't know where you been. Don't know where to go. Just know that you got to move on."

When they had picked her up from the police station, her parents had been cordial to the officers. She overheard the whole story again, her story. "Oh, how very sad. Her son killed in a car accident. Young boy too, ten years old." Her mother shedding just enough tears so that the officers would forego a psychiatric evaluation. Their little girl just needed some time to get through this terrible ordeal.

It had been two months since she had killed her son with her wish, and Liz had stayed in bed with the blanket over her head. She rode the train in the back of her mind for the next few weeks before getting in her dad's car and leaving. She'd loved where she had been. She was lost where she was now. The only thing left was to move on.

Ted was gone, and Josh the attendant was back in her window. "She runs okay. I suppose I could give you twelve hundred for her."

Liz couldn't believe that this strange man was offering to buy her dad's car. She couldn't bring herself to make a move. *Where am I?* She knew that one of her son's action figure toys was lost somewhere in the back seat. She also knew that she couldn't bring herself to go back there to find it. There was magic in that toy. It held the fact that her son had truly existed, but it would go on lifeless forever without his little hands to give it a history. Without Sean, Liz was lifeless just like the toy. *Who am I?*

The attendant, Josh, was leaving, and she wanted to call him back. She had nothing to say to him, not really, but he had been a distraction to her and all the madness swelling in her head. He had offered to take her car and her reason to go any further. The driving was useless, and she knew it. With the car, she would keep going until she found a cliff and then the rest would be between her and God.

"That seems a fair price," Ted Barlow drawled from over by the pumps before returning to his bench.

Josh disappeared into the store for a minute and then he came back out. As he walked toward Liz, she noticed that he avoided eye contact. He had hardly looked at her at all. He seemed aloof to everything. In the store, he had watched her reactions like he was a bystander and not the person who she was yelling at, and since he had come out of the store, he had mostly looked at her car or at the ground or into the trees off the side of his lot.

"Here's $138.94. It's all I've got. I'll have to get the rest to you, and if you want to buy your car back before I sell it, then just pay me what I've given to you at the time. Is that all right?"

Liz didn't answer so he tried again.

"Like a down payment. I have $138.94 now, and the rest later." He held out the money. The coins were perched on top of the bills like children on a downhill sled about to fall out.

Liz looked out the windshield and tried to focus on her options. She could call her mom and get the money she needed to go back home, but that didn't seem right. Her mom did what moms do which made going home an impossibility. She loved her daughter and wanted to care for her and protect her. But Liz was aware that she might need the stillness of this small town, even if just for one day.

It was ridiculous and crazy. He was giving her money for her car, and she was taking it and walking away. She shoved the cash in her shirt pocket and immediately forgot about it.

CHAPTER 3

*J*osh found himself babbling just to fill the silence, a silence he normally didn't mind. This woman was crazy and intriguing. Josh had given her all the cash that he'd had in the register, even though he didn't know her name nor have the title to the car that he'd just given her a down payment on.

He wasn't sure why he had offered to buy her car. He repaired and resold cars for extra money over the years, but her car was in decent shape and only needed a wash and a tune-up. He'd offered more than he would have typically paid, but there was something else too. It wasn't her looks, well, not completely. Josh wasn't dead, and Billy wasn't the only one who had noticed how pretty she was.

There was something about her, a loneliness maybe, which he recognized when he saw her asleep in the front seat. He saw tears on her cheeks. And the way she looked up at him blankly without even really noticing what was going on around her; it seemed familiar to Josh. It was as though he could see the storm cloud over her head, and he'd wanted to clear it away if he could.

She had yelled at him in the store like she had really seen him, like she knew that he was a fellow human being. Josh was aware of what most of the town thought, that he was weird or that he was retarded, and most everyone had ignored him since he was a teenager. But this woman had looked right at him and demanded action, and he liked it. She must have needed him. He felt that's what it was about her that was so compelling. Standing in the parking lot watching her move on with his money made Josh feel an accomplishment. He had helped.

He almost called out to her as she walked away to ask her name and where she might go. He wouldn't know how to speak up though. Josh never usually talked much, and although he had only asked about her car, he had found himself trying to be chipper and cordial. Her medium brown hair and light brown eyes distracted him, and he'd had to pretend to wipe his clean hands with his rag to pull himself together. He'd had thoughts of a different future when he saw this woman, a daydream of holding her hand and leaning in for a kiss, but as she walked away, he jolted himself back into the reality of who he was and who he would always be.

Josh opened the back door of his new purchase and slid over the brown vinyl into the center of the back seat. He wondered where this car had been and what had haunted its owner so powerfully. There was no luggage in the car or any other belongings to be seen and it was eerie, as if without the car, that woman might not have existed. But he could still see her, walking slowly into town like an animal that had been beaten into submission. The void in this woman's eyes reminded him of his mother and all the tears shed when he was a child. It was the same dead look his mother had carried on her face after Josh's father had died.

Josh felt like a child sitting in the back seat of this Saturn station wagon. He remembered sitting in the grocery store parking lot and waiting for his mother to come out. He had been the most patient child since his father had died, his only concern for his mother. She let him go about life as he pleased, always trying to find a smile for him even when her eyes were red from crying. She was always very supportive of her son. Family had helped to keep the gas station open until Josh had graduated high school, and he had been there every day since. Of course, his mother had voiced her concerns, too. There were years when she was worried about her son fitting in and living a normal life.

I do lead a normal life, he thought. Josh pulled the keys from the ignition and locked up the station wagon and headed inside. This gas station was his place of business, owned by his mother and run by himself, and this was a normal existence.

Josh put the keys in the cash register. Billy Noodles was off his stool with his notepad in Josh's face, and Josh read the last two tiny lines on the page.

"Yes, Billy, you've got that right. But I'm sure she'll be back for her car."

Josh should have been in back working on the cracked head of that pickup truck he'd promised three days ago would be ready in two days. Instead, he and Billy sat in the store and stared at the cars that came and went. No one came in the store to pay. They all had credit cards, and Josh knew that the locals stopped trying to come into the store for anything else years ago because he couldn't be trusted to be there on time.

On time, he thought. What a joke people played on themselves. There was only birth and death and the struggle in between if you lived and died by the clock. Josh didn't though. There was no way to truly be on time. There was no way to make the future happen until you got there, and there was no way to fix past mistakes. There was only this second and what you would choose to do with it. That thought made Josh look up at the clock on the wall, and he could see that Billy had set it to the time on his wristwatch. Billy watched Josh who shook his head, and Billy wrote in his notebook.

Josh wondered if the girl had been real after all. He wondered if she was cold or hot or thirsty or hungry, but he had no answers. When the sun was below the tree line, he closed the shop. He drove through town and looked around for the woman in case she was headed back to pick up her car, but he didn't see her anywhere.

He thought about her on his drive home. The way she had yelled at him, it had woken a part of Josh that he'd forgotten about. Josh hadn't thought about keeping time for years. He wanted to help her, but he had no idea where to start. So, he'd bought her car, or at least he'd given her all the money he'd had onsite because it was all he could think to do at the time.

And now her words gnawed at him. When Josh pulled up to the old farmhouse and parked the truck, he didn't get out. He looked at the front porch where he'd last seen his dad alive. He bit his lip and then cursed and shook his head as everything he'd tucked away flooded back.

If eleven-year-old Josh Davis would have known his father would die that afternoon, he never would have ignored his mother's call as he ran out of the house to play with his friends. There was nothing unusual about that summer day in 1989 in Sycamore, Illinois. The sun shone on time, the birds sang, the wind danced in the trees luring Josh and his friends to their branches.

"I'd like to talk to you a minute, son."

Josh barely glanced at his father as he ran past him and out the front porch door. He heard the screen door slam closed as he jumped off the third step. He didn't notice the old man's hunched posture or the gray color in his cheeks.

"Mom's upstairs, Dad. I'm going to Sam's." Josh was eleven years old, and he felt that he was practically a man. He could drive Mr. Thompson's tractor and his cousin's dirt bike. He and his friends had the run of town in the summer from the swimming pool to the library to the Confectionary candy store. He knew almost everything there was to know. His father could wait until later.

For years to come, Josh would berate himself for not realizing that his father never came home early from work, especially not on a busy Tuesday afternoon, and his father never parked his truck out in front of the house.

Josh and his friends went north of town to play in the small lake and climb trees. It was a perfect afternoon as temperatures remained in the high eighties. The small lake had been heated for the past two months by the summer sun, and when he dove, in the nip of winter cold was gone. If he'd known that this was the last afternoon the world would seem right, Josh might have savored his swim or his view from the top of an oak tree.

He returned home twenty minutes past supper time, not a crime for a Midwestern boy in the summer, but something he knew that his father would scold him for. As the door creaked closed behind him, he was surprised to see the table empty of food and the room without his parents' disapproving faces.

"Mom?" Silence.

Louder now. "Dad?" Fear.

There was a sound, an unfamiliar noise carrying down from upstairs. "Mom?" Josh called. He climbed the stairs slowly, unsure of the sound he heard. The moment Josh discerned that it was his mother crying, he was off in a shot. At first, he thought that maybe she'd broken another antique trinket given to her by her grandmother, something brought over from the old country. The last time she'd broken a china serving dish, she'd been sad for over a week. But as Josh drew closer, he knew this cry was different. It was a low desperate moan, and it sent crackling chills through his bones.

He found his mother in his parent's bedroom. His father laid on the bed in his work clothes, his boots still on, his lunch box tucked underneath his right arm. Josh's mother was lying on the bed slumped over and crying, her head on his dad's chest and her arm wrapped around him.

"Mom?" Josh asked three times from the hallway before she

noticed. Josh slowly approached, blinking away the tears that would fog his vision for weeks to come. He watched his mother from just inside the doorway, a space that seemed miles away in his mind. He had never paid much attention to his parent's bond. He never needed to notice it because he always felt secure in his home. And now his mother was lost, and his father was found, and Josh's confusion made him sweat.

The curtains blew in the room and a door creaked, and Josh watched all of this with the fascination of seeing a slow-motion film for the first time. He noticed the way his father's huge fingers cupped the lunch pail as they had Josh's whole age of remembering.

"He wanted to tell you he loved you. He wanted to make sure that you knew," his mother said between sobs.

Josh didn't move.

Somewhere in the distance behind his own grief, Josh should have been able to hear his mother's words, but he couldn't understand. There was only his father asking to speak to him and the slam of the door and creak of the steps as Josh had run from the house.

Josh moved to the lifeless figure. "Dad!" he yelled over and over begging his father to come back. His tears made him angry, and he yelled until his mother grabbed his arm and pulled him over his father's chest toward her. Josh stood next to the bed and lay across his father's chest as his mother tried to hug him. They stayed like that for a long time.

Josh's anger transformed into the pain of loss. He cried so long and hard that he didn't remember falling asleep. When he awoke, he was still with his father, kneeling on the floor, his arms and head laying on the old man's blue work shirt, the smell of the gas station repair garage filling his nose. His mother was seated next to the bed, now removed from her own grief and alert and ready for her son.

Josh looked for the hope in his mother's face and when he

couldn't find it, he watched the clear white curtains sailing in the window. It seemed funny to him that the curtains could have more life in them than his father. He noticed the clock, the face tipped on its side from Josh's horizontal view, staring at him beyond the hill of his father's chest, a hill that should have been moving up and down with the curtains.

For a moment the clock made Josh forget his pain. He focused on these hands of time that had cheated him. Josh got to his feet and willfully stared at the time. He moved around the bed as his mother held out her arms to receive her son, but Josh went to the nightstand and picked up the clock. He was angry enough to smash it. He turned the hands back an hour and then watched his father, but nothing happened. He turned the hands back once more as his mother looked on in dismay. His second attempt to cheat time failed, and before his mother had wrapped her arms around him and guided him from the room, he had already decided that time did not exist.

Josh sat in his truck looking at the front porch. It was the last place that he'd spoken to his father. The pain of that day came back sharp in his gut, and Josh realized that was the day that had ruled his decisions for the next thirty-odd years. His world had turned upside-down, and he felt sorry for the boy he'd been. His life had never been the same. Josh hadn't lashed out or pushed his friends away. They had all given up on him when he'd stopped keeping time.

Josh wondered about the woman with the Saturn station wagon who had yelled at him. She had issues; he could see that. People didn't simply run out of gas in a random town and sell their car and walk away. She'd looked tired and anxious but sane enough to know that people didn't just turn the clock back whenever it suited them. He assumed she would be back for her car, and mostly, he wondered where she had gone.

CHAPTER 4

*L*iz walked five blocks from the gas station to the center of town and sat on a bench across the street from what looked like a hardware store. There was a short stack of blankets neatly folded on the other end of the bench, and she waited for their owner to show up to collect them, but no one did. She looked up and down the street and noticed that downtown Sycamore mostly consisted of three blocks of two-story brick buildings. There were store fronts on street level, and at the end was a 7-11 convenience store. It was small-town America. She had only seen it on television before.

She sat there for a couple of hours in the shade and watched the cars and the people. She thought about her cell phone and realized that she never used to manage to sit this still. Liz was sorry that she was making her parents worry, and in the same instant knew that she needed her independence from the world that knew her before. Liz didn't think she would ever have a cell phone again.

She didn't allow herself to wonder what to do next. The anger she had felt at the gas station had run out of her. Liz sat down on the bench in midafternoon, only in her mind it had been days and years that had gone by as she relived her son's life. She was in and out of daydreams, sometimes floating in outer space where she felt nothing, and then back to her parent's house in New York where she and Sean had lived a small but wonderful life.

She rubbed her hands together and remembered how Sean would sit next to her on the couch. He would put his hand under hers, then softly tossing hers up in the air to clap down on his hand over and over as they watched TV. He would snuggle up next to her and put his cold feet under her legs to warm them up, their sharp cold causing Liz to jump a little, and his mischievous laugh would make her laugh, and he'd move his feet up and down her leg just to laugh at her reaction.

Then the couch was gone, and she was back on the bench. This bench that held her figure from falling onto the concrete in a heap. She was tired and a little confused. Liz had become a shell. She reasoned that this useless figure that she was now trapped in must have been the dream, and the flashback moments spent with her son in her trances were reality.

Liz wondered if she had even blinked once since she had sat down, and for some time she had even wondered what her name was or if she had ever been given one. She was only reminded of reality and of her name when a passerby looked directly at her on the bench. And for the third time in as many hours, an older man in a red apron was sweeping the sidewalk across the street. He would glance up at the bench several times as his broom massaged the pavement, and Liz wondered if he could see her. He stepped in front of the orange letters on his "Help Wanted" sign, the one her eyes had been fixed on. Liz wanted help, someone to get her back to her dreams and back to her son. None came.

Liz watched Ted Barlow, the drunk, swagger down the block. His long trench coat made him appear very tall. He was headed toward her, and she wondered if this, too, was a bench that he used to live his life. When Ted noticed her, he moved back across the street. The old man with the red smock stopped his sweeping and followed Ted into the store. When Ted came out of the store, he took a long look at her, and Liz thought he might come and ask her to pay him back. She'd forgotten about the money in her pocket, and she looked away. He didn't come over to talk to her though. Liz watched him move further down the block and around a corner.

The days were getting longer. At dusk, the streetlights finally clicked on in preparation for the moon. Liz became anxious so she pulled herself off the bench and headed toward the shopkeeper who was sweeping the pristine sidewalk for the fourth time this afternoon. He saw her coming, and like an exposed rabbit, he had retreated. She was through the glass door and heard the small tinkle of a bell. She was at the counter waiting and looking out across the street. Liz thought that she could still see the ghost of herself on the park bench.

She noticed that the store clerk had a full head of gray hair. He put the broom in the corner and watched Liz as she looked back out the window.

"How are you today? Can I help you with something?" His questions brought no reply, so he took another tack. "You've been sitting outside for quite a while now. Did you take the day off to relax?"

Her stare moved to the "Help Wanted" sign which was backwards now but still accurate enough in her mind. "I was waiting."

"Well, I hope you haven't been waiting for the bus because that hasn't been a bus stop for over twelve years."

She looked across the street noticing for the first time the old metal pole which held a painted placard. Like a bodyguard, the pole had been planted next to her the whole time and she hadn't even noticed it.

"Can I help you find something?"

"A job," Liz said before the shopkeeper could finish his thought. She wondered why she had responded and hoped that she didn't sound desperate. She felt a glint of a future that didn't encompass her in grief, and that would have to be enough to keep her heart pumping.

The old man looked Liz up and down. She was embarrassed almost immediately because she hadn't looked in a mirror for days. Her embarrassment brought some color to her cheeks, and the New York fighter in her rose to the surface. She could do this.

"Can you run a register?" He pointed at the large brass machine in front of him. It was very old, with the white numbers on the black steel keys. This was the kind of antique that sounded like it was putting numbers through a grinder before the total popped up in the glass. The heavy slot machine looking register fit perfectly into Liz's idea of small-town life.

"I've been a cashier before," Liz said defensively. She pointed at the gold hunk of steel. "Never used one of those."

"No one ever has." The old man smiled and offered a hand-shake. "My name is Jim Thompson, and I'm the owner of this here 'Thompson's General Store'. That's my wife, Dotty." He pointed to a woman who had been standing in the first aisle rear-ranging items, and Liz was surprised to see there was someone else in the store with them. The woman had curly, reddish-brown hair that perched above her shoulders. She was short. She didn't smile. She only stared and squinted at her husband in obvious disapproval of his job candidate.

Mr. Thompson looked directly back at his wife as if staring down a bull and then smiled at Liz. "You've got the job. Can you start tomorrow morning?"

Mrs. Thompson made a loud grunting sound. She stormed down the aisle and disappeared into the back of the building. The old man let out a chuckle. "Don't worry..." he waited for her name.

"Liz... Campbell... Liz Campbell." She repeated her name slowly as if she had been making it up on the spot and was trying to get used to the sound.

"Well, don't worry, Liz Campbell, you'll do fine. My wife is just angry because I gave you her sister's job. The old bat never shows up to work. She thinks she'll just get paid because we're family." He laughed loudly, reminding Liz that somewhere in the world happiness still existed.

Mr. Thompson gave Liz a job application, but when she just stared at the paper, he encouraged her to take it home so that she could write down her personal information and bring it back the next day. She slowly walked out the door, the bell ringing behind her. Liz stared across the street and wondered where home might be for her. She could no longer see herself sitting on the bench, so she stood on the sidewalk clinging to the prospect of belonging somewhere on this planet. She heard the bell ring as the door opened behind her, and she turned around to see Mr. Thompson.

"Go three doors down on your right to The Frame Shoppe. Daniel is waiting for you. He has a room for rent above the store." Mr. Thompson winked before closing the door, and Liz thought that this man must have been Santa Claus, giving gifts to the world with a rosy smile, a wink, and a twinkle in his eye.

Liz wandered three doors down and hesitated on the street. She wasn't sure what was happening, but it was getting dark out, and she should find somewhere to stay. Mr. Thompson had seemed genuine, so she turned to open the door of the shop, but a thin, young man pushed the door open from the inside.

"Hi, I'm Daniel. Mr. Thompson just called and said that you were taking the apartment," he told Liz, flipping the open sign to closed. He held his hand out to the left and Liz stepped back, following Daniel to the door that was between his store and the next.

Between the front door of his shop and the apartment upstairs, Daniel managed to fit in his life story. He had lived in DeKalb, the next town over, for five years while he earned his bachelor's degree at Northern Illinois University. There was a year in the middle where he hadn't been focused, but don't ask him about that. Then it was off the to the big city of Chicago for two years to try his hand at life. But he had loved Sycamore and the small-town way of life and had moved back to buy the frame shop when it had come up for sale. He loved photography and art, so Daniel had stepped in, and here they were.

At the top of a tall flight of stairs, he opened a door and led Liz into a sparsely furnished two room apartment that was the perfect size in which to lead a tiny existence. Daniel chattered on, explaining that the rear apartment was larger, but it was already rented by a young couple who were putting themselves through grad school.

Although it was already dark out, Daniel opened the curtains to show off the 'magnificent' view of downtown Sycamore. The most Liz could see from the center of the room was her reflection in the dark window. She turned her head to avoid her image and instead looked at the full-size bed, a chair, and a lamp. Daniel clicked on the lamp as Liz stepped back into the small kitchen, and he joined her while he continued the efforts of his grand tour. There was a small, ancient stove, and Daniel showed Liz the spare pots and pans and tableware that came with the place.

This was a very old building, and there was one bathroom in the main hallway that would need to be shared between the two apartments. Daniel explained that he didn't care if they made a schedule, just as long as everyone was happy. The pictures in the apartment were chosen and decoratively framed by him in the frame shop, and the comforter on the old bed perfectly matched the valence above the window. A couple months earlier, Liz would have thought the place charming, but now she just wanted to lay down and die on top of the afghan blanket that Daniel's grandmother had knitted.

"I don't have much money," she told him.

Daniel smiled. "The first two months are already taken care of, and if you get hired on with Thompson, I know we won't have any problems. I'll leave the key on the table." He smiled and left, pulling the door closed.

Liz stood still, her zombie brain playing tricks on her. He'd said that the apartment was free for two months if she was working. She thought she must be in an alternate universe because things like this didn't happen in real life.

Fully clothed, Liz did lay down on the blanket and for a few minutes, she tried to convince herself to die. Then she thought of the others who might have sat in this room as she was now, and the people in this town and in this country and in the world, who were somewhere in a room not even noticing their lives going by. The whole world might be aloof and trapped inside man's handiwork. Then she thought of the man at the gas station who had bought her car. His actions had started a very strange afternoon for Liz, one in which she wasn't as lost and alone as she might have thought. Liz wondered about the room that he might be in at this very moment.

LIZ WAS guilty for everything that she had done. She felt guilty for getting married and then divorced, guilty for letting her son die, guilty for selling her father's car in this forgotten town, and guilty for letting herself go on. The guilt led to two days of self-loathing. She lay in bed hating herself for not giving her Sean everything he had asked for while she still could. There were video game systems that he had begged her for, and from lack of finances, she had denied him. When they would see a commercial on television for the high-priced vacation resorts, Sean would implore her to go, and Liz dismissed him. There were countless other things that Liz could not forgive herself for rejecting. Sean's wants should have trumped her own needs. He was her boy, and she loved him.

On the first night in Liz's trance of self-loathing, she dared to look herself in the face, and the small mirror that was hung next to the hall door paid with its life. She gave no attention to the blood on her wrist and arm as she dropped back into bed and passed out.

That night, Liz didn't know who she was. She was confused and exhausted. When she could think, it was of how to kill herself and rid herself of the guilt. She had woken several times thinking that someone was standing over her. In her stupor, she hoped that it might be the Angel of Death readying her soul for the afterlife. She couldn't feel her soul anymore. Liz was pale and weak, and all she could do was lie in bed and listen to her lungs pull and push on the air.

The walls turned red and then black with sunset. The next day came and went and she spent most of it trying to lie as still as the furniture. When she slept, it was for a short period of time, and she would always wake up in panic.

There were dreams and there were nightmares, and Liz didn't want to wake from either. The dreams were wonderful, fanciful pieces of art where Liz danced around with her son and showed him the world and they both smiled through and through. The nightmares were hell: black and white faces full of tears, mother and child trying to reach one another, both terrified and both alone.

She should have jolted awake when her subconscious showed her son getting hit by a car. He was thrown bloody on the pavement, his life spilling out of him. But she knew that she was making that part up because she hadn't seen the real accident. So, Liz waded on through the unspeakable images of the accident because each time she allowed her mind to show the pictures, her son played happily and stopped to look back and smile at his mommy one last time. She felt his spirit in that smile in her dream, the moment before his death.

Finally, Liz woke from the conflict in her mind, and although this should have meant relief, it was bittersweet. She was like so many soldiers who spent time between battles dreaming of a home they would never know again. Either they would die to protect it, or upon return, the home they dreamt of would be dead and gone, the perfect picture erased by the demons in their recent memories.

It was dark, but Liz didn't know the time or the day of the week. She knew that she had laid in bed for at least two days because the sun had come and gone. She rose and moved to the window. The street was lit by lamplight, but all the lights inside of buildings were out, and she reasoned that it was the middle of the night. She was cold, but she didn't pick up the blanket. She would suffer in the cold. It was only right that she suffer.

She saw the headlights of a car and watched as it crept slowly down the street. She thought it might be a police car patrolling the area, but the car stopped halfway down the block, and Liz could hear the low rumble of a sports car muffler. She watched as a lady got out of the car with a blanket. The lady walked up to the bench across the street, and it wasn't until then that Liz noticed the shadow of a figure slumped over in the dark. The woman's blonde hair glowed under the streetlamp as she gently placed a blanket over the figure and then got back into her car and slowly idled down the street, turning the corner out of sight.

Liz remembered sitting on that same bench, the short stack of blankets an enigma in this small, clean town. It must have been someone homeless sleeping outside on this cold night. She was caught off-guard by the empathy she felt for the sleeping figure on the bench, and for the person who had slipped the blanket over them.

Liz pulled her sweatshirt over her t-shirt and stepped over the broken pieces of mirror by the front door. She wondered what had happened, and then remembered and tried to make herself forget. If she allowed herself to plunge back into her thoughts, she might not make it out again.

She grabbed her key and slipped into the hallway, creeping

into the bathroom, and making sure to not wake her new neighbors. She washed the side of her hand where dried blood had formed a crust. Once she was sure that the wound wouldn't open again, she splashed cold water on her face and ran her fingers through her knotted hair. She hardly recognized the person in the mirror, but she didn't stay long enough to care. When she stepped back into the hallway, Liz noticed a box next to her front door. She went to it, and in the dim light from the single bulb on the landing, she saw some clothes inside. She unpacked a couple of shirts and held them up in the dim hall light. They were her size. There were some toiletries and a note that said in careful lettering, "Just to get you started."

Liz stepped around the glass and put the box in her apartment. She stopped contemplating who might have given her the box when she remembered the figure on the bench across the street. Curiosity got the best of her. She moved down the stairs and looked out the window interested as to who might be sleeping on the bench. The street was quiet, and just before she turned the knob to leave, a figure passed by the window and startled her, causing her heart to jump into her throat.

Liz waited with one hand on the doorknob and the other over her heart, listening to her quick breath and inwardly laughing at her stupid self. She gently pushed the door open and looked to the right. She could see that it was a man. He had his hands in his pockets as he walked, and the night was so quiet that Liz could hear his steps under his soft-soled shoes. She quickly forgot about the person on the bench across the street. Liz held the door as it closed behind her to stop any sound from escaping into the silent night. As the cold wind hit her, she put her hands in her pockets and followed.

Liz was half a block back, and when he crossed the street to his left, she didn't follow him across. He whistled to himself, and Liz wondered who he was and what he was doing out at this time of night. In another life, she might have wondered the same of herself, but novelty caused her to march on after this stranger.

The man stopped suddenly, stopped walking and whistling, and he stood very still for some time. Then he pulled a large key ring from his coat pocket and stepped up to the building. Liz heard the keys jangling as he flipped through them in front of the glass door. She looked at the sign on the building to see where he was headed.

The State Theatre was a throwback to when movies first became popular a hundred years ago. The marquis read "STATE" in large letters mounted horizontally. The single box office stood out from the front doors. He turned the key in the lock and Liz heard the steel bolt click, and then the man turned to face her. She wondered if she should hide, and then she laughed inwardly again at her stupid self.

"The movie is about to start. Are you coming?" he asked. Liz could see his face in the streetlight. It was the man from the gas station who had bought her car. She fought her memory for his name. It was Josh. This man was named Josh. He was dressed in jeans and a warm looking mechanic jacket, and his neatly combed hair was parted to the side and almost shined under the overhead light. *He was a clean mechanic*, she thought. He was still staring at her across the street, so Liz stepped off the curb toward him.

"My name is Josh," he said.

She nodded as she closed the distance, but she didn't offer her name. She didn't want to be Liz for a while, and this might have been a dream, for all she knew.

He held the door open, and she silently stepped into the darkness and waited for Josh to lock the door. He walked past, and she followed him through to the lobby. There was not an instant that Liz second guessed her situation. He was a stranger, but there was something about his kind eyes that made her feel at ease.

"Wait here," Josh said. She could see him walk away in the red glow of the exit sign and then he disappeared in the darkness. Most people would get an eerie feeling standing in a foreign and pitch-black space, but Liz was calm and passive as she listened for Josh. It was a refreshing distraction from the noise in her head.

The lights came on in the lobby and Josh reappeared. "It's that door," he pointed to the left. "Go ahead in and sit wherever you want," Josh said as he walked in the opposite direction. He turned back and then looked down at the floor when he saw that she was watching him. It was as though he was apologizing for not escorting her into the theatre, and she thought that this man had no idea how to be in the presence of another human being. Not that she knew how to interact right now either.

Liz walked on the carpeted floor and noticed the wood paneling. It had small vertical slats that ran halfway up the wall with movie posters neatly spaced throughout the lobby. They were framed perfectly, and Liz wondered if Daniel had a hand in it. There were some small tables and chairs arranged in front of the posters opposite the long candy counter. She could hear Josh opening cabinets to her right, but she didn't look. Instead, she went to the door on the left and entered a small theatre.

Liz walked halfway to the front and sat down in an aisle seat on the left. The screen was blank, and the theatre was dimly lit by sconces hung around the side walls. She could see large columns and ornate framing in the sconce light. She thought she saw Egyptian images painted around the huge open space, and Liz could see that this theatre was as old and grand as some in New York City.

In a few minutes, Liz's mouth watered as the aroma of fresh popcorn filled the entire building. She closed her eyes and breathed in the smell and when the trailers started, Liz watched new movie previews as the theatre lights slowly dimmed to black.

She wondered why she wasn't creeped out by the fact that she was in a strange town and with a stranger in an empty theatre in the middle of the night. It didn't seem real. She shrugged and watched the screen, trying not to think of the last time she had taken Sean to the movies. The theatre was like a womb: dark and enveloping, closing out the harsh world to one of fantasy. Laughter, romance, and action filled in the blank spaces, distracting Liz from real life.

During the last preview of coming attractions, Josh appeared and handed Liz a huge bucket heaping with hot popcorn. He gave her a small cup of bright orange butter and a soda. "I hope 7up is okay," he said as he walked back up the aisle. Liz didn't want to eat. She wanted to forget that she was human and needed food, but the smell of the popcorn overcame her, and she poured the warm oil over the top of the bucket and began scarfing down the fluffy kernels.

Josh had been surprised to see Liz following him to the theatre, and he wasn't sure of the etiquette. He invited her to watch the movie and wondered if the word etiquette had ever crossed his mind before.

He had found a name in the glove compartment of her car, but it was a man's name, and he wondered if she was married. He was jealous when the thought crossed his mind. He waited at the station the rest of the afternoon and even washed and waxed her car in case she did return for it. There was something about her sad eyes that made Josh want to take care of her.

He had returned to the station in the evening so she could come get her car and drive away. He'd only given her one hundred thirty-eight dollars for it so far, and that was ridiculous. But she didn't come for the car, and that made him continue to wonder who she was and why she was here.

Ted Barlow told Josh that her name was Liz and she'd borrowed some change to call New York City, and that she had talked to her mother. When Josh pried, Ted said in his matter-of-fact drunken manner, that he couldn't offer any more information than that. He told Josh that it was a conflict of interest to the privacy of his payphone customers.

Josh held his own popcorn and took a seat across the aisle from her to watch the movie. From the corner of his eye, he watched Liz, too. She had eaten much of the popcorn, but he didn't approach to see if she'd wanted anything else. There were times when he thought she might be sleeping because her eyes were closed, but she would suddenly open them wide like she was afraid of what she'd seen in the darkness under the eyelids. Sometimes Josh forgot that she was even there, and then something on the screen would make her jump or laugh, and he'd be startled by her presence.

Josh was comfortable with his mother and Billy Noodles and Ted Barlow in his life. He liked Mr. Thompson and Dotty, and some of the locals, too, like Mr. Johnson who was always bringing Josh fixer-uppers to flip. Josh wasn't quite sure he had intended to build this lifestyle. It had just happened in the years after high school. His classmates had gone from understanding to unforgiving, and Josh didn't spend time with many of them anyway. He had started avoiding society, doing what he wanted as a young man, and his late nights had gotten later and later until he'd gotten so used to it that it felt completely normal to be mostly alone and around town in the dark of night.

Most of the rest of the town didn't badger him, and Josh tolerated them just as the town tolerated having to use a credit card or debit card to fill up on gas at his station. Outside of the garage and home, not many understood his aversion to clocks. And clocks or not, he had turned his life into mostly living at night.

When he constantly showed up late, many people had asked

Josh, "What, are you stupid?" But it was only late in their minds. Josh knew that they were the stupid ones. There were few things in life that could be done *on time* and even less things that mattered in the big picture. Life was finite, and the hands of a clock could not change that.

The credits rolled, and Liz stood up and looked at him. "Thanks."

Josh stood too, and he looked across the aisle in the dim light of the credits rolling skyward on the black screen. He nodded. He wanted to say something so she wouldn't turn away. He wanted to see her chocolate brown eyes, but the shadows were dense, and he was too slow with words, so she turned and walked up the aisle. She dropped her cup and bag in the trash and left the theatre.

Josh left his trash on top of the garbage can and followed her to the front door of the theatre. Liz pushed the handle on the door and stepped out into the night. He wanted to tell her to wait so he could walk her back to wherever she had come from, but the words got stuck in his throat. Downtown Sycamore was mostly crime free, and he had never been concerned for his own safety, but something in his gut was telling him to protect this woman. He watched as she walked down the street under the lamplight, and the overwhelming need to make sure she was safe pulled him out of the theatre. He stayed on his side of the street for two blocks. When he saw which door that she opened and disappeared behind, he understood why she hadn't come back for her car. Josh glanced at the dark pile that was Ted Barlow passed out on the bench under a blanket, and then he returned to the theatre.

Josh thought of Liz the whole time that he took their trash out back to the dumpster and cleaned out the popcorn machine. Like usual, Josh was making sure that there was no evidence of him left behind, aside from the neat pile of cash that he left on the counter with a napkin that held his tally written on top. For the first time, there were two tickets to tally, and snacks for two. Josh smiled as he wrote on the napkin. He wondered if Steve would be curious as to who Josh might have brought with him to the movies tonight. Josh stared at the napkin for a long time before locking up and going home.

CHAPTER 5

*B*ack in the apartment, Liz thought about the movie and how everyone shot in all directions and drove recklessly and jumped from impossible places to catch themselves in the nick of time. She closed her eyes, and she could see the actor dangling from a helicopter skid. She again imagined herself dangling from a thread high above the earth, although Liz wasn't acting. She was pulling away from the planet, and the tiny thread was the only thing keeping her from slipping out into space. She was holding on to an almost invisible piece of string, her grip getting weaker and weaker. She looked down and saw the earth which had always been her home, but she wasn't afraid of letting the void take her to her son. She tried to let go of the string, but she couldn't, not yet. It was funny watching the earth below her, knowing that all the humans were scurrying about their business. She had nowhere to run to, and in her daydream, Liz felt at peace.

The sun rose with Liz looking out the window and down onto State Street. This wasn't New York City where you could look down from a tower at the little ant people scurrying about. In this little town, few people walked or drove by, and then the store owners showed up. Even strangers nodded at each other. In the Big Apple, civilized recognition amongst humans was minimal as all comments were saved for the jerk who cut you off in traffic. Only the beggar sees everyone, Liz thought. Her eyes went to the bench across the street, but the dark figure was gone, and the tidy stack of folded blankets was one higher.

Liz watched until the sun was blaring and started to hurt her eyes. She noticed a piece of paper on the floor by the front door and went to it.

Liz,

I don't know what it is, but when it's gone, feel free to come in to work. Your register awaits.

Your friend,

Mr. Thompson

Liz's hand involuntarily flew to her chest as she read the note two more times. Lost in her grief and exhaustion, she'd forgotten about the job. She couldn't understand how a stranger could allow her to not show up without a word and then invite her back. It appeared that Mr. Thompson understood something about the world that Liz could not fathom.

She walked to the bathroom and ignored her reflection in the mirror. Liz stepped into the shower and washed her confusion away, and then borrowed the body spray from the drawer to spray her clothes. Back in the apartment, she remembered the box of clothes and pulled out a pair of gently used blue jeans and a button up shirt. She walked into Thompson's General Store an hour later as if she was walking into the store for the first time and having an overwhelming feeling of déjà vu. The bell rang overhead, but no one was at the counter, so she looked at some of the merchandise for a minute.

"There you are, Liz. I didn't hear you come in." She watched Mr. Thompson as his tall, wide frame moved to the third aisle. He wasn't heavy, but he was solidly built, and Liz wondered if he had been a football player in a past life.

"We've been busy, so we can really use the help." He slowly stocked up more light bulbs on the already bulging shelf.

Liz looked around and there were no customers. She didn't know what to say, so she remained silent, but he didn't wait for her to respond. He disappeared into the back while she wrestled with her guilty conscience. She didn't know what she was doing here, but she hadn't known what to do with herself for months, so this seemed like the place to be at the moment.

"Dotty will be in this afternoon, so let me get you up and running before she comes in." Mr. Thompson handed Liz a red smock with the store logo embroidered on the center pocket. She put it on and moved behind the counter to run through the workings of the massive register. She wasn't sure if she could think straight right now, but despite her nerves, Liz caught on quickly. Mr. Thompson had chuckled when she was able to complete a transaction on the third attempt, mentioning that Dotty would be surprised because Liz already understood the register better than Dotty's sister had after months.

Mr. Thompson patted Liz's hand as it rested on the counter. "Don't you say anything to Dotty about my note. I told her that you were sick and you'd be in soon enough. I didn't want her getting any ideas about calling her sister back." Mr. Thompson smiled and left Liz behind the register in her red smock.

The morning was slow, and time went by in a daze of memories. Liz spent hours just standing behind the counter. She found that she liked looking out onto the small street outside and the way the sun shone through the window. She liked this place in the world. No one expected anything of her. She was just the lady behind the counter at the local store. No one knew her past or expected her to have a future.

Liz's eyes fixed on a point as she thought of Sean's smile and his laugh. This memory had been destroyed by her grief since his death, but this time it made her smile. It was strange that only weeks ago, this same memory could make her want to destroy her own life. Now it seemed as beautiful as a sunrise. She choked back tears when she realized that she had done an injustice to Sean all these months. He was pure love to her, but she'd boxed out that love and, in her grief, had become selfish with his memory.

Liz noticed a Hershey chocolate bar, and she didn't fight the memory of Sean eating his first s'more. She'd been distraught that day over an argument that she'd had with Darren. They were finalizing the divorce, and Liz had shown up at her parent's house with Sean in tow. While Liz vented to her mom, her father took Sean out to the yard to do "man's work" he'd told Sean. He taught his six-year-old grandson to cut small branches from large bushes and pile them up next to the garage. Then they took dry kindling from the shed and made a small fire while Liz's mother prepared a plate of marshmallows and chocolate bars. Liz was lost in her own conflict, but Sean's excitement over learning to use a saw and learning to light a campfire made her smile and pulled her from her reverie. Sean had joined Boy Scouts that year.

A middle-aged woman looked in the window and her eyes froze on Liz, and then she turned and continued down the street. Liz was relieved because she didn't want anyone to see her crying, and she didn't want to answer any questions. As long as she stood behind that counter and did her job, her son could be somewhere out in the world playing with his friends until suppertime. It didn't matter to Liz that this was a lie. It had been the truth at one time, and she was content believing it. She knew that the lie might haunt her to tomorrow, but today she was able to stand upright in public. For the first time in a long time, Liz wanted to see what tomorrow might look like.

Liz noticed movement in the back of the store, and she turned to see a short woman with curly hair looking her up and down. Her pointed chin seemed to be accusing Liz of what, she wasn't sure. Then Liz realized that this was Mrs. Dotty Thompson. Liz tried to smile but her face was out of practice, and she managed a grimace. Dotty returned to the back of the store and Liz could hear muffled voices, but she didn't mind.

After a while, Dotty walked through the store without more than a polite nod toward Liz, but Liz paid no attention. She was glad that Mr. Thompson had mentioned Dotty's sister losing the cashier job. Liz told herself that the silent treatment was nothing personal. She'd been married too, and she knew that Dotty was trying to prove a point to Mr. Thompson more than she was trying to slight their new employee.

Business trickled in and out of the store throughout the day. Men usually shopped on the right side of the store which contained mostly hardware. The women typically went to the left side which had cosmetics, magazines, some arts and crafts and sundries and food necessities. Liz was used to small grocery stores in New York, but she had assumed people in the country shopped at big supermarkets and big box stores. She watched the Thompsons interact with their patrons, and she realized that these were loyal customers. A few people who interacted with Liz told her that these prices couldn't be beat. Liz wasn't sure about that, and she realized that some women were just trying to strike up a conversation to find out more about the new girl in town. Liz sidestepped the indirect questions and rang up the purchases as fast as she could.

Midday, Liz noticed a man appear in front of the store with a picket sign. He slowly walked back and forth in front of the door, his giant belly marching in front of him. The tattered cardboard sign was attached to a piece of wood that looked like it would split at any time. "On Strike for Fair Pay" went round and round, putting Liz in a trance. She wondered how such a fat man could walk back and forth so tirelessly.

Liz wasn't sure what to do, so she stood at the register until Mr. Thompson finally reappeared. She waited for Mr. Thompson to show some outrage or offer an explanation, but there was none. Thompson waved to the man picketing his store, and the man looked back with a straight face and continued at a faster pace.

"You can take your lunch break now, Liz," Mr. Thompson said with his ever-present smile. She wanted to ask about the man in front of the store but didn't know how. "You're wondering who he is?" Mr. Thompson asked. He seemed to read her mind. "That's Sam Waters. He makes pick-ups and deliveries near Chicago a couple times a week for me."

"Why is he on strike?"

"Unfair pay," Mr. Thompson chuckled as he pointed out the sign that Sam was carrying. "Don't worry, Liz, I pay fairly, and I give raises to deserving employees. It's just that Sam, well, he doesn't really know how to ask for a raise, so he pickets the store instead."

"He doesn't know how to ask for a raise?" Liz asked, trying to understand Sam Waters and his tactics. Then she realized that she had no idea how much she would get paid, but she shrugged the thought off. Having somewhere to go each day where she was expected was enough for her right now. And if she was remembering correctly, the apartment was paid up for two months.

"Sam has been doing odd jobs for me for about ten years. He's a nice man, but a little slow on the take. I think he occasionally needs to feel a bit of a fight in life. Like people who take on a cause to feel important, more than believing in the cause that they're championing. He won't bother anyone out there, and if he comes in the store for a pop, just give him one."

"He's picketing your store and you're going to give him something to drink?" Liz was used to the hardball tactics of the big city, and this generosity in battle was unfamiliar territory.

"Every few of years, Sam pickets the store. The first time he did it, I was angry, but by now everyone around here knows about Sam, and they don't pay any attention to him. I'll let him sit out there until Friday and then call him in for negotiations."

Liz wondered what day it was, but she didn't ask.

Mr. Thompson was quite pleased with his solution, but Liz was still a little baffled. She had seen beggars on the streets and in the subway and homeless living out of cardboard boxes. She had seen old ladies with shopping carts full of junk talking to no one as they pushed from street to street. But the people in this town seemed stranger to her than anything. She thought maybe it was because in this small-town America, there weren't millions of people living on top of each other while trying to ignore each other's existence at the same time. They were individual characters in their own little plays with the scenes from all their family and friend's lives intertwined.

"I'll need you to be here the next couple of mornings so that I can run some errands. Can you be here by eight?"

Liz nodded, and then Mr. Thompson reminded her that she could take a break for lunch. She took a walk to the 7-11 and bought a tuna salad sandwich. She wandered down a side street and turned a corner and found herself drifting down Main Street toward Josh's gas station. She saw the figure of a man on the bench next to the payphone, and she knew it was Ted Barlow. He was sitting up and his head was bent forward so she assumed he was sleeping.

Liz teetered on the curb and looked around the lot. Although a 'closed' sign was posted on the door of the gas station, a man stood at the pumps filling up his pickup truck. He was no doubt one of the local farmers who knew about the inconsistent man who ran the gas station. He pulled his credit card receipt from the pump and drove away.

Liz admired her dad's Saturn station wagon from across the lot. The car had been moved in front of the garage door, and the brown paint gleamed in the limited sunlight as though it had been freshly washed and waxed. Ted Barlow was still asleep on the bench, so Liz walked to her car. Upon closer inspection, Liz could see that the car had been cleaned up. She wondered if Josh was looking to sell it, but as of yet, there was no for sale sign in the window.

Liz daydreamed about her past life for a while and then shook her head. She wasn't sure how much time had gone by, and she didn't want to let Mr. Thompson down, especially with Dotty around. Liz retraced her steps in her mind and assumed that unless she had zoned out for longer, less than fifteen minutes had gone by since she'd left the store. Liz bit her lip. She wasn't sure if lunch was an hour or half an hour.

She walked over to the park bench and stared at Ted. She could see his chest rising with his breaths, and she wondered about this man. He wore a long, dusty, black, and gray wool coat, and Liz didn't think it was cold enough to justify the coat since spring was in the air. She wondered why he would have it on in late May.

She noticed his long legs stretched out in front of him. His short haircut and clean-shaven face was in such distinct opposition to his current state. He had a dimple in his chin, and Liz thought that he might have been a handsome man when he was still living a normal life. Liz peeled the plastic wrap from the top of the sandwich container and took half, leaving the container with the other half on the bench next to Ted. She ate as she strolled back to her job.

She walked by several houses that had been converted to businesses. She noticed that they were mostly law offices. She stopped at State and Main and looked at the three large brick buildings on the corners. The library across the street had an interesting rotunda on the front, and the brick was orange-brown. It was refurbished and eye-catching, but some of the design looked one-hundred years old. The other buildings on the corner gave Liz the same time capsule feeling. The post office was kiddie corner, and it had an imposing classical look, with brick surrounding the high white columns that ran across the front of the building.

Liz turned the corner and walked by the DeKalb County Courthouse which accounted for the law offices she had seen. It was a three-story building that looked like it belonged in Washington D.C., with its gray brick and columned front. A tall statue that went straight up like the Washington Monument drew her eye, and Liz walked halfway up the sidewalk to the courthouse and read that it had been erected in 1896 for the men who fought to preserve the union. Liz had walked by monuments before, but here in small town America, she felt that it might have really meant something to the locals.

Back in the store, Liz tried to familiarize herself with some of the products for sale in case anyone asked her questions. The two Thompsons were in rare form that afternoon. Dotty came out of the back a few times and walked around the store until Mr. Thompson commented.

"Stop staring at Sam," he'd say, and then Dotty would retreat to the back.

"I think she has a crush on Sam," Mr. Thompson told Liz. She thought at first that he might be jealous, but he was smiling a sideways grin.

Liz found herself wandering the streets before dawn. She sat down on a stack of wood railroad ties at the edge of a property and stared at nothing for a long time. When the sky showed signs of light, she stood up, and a bird chirped and flew away.

"I'm sorry. I can't sleep. But I'm in a new apartment, and I'm

sure I'll get used to the mattress soon. So don't worry about it."
Liz smiled as she watched the bird fly away, and the muscles on
her face reminded her that it had been ages since she had smiled.
She bit her lip and walked back to the apartment.

Liz was proud of herself for getting to work before eight
o'clock on the next two mornings. Mr. Thompson had been
waiting for her, and he stuck around for the first fifteen minutes
before leaving to run his errands. Liz felt strange being left in this
store alone since she had only worked here for one day. It seemed
strange that they could trust her alone with their goods and the
cash in the register. Liz knew that she was trustworthy, but how
did they know that?

Mr. Thompson had left her with one chore. He gave her a list,
and Liz was to pull the items from the shelves and put them in a
box and ring them up. It took Liz twenty minutes because she
wasn't sure where some of the items were located. She put the
total from the register and the list in the box next to the counter
and then leaned back and watched the town of Sycamore come
to life.

Ellison's Bakery across the street had the most traffic, and
Liz watched the people flow in and out. She wondered about
each of them. Who they were, if they had families or aspira-
tions, and if they were planning to ever leave this town? Liz
thought that people from small towns grew up to leave them
because she had met several people like that in college and at
work. She couldn't remember anyone planning to leave the city
to go live in a small town, but now as she watched the calm
morning, she knew that there must be people like that. After
five days in this town, Liz wondered if she was becoming that
kind of person.

Mr. Thompson stuck his head in a couple of times between
errands, but Liz had everything under control. She rang up about
four customers each hour, and the pace was enough to keep her
busy, but not enough to make her worry that a line might form as

she methodically pressed down the huge lever-like register buttons.

When it was time to leave for the day, Liz walked the half-block to her apartment. She changed into the shorts and t-shirt that were in the good will box, and she stared at the ceiling until she fell asleep. She heard a small voice telling her that she should be doing something with her life. Even Billy Noodles busied himself by writing things in his little notebook.

Most days Liz tried to ignore that voice. Sleep was easier, and it was the best way out of her misery. But when she woke up in the middle of the night in the quiet of darkness, her loneliness came back to her. She would remember why she was in Sycamore and her thoughts would move to Sean, and she would cry until it hurt and then cry until she ran out of tears. If she was lucky, she would fall back to sleep.

Still no luck, Liz thought as she climbed out of bed and went into the hall bathroom to wash her face. She looked in the mirror. "No luck, still stuck," she said out loud, quoting the book *One Duck Stuck* that she had read to Sean over and over when he was a small child. Liz rubbed her eyes and swallowed the lump in her throat. *Stuck* reverberated in her mind, and she couldn't bear to sit in the apartment until sunrise. She slipped on her jeans and shoes and went outside.

It would soon be summer, but it was still chilly at night. She didn't grab her dad's green jacket though. Liz felt the chill and rubbed her arms to keep warm. She crossed the street and walked over to Ted's bench. *Well, Ted's other bench*, she thought, but he wasn't there, so she sat down. She assumed that it was Ted who slept on this bench because she spent hours looking down from her window over State Street, and she hadn't noticed any other homeless people wandering the streets of Sycamore. Liz wished Ted was here, even if he was asleep, because Liz needed to know that she had woken from her dream and that she was a real person in the real world.

She had been sitting on the bench for a while when she noticed a shadow approaching. She wondered if the Veterans Club was closing, but Liz had no idea what time it was, and the club could have closed hours ago. She looked at the sky for the telling signs of dawn but there was only black speckled with stars.

Liz looked a half block down, and the figure turned into the light from the streetlamp in front of the bank. Although his base-ball cap shaded his eyes, she could see that it was Josh. Without thinking, she stood and walked after him. She turned the corner and saw him cross the street. She wondered if she should call out for him to wait, but the night was so quiet, and they were a block south and crossing into the residential streets.

She picked up her pace, but Josh stayed well in front of her. At one point, he looked back and saw Liz, at least she thought he'd seen her, but he didn't stop, so she slowed her pace as to not overtake him. Maybe he wanted to be alone. He'd lived all these years with these late-night habits, and maybe Liz was cramping his style.

When he turned to look back the second time, she was posi-tive that he'd seen her, but he kept on for another five minutes without slowing down. Josh turned a corner, and when Liz reached the spot where he had turned, she stopped in her tracks. Josh was at the door looking back. He was waiting for her. When he saw that she had seen where he was, he went into the building.

Liz swore out loud. It was a church. She noticed the backlit sign by the street that read 'St. Mary's Catholic Church' and she swore again. Liz stood on the corner for a long time. She hadn't been in a church since the day Sean had been buried, and she hadn't intended to return ever again. God had forsaken her when he had taken her son, and she knew now as she stared at the cross on the building that she had renounced Him in her heart.

Liz paced in a circle and felt the anger rise with the tears. She stood alone on the corner in the dark of night with her fists clenched, and she cried.

"Aaaaah!" she screamed, not caring that she was on a block of houses in the middle of the night. She paced in a small circle and tried to fight off the coming wave of shame and inadequacy. She swore at herself for being horrible, horrible, horrible.

"Aaaaah!" she screamed again, and dogs began to bark.

Liz punched her fists together and it hurt, but she didn't care. She cried furiously as she slowly melted down into a heap on the sidewalk, punching the concrete as it all came back to her. The screech of tires, the screams, the sirens, and the condolences. She had spent so many months numbed by the pain. Taking any action had seemed futile to her. She thought she was grieving, and she was, but she wasn't facing the truth. It all raged out of her on this street corner in the middle of the night.

Liz lost herself in the memories and the pain, and then she offered one last prayer to the God who had forsaken her that she might die right now. She hated the driver of that car, and yet she'd hated herself more because she was supposed to keep Sean safe. She was his mother, his protector, and his survivor, although at this point, she didn't really think that she had survived at all.

"God damn you!" she tried to yell at the cross on the church building, but her words were incoherent. "Why me? Why did you have to take my son?" Liz was angry and defeated all at once. She realized that she would never understand why, and the new reckoning of that was like flipping a switch in her mind. She lay defeated on the concrete, feeling her wet face and the pain in her hands from pounding the sidewalk.

"Liz," she heard in a whisper. She didn't respond as arms lifted her up and angels pulled her floating away from her pain. She thought she might be dead but then still tasted the salt of her tears. She opened her eyes and saw that it was Josh carrying her away. Squinting through her tears, she looked into his eyes and wondered who this man was. She put her head on his chest but was limp in his arms and her limbs swayed with his steps.

"Thank you," he said to no one, and then Liz felt herself being lowered. Josh laid her out on a wood bench, and Liz covered her face with her sleeve.

She lay there a long time and asked herself over and over, *What do I do now?* She didn't see her son in her thoughts anymore. It was only her and the darkness of her future.

Liz imagined herself in space again, floating above the earth. She was at the end of a string trying to let go, but she couldn't open her hand. Warmth enveloped her, and a tender spirit closed over her hand and stopped Liz from gently slipping away.

When Liz came to, she realized that she was curled up on a hard surface, and she slowly opened her eyes. There was a warm, colorful glow around her, and she wiped the dry crust of tears from her eyes and slowly sat up. She was laying on a wood pew in a church, and the stained-glass windows were coming to life under the guise of the rising sun.

She looked behind her and saw Josh seated with his head bowed low. Liz felt a dry pain in her throat. She had a thirst that a gallon of water couldn't quench. She tried to clear her throat and then she noticed a figure in black walking toward her. Liz looked back at Josh again.

"I asked the pastor for help because I wasn't sure what to do. I didn't know what you were…" Josh's voice trailed off, and Liz remembered pounding the cement on the sidewalk and that she had begged to die outside in the darkness. She looked at her hands and they were soar and scratched but not bloody or broken.

The older man approached and smiled gently at Liz. "Can I help you?"

Liz shook her head slightly, and the priest waited. She stared at the white square of collar below his chin.

"Can I pray for you?" he asked.

Liz rubbed her face and wiped away the tears that were forming. She let the guilt wash over her as she accepted the fact that she would go on in this life without her son. She sighed and croaked, "Can you pray for my son? He died three months ago."

Liz's hands shook as the priest asked, "What is your son's name?"

"Sean. My son's name is Sean."

The priest nodded and then he sat in the pew in front of Liz and turned to face her. He closed his eyes. As his words ran over her, Liz prayed for Sean, too. And when his words stopped, she closed her eyes and her own words ran on in her mind, and she said all the things that she needed God to hear.

God, take my Sean into your heaven. Let him rest in peace, Lord. Forgive me. Forgive me.

They sat in silence for a long time, and then Liz made the sign of the cross and opened her eyes and tried to force a smile at the priest, but her lips wouldn't curl that way.

"What is it?" he asked.

Liz bit her lip and then she croaked, "All I can think of is the pain that Sean must have felt when he died. He was hit by a car. It must have been awful, and I couldn't help him." Again, tears streamed down Liz's face. The priest nodded slowly, and Liz looked at the floor and wiped away her tears on the back of her hand.

"There's no way of knowing if your son suffered. As a mother, you want to take away all your child's pain. His pain is gone now, and it's gone forever."

The words gave Liz some relief. Sean would never feel pain again. And Liz would never feel the touch of his hand or the softness of his cheek as she kissed him goodnight. But that was her pain, not Sean's pain.

"Thank you," Liz whispered before standing up and leaving the church.

She crossed the street and walked back toward downtown

Sycamore and her apartment. Liz walked slowly in the light of day. The one time that she looked back, Josh was twenty steps behind her, walking with his hands in his pockets and his shoulders hung low like a dog that had been kicked and still couldn't help but follow.

CHAPTER 6

*J*osh liked the church. It was quiet and even in the middle of the day no one would disturb you if you were sitting quietly. He had been so deep in thought as he walked through the dark streets that he barely noticed the shadow of Ted Barlow on the bench. When he sensed someone behind him and turned back to look, he was surprised to see the small outline of a woman, and he guessed that it was Liz. No one had been out in Sycamore at this hour for years besides lost college students from DeKalb looking for the next open bar. Josh would have told her to turn back if he'd had any idea of the effect a church would have on her. His heart broke when he heard her talk about her son.

He knew there was something very wrong with Liz when he'd first met her; or not something wrong with her, but something very off in her life. Beautiful women didn't just show up at his gas station and sell him their car for a hundred thirty-eight dollars cash. When Josh saw Liz crying on the sidewalk, her hands scarred and red from pounding the pavement, his suspicions were confirmed. She was broken.

He picked her up, and she was as light as an angel in his arms.

He liked the way she rested her head on his chest and then scolded himself for even considering that as he laid her on the church pew.

Josh liked to go to the church a couple times each month. He always liked the quiet reverence that he felt there. He believed in God. He knew that he did because he asked God for things sometimes. But when Liz spoke of the son she had lost, it cut Josh to the core. For the second time this week, he'd been brought back to the day his dad died.

There was something about loss that seemed to break people. But now it was less about people in general and more about this particular woman. He wanted to help her. He wanted to take away her suffering. He wanted to tell her that everything would be all right, and he wanted her to know it as sure as she knew the sun would rise. There was a whole depth to life that Josh hadn't even known about until he had seen her for the first time. He'd looked into her eyes and looked past her pain and heard a whisper in his heart. He thought it might be love, but he told himself that was impossible. As he watched Liz sleep and looked upon the stained-glass windows of saints past, Josh started to see the cracks in the life he had made. He had the creeping feeling that he, too, might still be broken. It was unsettling.

Josh watched Liz safely back to the apartment, and when she entered the building, he turned and made his way toward the gas station. He walked with his head down and didn't notice Mr. Johnson wave as he picked up the newspaper from his front porch. Josh was shaken.

He'd read in Billy Noodles' notebook that Liz had come by the station and left a half a sandwich on the bench next to Ted while he slept. She was broken but was a kind stranger.

Ted said that she was working at Thompson's and staying in 'the apartment'. Josh was glad that the place was of some use in the world if Ted wasn't going to sleep there.

Josh looked at the Saturn station wagon parked in front of his shop and rubbed his chin. He now felt like he understood how Liz could walk away from this car. It probably reminded her of her son, although he'd only found one small toy superhero under the back seat. He'd looked at it for a long minute before putting the toy back where he'd found it, and he knew it was under the seat in the car still. He wanted to pull it out and turn it around in his fingers to see what secrets it held about Liz's past life, but there was nothing a toy could tell him that her own words hadn't already said.

Josh unlocked the station door and turned the lights on. He sat on the stool behind the counter and tried not to notice stares from the patrons who filled up on gas at the pumps. A couple of townies came in for a random pack of gum. Josh knew them from back in high school, and he knew they came in to see him up close because this morning was an anomaly. Josh was never in the store before the sun was already pretty high in the east.

He nodded and made change for their small purchases, but no one spoke.

Life in this town had been difficult in high school. Josh had watched the others live as they had been taught, but he couldn't bring himself to worry about the clock. He understood time the moment he'd seen his father's lifeless body. There was no such thing as time. We were here, and we were gone. *Dust to dust.*

We were files in a cabinet, and God could pull any drawer open and thumb through the moments, past, present, and future, and time didn't truly exist. But the last five hours were real. He'd picked Liz up like a wounded animal and took her to shelter. He watched her sleep. Not with affection, but like a sentry posted to protect in the night. He knew he was doing the right thing, but he couldn't look at Father Brown the few times he'd stopped in to see if Liz was awake yet.

Candles lit in front of Blessed Mary burned low, and the lights on the altar were dim as to let Liz sleep it off. Josh watched her and felt helpless and ashamed. Was he looking over Liz the way his mom had been looking over him all these years? Like she was waiting for something to happen? Like she was waiting for him to snap out of it?

And that was why he was shaken today. It was Liz's utter grief that had brought him back to the day his father had died. Josh tried to ignore the feelings that came back to him so vividly. He recognized the stabbing pain of emotion. It was the same feeling that had ravaged him before he'd first turned back the hands on the clock. It was a thousand questions all wrapped up in help-lessness.

Billy arrived at the gas station and stood outside the front door for a few minutes. He eventually looked inside, and when he spotted Josh, his round eyes bulged behind his round glasses. He scribbled in his notebook and then pulled the door open.

"I thought you left the lights on by accident," Billy said as he placed his backpack on the floor in the corner and perched his thick body on top of his stool.

Josh was surprised to hear Billy talk because the boy usually preferred to write his thoughts, but Josh ignored it. He was in no mood for conversation, spoked or written. They sat on their stools and stared out the front window. Ted showed up and his tall figure leaned sideways in the window. He cupped his hands and looked in like he couldn't see through the reflection on the glass, but Josh knew he could see inside. Ted was making a point this morning because for the first time in years, Josh was in the store before lunchtime. Ted was saying without saying, "What the hell happened to you?"

Josh was glad that Ted didn't come in and ask him to his face, because he wouldn't know where to begin.

~

LIZ WAS FLOATING in space again, holding on to the string for dear life. She was closer to earth, and she could feel the heat of re-entry burning her skin. Liz loosened her grip and slipped back out into space where the atmosphere couldn't burn her. For the first time, she wanted to go back down to the planet, but she was afraid. She wanted to live among people, but she wasn't quite sure how to do that without burning up in the atmosphere. So, she tied a knot in the rope where she was, and she clung to it for dear life.

WHEN SHE HAD RETURNED from the church two mornings ago, Liz had the presence of mind to leave a note on the front door of Thompson's General Store that she was feeling sick, and she wouldn't be in for a couple of days. She felt bad since she had just started the job, but her body felt as though she'd been on an all-night bender. She dragged herself up the stairs to write the note and then back up the stairs a second time. She laid down on the bed to sleep, and she woke up twenty-four hours later.

It was as though her body was recovering from an illness which the blood in her aching heart had pumped into her cells. Liz lay in bed the second day and listened to the sounds of the small downtown. She heard the swoosh of tires on concrete and heard the occasional voice that drifted up from below. There were three honking horns that day, but they weren't the long angry sounds of New York City drivers. These were the short bursts to alert someone that they had arrived to pick them up, or to get a passerby's attention to wave hello.

Liz thought about the pastor praying for Sean. He's said Sean's name with such care like he was devoted to a boy that he'd never met. And he'd seemed devoted to Liz, too. His prayers gave her hope that her son was okay.

She showered and walked down to Thompson's and peeked her head in, letting them know that she was all right and that she would be there in the morning. Liz was glad that Mr. Thompson was manning the register, and his easy smile and good wishes put her at ease.

She arrived at work the next morning with little fanfare to her absence, and Liz was glad to be back behind the register. She felt clean in a way. It was as if her soul had been showered clean. She wasn't over Sean's death, and she never would be, but she could see tomorrow clearly now. She was alive, and she breathed in deep gulps of clean Midwest air. She couldn't remember ever doing that in New York City because of the constant car traffic and random smells of cooked food mixed in with trash.

Sam was back that morning, and Liz watched him waddle back and forth in front of the store until Mr. Thompson finally went out to discuss labor disputes. The two men talked for less than a minute, and then Sam picked up his sign and was gone. Business went back to normal after that, and Liz found herself in a pattern of working, walking, and sleep. She ate some canned and boxed food, but just enough to sustain her daily regimen. Some days on her lunch break, she would buy a sandwich and walk the few blocks to the gas station. She would see that her dad's car was still there, still with no "For Sale" sign in the window. She would stop at Ted Barlow's bench and watch him sound asleep. She would sit in silence sometimes, or she would tell Ted stories about her life, and she would leave him half of the sandwich for when he woke up.

Weeks passed as Liz watched the small town come to life each morning from her window above the storefront. She slept fitfully and somehow made it in to work each day that she was scheduled. When she wasn't scheduled, Liz usually spent the day in bed in a fog of memories. She liked the fog because it kept her company. There was a gray haze protecting her from the rest of the world. She had thought that the expression "misery loves company" meant that a miserable person loved to drag down someone else so they could be miserable together. Liz now understood the true meaning. Misery was a living being, a black shadow seated at the foot of the bed or sometimes over in the corner chair. Misery loved Liz, and she bathed in its power. It started with a thought tightening her throat and it gave way to roiling in her stomach and a stabbing pain in her chest. Misery held the sharp pain on her and kept the haze around her mind to protect her. Somehow misery was alive, and it was keeping Sean alive too. Misery loved Liz, and misery loved her company.

Some days there was no haze, and Liz felt guilty about wanting to live again, but slowly, she did anyway. She wondered about Josh who lived in the same town but lived a unique life. She wondered how he could exist on his nocturnal schedule, and how he had come to know Ted Barlow and Billy Noodles. It was a very small town, a place where she assumed everyone knew everyone else, but she wondered how these three strange friends had come together.

About a month after she arrived, a large, pale woman came in the store and made a loud huff. She looked at Liz and waited to see if anyone else had heard her, and when nothing happened, she opened the door and let it close so that the bell would ring again. She waited, staring at Liz who stared back. Then the woman came to the counter, and Liz could tell that she was going to have a problem.

The woman's cheeks were puffy, and her chin seemed to point at Liz in conviction. "Move," the woman told Liz.

Liz's pulse quickened and her cheeks flushed. She froze.

The woman leaned her bulk forward and put her hands on the counter, eyeballing Liz for another go. "I said move."

Liz was lean most years, but this year with less eating and no physical activity, her frame was practically waif. Still, she wouldn't move for anyone. The woman didn't project 'thug' to Liz. She smelled nice, and her short curly hair was round and shiny like her face. Liz could see deep lines setting in on her forehead and around the eyes, and Liz guessed she was about sixty years old.

"Can I help you find something?" Liz barked in her thick New York accent. She crossed her arms and leaned back on the divider behind her like she had all day.

"You can help me by moving out of my way. That's my job you're doing there. Your help is no longer needed."

So, Liz thought. This was the sister-in-law that Mr. Thompson had told her about. She was charming. Liz tutted and rolled her eyes, ready for the confrontation. The city girl in her was born for battle.

Liz smiled. "Say please," she purred, and the woman's eyes opened wide. She pushed her knuckles off the counter and took a step back, and Liz readied herself to slide sideways if the woman decided to lunge across the counter. There were a tense few seconds and then Dotty appeared.

"Becky, what are you doing?" Dotty grabbed her sister's arm, and Liz could see the resemblance only when they stood side by side. They both had a pointed chin, and their brown eyes were very light and in the same rounded shape, but the sister was a full head taller than Dotty and their personalities were worlds apart.

"I'm here to work, Dotty. Tell her to go home."

"Sorry, Liz," Dotty said over her shoulder as she tried to pull her sister's bulk toward the door.

"Becky, how could you?" Dotty rasped in a scathing whisper. "You're embarrassing me."

"Come on, Dotty," her sister pleaded.

"You had your chance. You had three chances and it's been over a month already. Now go home and leave this poor girl alone. I'll give you a reference if you find another job."

"Wait," Becky said, her tone appeasing. "Just wait a second." They stopped near the front door, and Dotty took her hand off Becky's arm. Liz watched the sisters and wondered what it was like to have a sibling. She had friends who were close to their brothers and sisters and others who never spoke. Liz wondered what kind this family would turn out to be.

"You can't keep doing this, Becky," Dotty begged.

"I know." Becky's face softened. "I'm sorry, Polka-Dot."

The sisters nodded at each other, and then Becky grabbed three boxes of packaged cupcakes and walked out of the store. Liz could hear Dotty sigh. She walked past Liz with an embarrassed shrug, shaking her head before retreating to the back of the store. Liz was glad that Becky and Sam had been the most exciting things to happen this month. She'd had stranger days as a teenager working at the local movie theatre.

A couple of mornings each week, Mr. Thompson gave Liz a list of products to pull and box up with a receipt. The writing on the paper was neat, and there was something particular about the way each word was printed separately yet evenly with the one before. The letters were written as if from a typewriter, all the e's looking the same, all of the t's crossed in exactly the same place and manner. Liz wondered what hand could have given so much care to a basic shopping list which was typically something that was scratched onto the back of an old envelope or ripped from a notepad.

The box would be left on the floor next to the register, and the next morning it would be gone, and the exact amount owed would be left on the counter with the receipt. A couple of times, Mr. Thompson had Liz make change and put it in an envelope to leave on the counter. She was curious about the box but didn't ask the Thompsons about it. Then one day, she saw Mr. Thompson write "Josh" on the envelope and drop it in the box of goods.

When Liz saw the name on the envelope, she knew that it was her Josh from the gas station and the movie theatre and the church. The Josh who had bought her father's car but hadn't paid her in full yet. That transaction was currently in limbo. The car was still at the gas station, and neither she nor Josh had bothered to broach the subject.

"What's wrong with him?" Liz asked Mr. Thompson.

"With whom?" Mr. Thompson said, looking around the store.

"What's wrong with Josh?" Liz didn't know why she had asked, and she didn't want to explain herself, so she quickly added, "Never mind."

"Oh, that's okay, Liz. Josh is a friend, and I've known him since he was a baby. I was good friends with his father before he passed away." Mr. Thompson looked at the floor. "God rest his soul," he added, and Liz could see that the men had been very close.

"I don't mean to pry."

"No, it's all right. It's just that, when he was young, if I remember right, Josh was somewhere in middle school, his father died. Josh was never the same after that."

It wasn't an explanation, but it was all Liz needed to hear. Being the survivor changed so many people, and she was no exception.

"Josh leaves a list, and I pull it together and he swings by to pick it up. I also have Sam get some supplies for the gas station that Josh picks up here, too."

"He does?" Liz asked. She'd hadn't seen Josh in Thompson's store since she'd started here, but the box next to her register had been filled and emptied several times.

"He comes around when he has time."

Liz remembered the loud jingle of keys when Josh had unlocked the movie theatre in the middle of the night, and she guessed that he also had keys to Thompson's store. She was lost in thought when she noticed Mr. Thompson looking her way.

"I didn't mean to pry."

"It was a long time ago, Liz. Some people you just never forget. You know?"

She knew all too well. Liz nodded and tried to smile, but she felt a frown pull at the corner of her mouth and she shook her head to try to shake loose the impending thoughts of her loss.

Dotty came in the front door. "I'm back. You can go to lunch now if you want."

Liz was glad for the distraction. She took off her apron and put it under the counter.

Dotty smiled at Liz, and Liz tried to smile back, but in the month since Liz had been hired on, Dotty had met Liz's gaze only a handful of times. Liz had heard Mr. Thompson chiding his wife about being nice to the new employee, but Liz assumed that Dotty still had her feathers ruffled about replacing her sister as the cashier. The confrontation with Becky must have eased Dotty's mind because she was looking straight at Liz with a gentle smile.

"Okay, thank you," Liz replied even though it was early.

Liz decided it was too early to eat, so she walked the few blocks to the gas station to look at her car. It was still there, parked in front of the single bay door, shined up and ready to hit the road. Liz wasn't though. She had no more road left in her. Besides, her curiosity in the inhabitants of this small town had kept her from curling up into a ball and dying.

She walked over to Ted Barlow who was in his spot on the bench by the payphone. He was awake today, and Liz speculated that perhaps Ted was awake in the morning and then took a noon siesta, because usually when she came by on her lunch break, he was sound asleep.

"Hi." Liz nodded at the payphone. "How's business?"

"It's slow today." Ted scooted to one side so Liz could sit down.

They sat in silence, and every few minutes a car would drive by. Liz looked across the street and studied the buildings. This was the edge of the downtown area, and to her right she could see a large metal circular tower. She wondered if it was some sort of granary for the surrounding farmland, but she really had no clue when it came to farming.

She scanned the few small buildings to her left, just before the small river. There was a liquor store, but this one was different than most. It was a long rectangular building with a drive thru, and Liz couldn't ever remember seeing a drive-thru liquor store in her entire life.

"You've been the one leaving me the sandwiches then," Ted stated. Liz looked over at him, but she neither confirmed nor denied. "Thanks." Ted sighed, and then his somber mood turned festive. "So, let's talk about you! From the big city to the small town." He waved his arms up and down the street. "Must be quite a change."

Liz agreed. "It is. I think this is the smallest town that I've ever been in."

"Oh, it's not that small," Ted disagreed. "We have over fifteen thousand people now, and there are some subdivisions being built outside town. We're booming!" Ted was up off the bench and pacing. He walked to the payphone and put his finger in the change return slot, but he came up empty.

"Booming," Liz repeated, and although the town was growing on her, it was extremely slow paced. It probably wasn't even on many maps.

"Sure, it's not New York City, but we have our gems here."

Liz knew in her heart that Ted Barlow was one of those gems, but she didn't say it out loud. She turned her head back to the gas station and noticed Billy Noodles watching and taking notes on his notepad. She wondered what he was writing and decided that it probably didn't matter. She let out a long breath and wondered what life was all about. *Are we just like the rodents, left here to scurry about for food and shelter until we die?* she thought.

Ted paced in front of the bench, and just when Liz thought he would continue his small-town pitch, he noticed a car rolling slowly down the street. He watched it coming closer and then quickly sat back down on the bench like a boy who knew that he was about to be scolded.

Liz looked at Ted who was trying to keep calm. She couldn't

tell if he was embarrassed or angry. She turned away to look at the car. It was a collector's car, a fast-looking muscle car, and probably from the sixties. The exhaust panted out its low rumble, and Liz thought this might be the same car she had seen in the middle of the night when she'd first arrived in town. This might be the same person who had covered the vagabond with a blanket on State Street the night she had ended up at the movies with Josh.

The green car idled by, and Liz locked eyes with the beautiful blonde woman who was driving. She eyed Liz and Ted on the bench.

Liz looked at Ted for a reaction. "She's pretty."

"Yes," Ted croaked.

"You have an admirer."

Ted nodded as the car sped up the street and moved on. "You have an admirer."

"I don't know her," Liz said.

"I'm talking about Josh. He's been here the last couple of weeks by eight in the morning. He hasn't been here that early in the last ten years."

Liz felt her chest swell with nerves, or maybe it was the start of a tender curiosity. She turned toward the gas station, and Billy Noodles was still in the front window. When he noticed her noticing him, he quickly moved away.

Ted saw Liz looking at the station. "He's out back working on a truck."

"I don't own a truck, so I must not be the reason he's been at work early." Liz was trying to sound aloof, but curiosity burned pink on her face. She looked up the street so Ted wouldn't see.

"I know it. I think he's just trying to go through parts, so he has an excuse to go to Thompson's."

"That's a stretch, Ted. I've never seen Josh in the store." Liz stood. "I've got to get back to work."

"I'll walk you," Ted said. He stood up and although she wasn't short for a woman, he towered over her.

"How tall are you?"

Ted smiled. "Tall enough that I don't hardly ever have to stand on my tippy-toes."

Liz assumed that he was drunk, but he moved quicker than she thought he would, and she had to skip a little to keep up. She realized that she had formed a conclusion that Ted was always drunk because the morning she'd met him he'd been drinking from a bottle in a paper bag; and these last few weeks as she left sandwiches, he was always napping on the bench.

"Wait. What time is it?" Ted stopped walking.

"It's still early. Around ten-thirty, I think," Liz answered.

"Go ahead then. I'll walk you back next time. I'm waiting for a phone call."

Liz grinned and walked away. When she got to the corner of State and Main, she turned right and saw the green, muscle car a block up, parked across the street from her apartment. Liz watched as the blonde woman took the blankets from the bench and dropped them in the trunk, slowly backing out of the angled parking spot and driving away.

CHAPTER 7

From inside the gas station, Josh inched his head to the left enough to peek out at Liz and Ted. He wanted to join them out on the bench, but he hesitated. He crossed one arm over his stomach to prop up his elbow as the other hand slowly rubbed his chin. He shared a look with Billy who scooted off his stool and went to stand in full view in the window where he scribbled on his notepad as they both ogled the pair on the bench.

Liz stood and talked. She sat. Ted rose and paced back and forth. Then they sat together. Josh was curious as to what they might have to talk about, and when Liz turned back to look at the building, he wondered if they were talking about him. His face burned pink at the thought, and Josh was glad that Billy wasn't looking at him close enough to make a note of it.

Deep down, Josh hoped they were talking about him. He was a little jealous that Liz visited with Ted, and he wondered if she liked Ted as more than a friend. Josh was trying to convince himself that it was a ridiculous notion when he heard the rumble of a classic car from up the street.

Billy eyes were wide as he showed Josh his notepad and then

rushed back to his seat in the corner. All the tiny writing was perfectly in line except the last two words which had been scribbled in haste as Billy scrambled to safety. *She's here*, it read.

Josh watched the green car pass by slowly like a land shark. He knew it had been a long time since he was in the gas station regularly in the morning, but he could hardly believe that she still drove by to see Ted on the bench outside. Could she still be coming there every week? Ted had been back from Afghanistan for two years.

Liz and Ted's heads turned and followed the car, and then they were up and walking down the street together. Josh ignored his pang of jealousy.

Do you think they are going to have lunch together? Billy's notepad read, and Josh shoved it out of the way.

"No," he said a bit too begrudgingly.

Aren't you curious about what they are saying?

"No." Again, Josh pushed the pad out of the way.

Josh was irritated with Billy, and he was regretting coming in so early each day. Billy was usually helpful, but when it came to Liz, he'd become a bit obsessed. Billy was constantly writing to Josh when Liz came around, and it was getting harder for Josh to brush off Billy's sentiments.

I'm very curious, Billy's notepad read.

"Well, I'm not," Josh lied. He walked to the large window and looked down the street, and he was relieved to see that Ted was already back and waiting at the payphone. "See, Ted's right there," Josh pointed. Billy jumped up and looked out the window and wrote something in his notebook. Josh could see that Billy was almost as relieved as he was.

"I'm going outside to work. Hold down the fort, will you?" Josh looked at Ted and saw that he was talking on the phone now. Josh shook his head. Ted's social life was busier than Josh's any day of the week. Josh wondered if he had the courage to change that. He went outside and looked at Liz's car. Maybe he'd move it to the back of the lot so she would have to come around back to look at it, or maybe he would have to start working on cars inside the garage.

A pain poked at his chest, and Josh knew that he still wasn't ready to work in the garage. He'd gone in there to swap out tools, but he still couldn't bring himself to pull a car inside. His uncle had words with Josh about that every year, but it still didn't feel right to Josh. The memories of his childhood lived in that garage. Memories with his dad. Memories that Josh wasn't ready to touch.

Josh took a deep breath and went out the front door. He saw Billy jump off his stool to watch. Josh went to the garage door and looked in through the rectangular window. It was his dad's shop, and his uncle had used it but had left it mostly unchanged. All these years, Josh had chosen to brave the elements and work out behind the station instead of facing the memories of his childhood inside. He considered opening the big door and working in the shop. If he did, Liz would see him when she came by to look at her car.

Josh swallowed the ball of guilt down. Either way, he needed to make a move. Liz always stopped to look at the car when she came by. Josh had read that in Billy's notebook.

LIZ WOKE up when she heard singing. It was dark in the apartment, and it took her a minute to remember that she was in Sycamore, Illinois. She had laid down in bed to go to sleep the minute she returned from her shift at Thompson's store.

She heard the voice again. It was a man in the street, and although she couldn't decipher the words, the melody was unmistakable. He was singing "Happy Birthday" at the top of his lungs.

Liz moved to the window and looked out. She could tell by

the few cars parked in spaces that it was very late. Across the street, a tall figure swayed toward the bench. She could see his arms raised as though he was on stage in front of a large crowd. It was Ted Barlow belting the slurred words to the timeless song.

Liz pulled on the jogging pants that she had bought at the Salvation Army store and although it was June, she slipped on her dad's green army coat in case the night was chilly. She stopped in the bathroom and ran a brush through her straight, brown hair that had grown to her shoulders. Then she looked deeply into the reflection of her brown eyes - the windows she had been avoiding for months. She had carefully brushed her hair, and she reckoned that it must mean something about her future. Then she smiled pathetically and went outside.

Liz looked up and down the block, but there wasn't anyone else in sight. She could see some cars around the corner that were starting up, and she reasoned that the bar at the Veterans Club was closing for the night. She crossed the street and didn't think that Ted had noticed her, but she heard him say something out loud.

"Hi, Ted. What did you say?" Liz said as she stepped up on the curb. Ted turned slowly around and smiled wide.

"Hello, Elizabeth," he said very officially, and Liz shuddered to hear her mother's tone in Ted's voice.

"What are you doing?" Liz pulled the coat closed but didn't zip it. The weather here was very nice during the day, but at night the temperature still dropped, and it was a bit chilly.

"I was having a drink!" he announced. "I have a drink at the club every night." Ted was swaying as he talked.

"You look like you had all the drinks," Liz said and smiled, and Ted laughed.

"I had all the drinks!" he called to the empty street. Liz looked around, worried that someone would open a window and yell for them to shut the hell up, but they weren't in New York City, and there was no one to be angry at them on this little street.

"I thought you were saying something to me," Liz said quietly, hoping Ted would follow suit.

"Awe, never mind. I was just talking to myself. I do that a lot these days. I guess maybe I think I'm the only one worth talking to." Ted threw his head back and let out a huge guttural laugh.

Liz thought about going back inside because Ted seemed a little insane tonight, but something kept her there talking to him. She thought it might be his loneliness that made her stay. Or perhaps it was her loneliness.

"You had a birthday party?" Liz asked. She took a step back as Ted took a hesitant step forward. She was worried that he would fall on his face if he didn't sit down, but he lingered between the bench and the storefront. Liz saw the neatly folded blanket on the bench, and she remembered the blonde woman taking the rest in her trunk. She realized that she had assumed correctly, and this was Ted's bench, and the blankets were for him. Liz wondered who the blonde woman was to Ted.

"It wasn't a party," he slurred. "I was singing 'Happy Birthday' to Gus, but he doesn't get any more birthdays." Liz nodded and thought of her son, but she didn't say anything because she didn't want to talk about herself tonight.

"Why not?"

Ted walked away from Liz, and she watched him stagger to the end of the block.

"Get your popcorn here!" Ted yelled, and then he staggered sideways into the light pole which kept him from falling into the street. Liz strode quickly toward Ted, but she didn't get too close for fear that his towering frame would collapse like an old building, and she would be trapped under the rubble.

"Are you hungry?" Liz asked. Ted pointed to her right, and for the first time, Liz noticed a small red popcorn stand. It was a tiny red shack with a 'Popcorn' sign on top, and Liz couldn't believe that she hadn't noticed it before.

Ted was almost incoherent. "It used to have wheels, back in

the 1800's. It used to go places. But since the 1920's, it's been sitting here with no wheels. It doesn't get to go anywhere anymore. Gus doesn't get to go anywhere anymore either."

Ted pushed off the streetlight and staggered back to the bench. He circled it but somehow remained standing, and Liz remained steps away on the curb and tried again.

"Why not?"

"Gus died in Afghanistan!" Ted said boisterously, and once he realized what they were talking about, his bright face turned sour, and he teetered sideways and plopped onto the bench. "Gus died in Afghanistan," he said again reverently, and then he hit himself on the top of his head with both fists. Liz stepped forward to stop him and then realized that he was a very strong man and there was probably no way that she could physically stop him from doing anything.

"I'm so sorry," Liz said. She waited a minute to make sure Ted wasn't going to be swinging his fists again, and she sat down next to him.

"He was your friend?" Liz asked. She looked over at Ted and could see in the streetlight the tears that were starting down his face. She nodded as though she already understood. She imagined Ted above the earth, out in space, holding on to his own string, wondering if he should let go.

"He was my friend," Ted replied. "Only he's dead now, and he won't get any more birthdays."

"Were you in Afghanistan with Gus?"

Ted bit his lip like he was making a difficult decision. Then he jumped from the bench, and Liz watched him sing 'Happy Birthday' to Gus again at the top of his lungs. When Ted was done, he tried to smile at Liz, but the spell of the alcohol was broken, and he was left with his reality.

"Gus was my friend here in Sycamore, and we were in Afghanistan together. We were there twice. The first time it was for almost a year, and we were lucky. The second time it was for nine months, and only I was lucky." Ted walked over to the store window behind the bench and seemed to be looking at himself in the reflection.

Liz watched Ted floating above the earth, holding on to his string, but she didn't ask any more questions. Back home, she had been so tired of people asking her questions. For a while it was direct questions about Sean, and then no one talked about him again, like they didn't want to bring it up. As though they would be reminding her, like she'd forgotten about him. As though that would even be possible. There was no reminding her because her son was all she ever thought about. The only one who talked about Sean anymore was Liz's mom, but she went overboard, and it was too much.

Liz grasped that it wasn't the fact that her mom talked about Sean that bothered her. It was that her mom wanted Liz to get past her life with Sean that made Liz feel so alone. Liz wouldn't offer Ted any words of encouragement or reflection. She couldn't fathom the thought of her son's birthday. She would just sit on this bench and wait in case Ted needed to talk to someone.

Ted came back to the bench and sat down at the other end. Liz could hear him mumbling to himself, but she couldn't make out the words, so she just sat and waited.

"You know, Liz, the lady on the phone has been listening to me, and she thinks I need to get it together," he slurred.

"Maybe she needs to get it together," Liz said, because again she could hear her mother in his words.

"Ha!" Ted called into the night. He slid his torso down so his head could easily rest on his hand. "Maybe she's right. Maybe I need to get it together. Gus would have gotten it together."

"You don't know that," Liz whispered. Liz wanted to tell Ted that he didn't know what Gus would have done if their fates were reversed, but she sat in silence and listened to Ted mumble himself to sleep. When Liz heard snoring, she opened the blanket and gently placed it over Ted's inert figure.

~

Liz gently placed the blanket on Ted and watched him sleep before sitting down on the bench. She noticed again that for all his vagabond-like moments of sleeping on benches in this town, Ted's hair was neatly trimmed, and his face was shaven every few days. She felt hope for him in that. She had brushed her hair very deliberately before leaving her apartment tonight, and in that she felt hope for both of them.

"That was nice of you." A man's voice startled Liz and she jerked her head around. Josh was standing ten feet away under the streetlight. His hands were in the pockets of his blue jeans, and his light vest was zipped up over his short-sleeved t-shirt.

"Um," Liz countered dumbly. She stood up quickly as though he had caught her at something. Liz didn't have the energy to try to be cordial. She used all that energy up at work during the day. "It's late."

Josh nodded. "I came to check on Ted. It's Gus' birthday, and he doesn't always settle down. You seem to have a way with him."

Liz nodded slowly, unsure of what Josh was implying. "Okay," she replied. They stood in silence for a minute and Josh turned to walk away.

"Hey, Josh." She waited for him to turn back. "Why did you take me to that church?"

Josh looked across the street and then at Ted's limp figure. "I didn't take you to the church. You followed me."

Liz nodded. "But you knew I was following, and you led me there."

Ted started to snore again, and they both watched his lanky, limp figure poured out on the bench.

Josh met Liz's eye. "I like to go there and think. I guess when you followed me, I thought you might need somewhere to think, too."

"Do you take Ted there?"

Josh nodded. "He shows up on occasion," Josh admitted. "But there's no way I could carry him inside if I had to."

Liz bit her lip, embarrassed that she'd broken down in front of him. "Why did you think that I needed help?"

Josh shrugged, but Liz tipped her head sideways and looked at him with pressing eyes.

"Well, you showed up out of nowhere, and you left your car at the gas station and gave me the keys. You didn't even really know who I was. Don't you think that's even a little strange?"

Liz looked away. She could see his point.

"I was going to take Ted to the movies tonight to distract him," Josh said to the ground. Liz watched Josh rub his chin. Then he caught Liz's eye and nodded his head in the direction of the theatre. He pushed his hands deeper into his pockets and started walking away.

Liz watched him go for a few seconds and then followed. She didn't try to catch up to him, never quite walking at his side. They looked like two desert travelers in a sandstorm who might have tied a rope to each other, walking single file with their heads to the ground so as not to get lost in the blinding sand.

Josh pulled out his massive key ring and let Liz inside the lobby. Liz waited as he prepared the popcorn and drinks. He was a natural behind the counter, and she wondered if he had been coming here by himself for his whole adult life. She looked around the small lobby and wondered about the workers who had built this theatre so many years ago. She strolled along the rectangular glass candy counter and pointed to the smaller popcorn and smaller drink sizes when Josh asked. Josh handed over her popcorn and drink, and she took her snack down the aisle toward the front of the theatre and sat in the same area as she had last time. When the trailers started, she noticed Josh slip into a seat across the aisle from her. She wondered if her scene in front of the church had scared him away, but then she decided that if it had, he probably wouldn't have invited her along tonight.

A month of time had worked its wonders, and Liz took a deep breath and lost herself in the movie. It was a comedy with a huge group of characters, and she enjoyed herself. The dramas that were played out before her seemed so trite compared to real life these days, but she accepted them at face value. It was halfway through the film during a quiet scene when Liz heard crunching and looked over at Josh. Maybe it should have, but it didn't seem strange to her at all that they were here together and alone in the theatre late into the night.

She let herself look at his face turned up in the light of the screen, and she remembered the handwritten shopping list which she had found on the counter at work. She wondered again if this was how he lived, at night, no one in the world to notice him. Liz imagined a similar list on the counter at the theatre perfectly marking the letters for two tickets, two popcorns, and two sodas with the exact change perched on top. It was insane and endearing, and she felt herself getting caught up in this way of life.

Josh seemed like an actual nice guy, and although his lifestyle was extremely strange, he did care about Ted Barlow and that showed some character. Liz didn't know many men who cared much about other men. Everyone where she was from seemed to be trying to get ahead and it didn't seem to matter who they had to trample over to reach the top. Liz wasn't sure what the top was anymore.

The film was over too fast and as soon as the credits rolled, the theatre lights came on. Liz looked over expecting to see Josh, but he was gone. She waited a few minutes and then picked up her trash and walked up to the lobby. Josh appeared behind her from a small hidden door that was cut from the façade, and Liz realized that was the access to theatre lights and the projection booth. Josh reached out his hand to take the bucket of trash from her hands.

"Can I ask you something?" Liz said softly.

"Okay," Josh said and then turned to walk toward the lobby.

"What's with Billy Noodles? Is that even his real name?"

"Billy is a friend," Josh said, and Liz waited for an explanation. "It's a nickname from middle school. Something happened with a project involving noodles and the name stuck." Josh rubbed his chin. "You can see that he's awkward, so he was always picked on, but he's harmless. He just watches the world and writes down what he sees. It's his coping method or something like that."

"What exactly does he write down?"

Josh thought for a moment. "Well, when he eats a cookie, he writes down 'I ate one Oreo cookie' or whatever kind of cookie it is."

"Really? So, he's just there writing down a play by play of life?"

"Something like that."

"I don't believe you." Liz was smiling and waiting for the joke to be over, but Josh didn't return the smile.

"Sometimes things are really that simple, Liz. If you looked at his notepad from several weeks ago, you would see that he wrote 'Pretty lady yelled at Josh. Josh bought her car for $138.94. Not a good bargain.' You really got to Billy because he's usually a fact guy and he doesn't typically narrate. But he does now. He likes to narrate about you and Ted when you sit on the bench together. It's his new favorite hobby."

"Well, that might be a bit creepy."

Josh chuckled and Liz watched his smile. It was a wondrous and rare thing, and she shook her head to concentrate on the conversation instead of his face.

"It's not like that, Liz. He's observing, but he's harmless. It's actually nice to see. It's like, you are his therapy."

"Wow, you attract all kinds of broken, don't you?"

Josh smiled at that. "I guess I do. But I only fix cars."

"Well, you've helped me," Liz said before turning to leave. "Thanks for the movie."

"Thank you," Josh whispered.

Liz stepped out of the theatre and noticed that the sky was beginning to lighten. She walked up two blocks to her apartment and looked back at the theatre. Josh was standing on the curb watching her, making sure she got home safely. When she opened the outside door, she turned and waved, and he stepped back into the theatre building.

Liz didn't climb the stairs right away. She turned around to look at the bench across the street, but Ted was gone. She wondered about that bench and how many lives had sat on it. She was there on the bench when she had found her job, and that was the bench Josh had found her on tonight. The bench didn't move. It selected objects to catch and allowed the wind to pass unchanged through the green slats. The bench was silent, and like time, it kept the best secrets. Liz thought about the thread that held her as she floated in outer space. The thin thread became a sturdy rope, and in her mind, she tethered it to the bench.

JOSH WATCHED Liz return to her apartment building before closing down the theatre. He shut down the computer that housed the downloaded movies and shut down the projector. He cleaned the popcorn machine and made sure everything was in its place before writing a note for the items purchased and leaving money on the counter. He turned off the lights and locked the front door, taking a moment to look up and down the quiet street.

His car was at the gas station, so he crossed the street and walked by Liz's apartment. The light in her window was off, and he stopped to look up the dark staircase before quickly moving along. Josh liked Liz, but he didn't want her to think that he was some creep lurking around at night. He'd been called that before.

In his mid-twenties, Josh had been interested in several girls, but they had each gone their own way after telling Josh that he had no idea how to be a boyfriend. And the couple of relationships he'd had ended badly after he was told that he was unreliable, and his lifestyle was insane. But Josh liked his lifestyle. He ran a business, he had some friends, and he helped take care of his mom. Yes, he was mostly around town after others had gone home for the night, but this had become Josh's pattern in life, and he didn't mind it.

At the gas station, he walked to the back where the shed had been installed over a year ago. He used to leave the back of the shop unlocked in case Ted needed somewhere to stay, but he had learned the hard way that you can't leave your business unlocked next to a college town and across the street from a drive thru liquor store.

Josh slowly pulled the shed door open so it wouldn't creek. He'd learned not to shine a light in to see if Ted was there. He'd learned that the hard way, too. Once, Ted had jumped up and almost strangled Josh while in the throes of his nightmares. Now, Josh simply closed his eyes and listened until he could hear Ted's slow breathing and smell the liquor. He hoped that Ted had pulled the blanket on, but the onset of summer was warming up the small shed during the day, and Ted would stay warm enough as he slept it off.

Josh was grateful to hear Ted's slow breathing. This man had served three tours in the Middle East and seen things that Josh couldn't even imagine. Josh had watched many documentaries on war, and for all the footage that he had seen, he was certain he would never understand.

Ted's shed had some holes in it where the wood was splintered like a caged animal had been trying to punch its way out. There was one small window that had also been taped up after a sleepless night last winter. Josh listened to Ted sleep, and he was glad that there weren't any new holes in the shed. Perhaps after two years of sitting on the bench and watching the world go by, Ted was finding peace with the things he had lived through.

And this man who had served his country so faithfully was sleeping it off in a shed behind a gas station. But Josh was grateful for that too. There was a time after Ted had returned when he had told Josh that he wanted to "quit life".

That's the way Ted had said it. "I'm ready to quit this place."

"You're leaving Sycamore?" Josh asked innocently. And then Ted had given Josh a long straight stare that had chilled Josh's heart.

"I'm ready to quit life."

And Josh had stared back at Ted and wondered just what he should say to that. He opened his mouth, but no words came out. And then Ted turned to go.

"But I won't quit life, Josh, so don't you go calling anyone. It's a sin to take your own life, you know."

The matter-of-fact way Ted had said that let Josh know that many hours had been spent in contemplation on the subject. As much as he had thought about it, Ted wasn't planning to take his own life. Josh closed the shed and walked out front to his truck. The ride home was a short ten minutes.

Josh liked living in farm country. He didn't farm, but he'd lived in the same house his entire life. That was, aside from the six months that his uncle had made him move out to try to get a life. Whatever that meant. Josh knew that his uncle meant well, and he said a prayer for the old man as he turned into the drive. He closed the door on his old pickup truck as quietly as he could, but it was a heavy door and he still made noise trying to click it closed all the way.

The house was dark but for the light in the front window. His mom turned on the front room lamp in the falling darkness of the evening, and Josh turned it off when he was headed to bed. It was an unspoken signal they had worked out in his teenage years, after his dad had died and Josh had grown into a young man with a driver's license. Josh would leave the house when he wanted - when it was time to go do something and no matter the time of day. There was no time like the present, and so the time of day didn't really exist to Josh.

Josh always used the back door so as not to remember, but his avoidance of the front porch made him remember anyway. The way the spring on the screen door creaked when it was opened. The guilt rose, and he shook it off. He should have listened to his father. He should have stayed and maybe he would have been able to do something. Maybe his dad would be alive today. Or maybe he would have gotten the goodbye that a young boy might have needed instead of running off to hang out with his friends.

Josh rubbed his forehead and then ran his hand down to his chin. He didn't know why things turned out the way they did. He thought of Ted Barlow, a decorated war hero, sleeping in a shed behind a gas station. He thought about Liz losing her young son. Nothing really made sense in this world, so Josh turned off the light in the front room so his mom would know that he'd come home, and he went to bed.

CHAPTER 8

*L*iz pulled a sweatshirt over her t-shirt and left her apartment for the first time in two days. Her hair was neither washed nor brushed, but it was after midnight in a small town, and she didn't care if anyone saw her. The Thompsons had given her three days off in a row, and Liz hardly knew what to do with herself. She was feeling better than she had in almost five months. She could think about Sean without curling up into a ball and checking out from the world. Still, she felt an exhausting fog wrapped around her mind, so she'd spent the last two days sleeping.

It had turned out for Liz that there wasn't much to do in a small town. She didn't mind though. She couldn't imagine her old self liking this place. Time passed so slowly that Liz noticed each second going by in her mind. Her life before had been about doing the chores of day-to-day living; working, running errands, and getting each day over with, ticking off the to-do list. She'd wasted so much time in the hustle and bustle that could have been spent with Sean. She had a new perspective on life, and Liz liked noticing the minutes tick by here.

In the dark of night, Liz walked up Main Street away from the gas station and turned left after five blocks, touring a part of town she hadn't seen. There were blocks and blocks of houses, a little suburbia full of families and schools and the occasional church. It was everything good about the world. The moon was no help on this night, but Liz's eyes were adjusted to the dark, and she could see from the reflection of porch lights the tiny bicycles and swing sets spattered throughout the neighborhood. All the windows were dark as the residents of Sycamore slept, and Liz bet that a lot of the doors were probably unlocked.

The schoolyards were free of litter and the basketball hoops all had nets attached, and Liz couldn't believe how she had grown so accustomed to New York City. She had made it a habit not to notice the trash and it wasn't filthy where she lived, but here in this pristine town, she couldn't help but notice the absence of it. These houses didn't have an attitude or an angle on anything. They seemed to sit on the grass and say, "Come on in and live here. Everything is perfect."

Liz wandered aimlessly but never felt lost, which was one benefit of not caring. After an hour of walking up and down the blocks of streets, Liz made her way back to State Street where her current world was located. She was about to cross the street to her apartment when she noticed the shadow of someone sitting on the park bench. It was her park bench, the one that she had tethered her life to. She thought it might be Ted sitting there, but he was usually upright or flat asleep, and this person didn't have Ted's stature. Liz stopped in her tracks. Although she had been thinking about the people in this town as she walked among their homes, she had forgotten that they really did exist. This figure in the dark frightened her human senses.

She moved closer and tried to recognize the silhouette and what it was doing. She was three store fronts away when she realized that the figure on the bench was looking up toward her apartment. She wondered if they could see anything from the street and then remembered that she wasn't home. Still, she thought that she should feel mad or violated for someone looking at her darkened window. But she couldn't find the place within her anymore that lent to indignant anger or rage, and so she let it go.

Liz stepped into the deserted street and walked the last two storefronts. She approached the park bench startling its patron. She was dismayed to see in the yellow glow of the streetlight that it was Josh. They stared at each other for a moment as if figuring out what species of animal that they were facing and if they were friend or prey. Then Josh became embarrassed and looked at the ground before standing up and taking off his baseball cap.

"Hi," Josh said.

"Hi."

The minimal light from the store behind him kept Josh's face in shadow, and Liz couldn't read his expression. They both stood in silence, and Liz didn't know what to say. If he was out here looking at her apartment, then he was out here to keep an eye on her. Liz wondered if she was supposed to feel alarm, but all she really felt was contented.

"So," Josh said as he kicked the pavement lightly with the bottom of his boot. His hands were in his jean's pockets as he looked anywhere but at Liz.

"So," Liz concluded. At any other time in her life, when a man wanted to talk to her, Liz might have rambled on, taking the upper hand in the conversation. But she had changed, and life was different here. She had all the time in the world.

"We've got to stop meeting like this," Liz said to fill the silence.

"We do?" Josh asked concernedly.

"No, it's okay," Liz told him. "I guess that's just a thing people say when they keep running into each other."

Josh nodded. "Sarcasm."

A bright light from a store front hit the pavement half a block down, and Josh looked up the street. He kicked the pavement with the sole of his boot again. "I was thinking you might want to get a donut. The bakery will open in a while."

Liz bit her lip, and her hands went to her hair which she hadn't brushed. "I don't know if I'm really put together enough to go into a store right now. I was kind of just out for a walk."

"Oh," Josh answered. "Well, we don't have to go in. Come with me."

Josh started to walk away from the direction of the bakery and away from Liz, and she wasn't sure where he was headed. As though he read her mind, Josh turned back and put his hand out to her.

"Come with me, Liz," he said, his fingertips begging her forward. Liz took a few steps and reached out and slipped her hand into his. His hand was rough but warm, and Liz felt a smile in her heart. She squeezed her fingers into his, but Josh didn't respond, holding her hand so loosely that Liz wasn't sure he'd intended her to take it in the first place. For ten more steps they awkwardly held hands before Liz pulled away. Josh led Liz around the corner and up the alleyway, and she remained a step back, shaking her head in the dark and feeling embarrassed.

Halfway down the alley behind the row of brick buildings, Josh took the two steps up and knocked twice on a metal door and then turned the knob. He opened the door, and they were awash in the bright white light of the bakery kitchen. Josh stepped in, but Liz moved back into the shadows, aware of her disheveled hair and wrinkled clothes.

"It's okay. I know them," Josh said.

"I know. I just don't think I'm up to meeting anyone right now."

Josh nodded. "Be back in a second."

Liz waited in the darkness and thought about Josh's rough hands. She wondered how many girls he had held hands with before. She wished that she hadn't pulled away, but she had second guessed herself for taking his hand in the first place.

Josh returned with a white box. He opened the box and smiled at Liz, but it was hard to see the pastries in the pitch black.

"Looks great," Liz said. "Should we go sit down?"

"Sure," Josh said, taking a donut out and closing the box. Josh ate the donut in three large bites as they walked back around to the front of State Street and sat on the bench. Josh placed the box between them and opened it facing Liz. The donuts were large and looked delicious.

"Wow," Liz said. She took a donut that looked like a sugar coated cinnamon roll that was twisted together in a long spiral. She slowly pulled it apart, taking bite size bits off the outer ring. It was delicious. "I think I just gained ten pounds."

"One donut won't kill you."

"It's not this one. It's the one each day that I'm going to have from now on. I can't believe I haven't been in there before." Liz took a larger bite, truly enjoying the buttery cinnamon flavor as the roll melted in her mouth.

Liz was surprised to see Josh eat two more donuts. He was trim and fit, and she didn't see him as the sweet tooth type. She thought about inviting him up for coffee, but she bit her tongue. Her hair was a mess, she hadn't brushed her teeth, and she couldn't remember how she had left the small apartment.

They sat on the bench in silence until a local police car pulled into one of the parking spaces in front of the bakery. A tall policeman got out of the driver's side and stepped onto the sidewalk. His lights had washed over Josh and Liz when he'd turned in. The cop linked his thumbs inside his belt and looked toward the bench, and Liz thought his chin had jerked up in recognition, but Josh didn't say anything.

The cop went inside the bakery, and Liz and Josh sat in silence, the box of donuts on the bench between them. After deciding not to have another donut, Liz stood.

"Well, I'm going in then," she said.

Josh stood with the box. "Here, take one for the road."

He held the box open between them, and Liz chose a maple frosted pastry that had crushed peanuts on top. Her mouth watered, but she would save it for later.

"Thanks for the donuts."

"My pleasure," Josh said. "Goodnight."

"Good morning, I think," Liz replied as she stepped into the street.

When Liz reached the door of her building, she turned back, and Josh waved. She went upstairs, and once inside she turned the light on. She moved to the window and looked across the street. She was glad to see that Josh was still at the bench watching. He waved again, and then he walked away.

Liz couldn't believe that she'd actually held Josh's hand. It was rough and strong, and she squeezed her hands together trying to remember the moment. He was holding on so lightly that she'd become self-conscious so she had pulled away. She wished she hadn't. Since leaving her parent's house, Liz had no physical contact aside from the occasional customer at Thompson's who brushed her hand when they handed her cash. She didn't realize that she had missed that or needed it until she'd let go.

But it wasn't just that. Liz wanted to hold Josh's hand because it was Josh. His life was strange, but there was much more to him than the time of day. He was like a guardian for Liz at a time when she had needed protection from her own mind. He'd mysteriously moved her one more step forward when she couldn't see the path. Liz combed her thoughts of gratitude toward Josh, but there was something else, something deeper below the surface. She was attracted to him, and she'd wanted to hold hands with him, and she wanted to invite him up this morning for coffee. She wanted to ask Josh a thousand questions, but he'd let her hand go so easily that Liz tried to squash the thought. Besides, it was safer to talk to Ted Barlow because most of the time he was sleeping on the bench next to her as she rambled on.

Liz pulled the blanket over her head and still holding on to the small rope, she floated above the earth. She gripped it tighter now and felt a bit of panic that she might accidentally let go. She'd heard that people who came to the edge of a precipice were less afraid of falling than they were afraid that they might accidentally jump over the edge. There was a voice inside her head telling her that this meant she wanted to live. She knew it was true, but she shook the voice away and watched the earth rotate slowly below.

JOSH WATCHED until Liz's light came on and he saw her safe in the window, and then he turned and walked toward the gas station without a glance back. He felt like an idiot. He hadn't held hands with anyone in over a decade. He wondered how it had happened, and he was so self-conscious that he didn't really hold her hand more than cupping his hand around hers like a child holding a butterfly.

Liz had looked so natural the way her sleepy brown hair brushed across her cheeks as they walked. Josh was embarrassed when she'd first come upon him. He had been working on a white Chevy Cavalier in the single bay at his shop. It was Billy's uncle's car, and Josh had gotten lost somewhere between his aversion to working in the shop and his new daydreams about Liz and of what life could be. He'd been so mesmerized by his daydreams that he convinced himself that he would just go check to see if Ted was on the bench across from Liz's apartment. Never mind that he usually would have checked the shed behind his station first.

She had caught him, what, spying on her? He wasn't spying. He was just curious. Curious about everything she might be thinking or doing. Josh wondered where she'd been wandering alone in the night. He was glad that she had felt comfortable enough to come talk to him in a state that she considered unkempt. She hadn't wanted to go in the bakery. She didn't feel comfortable that way in front of strangers, and the fact that she had approached Josh meant that he must be a safe place for her to visit.

Josh opened Ted's shed and slid the box of donuts inside. He knew that Ted would eat one donut and give the rest of the box to Billy.

Josh thought that maybe he would go home and try to nap for a little while so he could still get back to the gas station before lunch today. He was sitting in the station with Billy more and more often, watching Liz visit with Ted on the bench next to the payphone.

Josh considered going into the station now. He could see that the sun would break the horizon any minute, and he had some work to do. Still, he lacked the patience to answer Billy and Ted's prying questions if they found him in the station before one of them was onsite. They were already prying about Liz and her car and what Josh would do with it. He cringed to think of what they might conclude when there were two less donuts in the box than usual, so he decided to go home.

When he got home, Josh sat on the front porch and looked over the fields where he could see the low straight rows of green corn stalks pushing out of the ground. He didn't know what to think or to feel. In fact, all he could think about was Liz. He wondered how, of all places, she had appeared at his gas station. He knew that she had been running from the tragic death of her son, and he wished that he could help. Somehow, Ted Barlow had caught her eye. Liz spent more time on that bench with Ted than anyone had in the last two years.

The screen door creaked open, and Josh's mom stepped onto the porch. She kept the door from slamming closed and took a seat next to Josh. He looked closely at his mom in the bright light of the rising sun, and he noticed all the wrinkles on her face. Josh could see that his mom was taking a turn with age, and that she would be the proverbial old lady soon enough.

"What's wrong?" she asked, watching her son.

"Why do you think anything is wrong?" Josh asked unconvincingly.

"Well, for starters, I haven't seen you sit on this porch since you were a boy."

Josh nodded and kept his eyes on the green shoots of corn. "I'm trying to figure something."

"Mmmm-hmmm."

"What's it all about, Ma?"

Josh's mom held back her chuckle. "Ain't it, though?" She shook her head.

"I'm being serious."

"I'm sorry, son. It's just that, you're asking the question that anyone aware enough about life eventually asks. I can't say there's one specific answer though. For me and for your dad, it was you. You were an answer to our prayers. For me, it's still you. I just want to know that my baby's okay in the world."

"And that's all you think about?"

This time she allowed the sound of her low chuckle. "No, son. I think about a lot of things. I don't suppose you'd understand until you're my age."

Josh let out a long sigh. "Okay. I guess I can wait."

"Oh, no," Josh's mom scolded. "Spending the next thirty years in that chair won't help you figure out life. You must go live it. There you find the answers." She squinted into the distance and when he didn't answer, she took a good long look at her Josh. He could feel her eyes, and he knew that she was waiting for him to tell her what had brought this on. Josh didn't want to talk about it, so he answered her with silence.

"Is it Ted Barlow? Has he been talking about life and death again?"

"No."

"Well, whatever it is, Josh, you've got to walk towards it. That's the only way to find the answer. Go and look for it."

CHAPTER 9

*L*iz was beginning to feel human again. She went to work, ate, and slept like the rest of the world. Mr. Thompson let her borrow his truck to go to Blain's Farm and Fleet when Liz had said she needed to buy some clothes. She shopped there and at the Salvation Army store to add to her odds and ends. She even opened an account at the bank on the corner to cash her paychecks.

After her second month in Sycamore, she had given Daniel a little money each week for the apartment, and Liz found that she even had a little money left over. It wasn't much, but after the scratch and claw of New York City, Liz was surprised on how little money she could live on. The utilities were included in her rent, and she ate very little. In her old life, she would have gone to purchase the newest gadget for herself or video game that Sean wanted, but in this life, she didn't even have a television.

The personal banker saw the paycheck she was depositing, and he went on for five minutes about the Thompsons. She knew better than to add anything to what he was saying. She wasn't going to be tricked into gossiping about the people who had given her a new chance at life.

He tried to get Liz to open a credit card so she could get gas at the local station. He'd leaned across the desk conspiratorially and commented that they only took credit cards at the pump because the owner didn't believe in telling time, so that the store was only open at any strange time of the day that he felt like showing up.

Liz felt defensive for Josh, but she held her tongue. She felt the small-town glare and remembered the conversations she'd heard Dotty have on and off with customers.

"He has a lacky there, a local named Billy Noodles, but you don't want to go in there. Personally, I get gas over at the BP on DeKalb Avenue, but you would still want a debit or credit card for that."

"I don't have a car," she told him, wondering if she still did have a car. Josh hadn't paid her, and yet he still hadn't asked her for the title. Liz had given the banker a hard stare after that, and he quickly finished the paperwork.

Even Dotty had finally come around to Liz. There was no more talk of her sister after Becky's first visit, and the encounter seemed to have pacified Dotty into accepting a budding friend-ship with Liz. In the mornings, Dotty would smile at Liz and lean over the counter to ask what Liz did the night before. Liz was glad that they were friends, but she always declined to mention her daily walks to the gas station or the time she spent talking to Ted or Josh.

A week after Becky had visited the store, Dotty started asking Liz personal questions. Liz didn't want to talk about herself, so she in turn asked Dotty questions about the town and the customers who came in. When Liz asked about Ted Barlow, Dotty's eyes had perked up.

"Liz, thank you for giving Ted lunch and looking out for him."

Liz wondered how Dotty could have known about that. "I like Ted. No thank you is necessary, Mrs. Thompson."

"Call me Dotty, Liz." Liz's hand was resting on the register counter, and Dotty patted it lightly. Dotty smiled, turning to walk to the back of the store humming to herself, and Liz thought she had seen for the first time the woman that Mr. Thompson loved.

Liz still didn't call Dotty by her first name. Day in and day out, Liz stood at the register and thought about the people she'd met over the months. At first, she thought that the whole town was filled with very nice people, and overall, they were. But she realized that people were just people anywhere you went. There were angry people, and quiet or loud people, and funny people, and people who thought they were funny. She had concluded that she had gone down the path to meeting the best people in Sycamore when she had first arrived.

Josh had offered to buy her car, and he put cash in her hand without even knowing who she was. Ted had lent her payphone money, which she really should pay back. Mr. Thompson gave her a job on the spot and introduced her to Daniel and the apartment. Mr. Thompson was perhaps the most genuine person ever. Liz was sure somewhere he had a fault, but until she found it, she thought that he could be the ambassador of good will for the entire human race. She had been exposed to those who were already looking out to help Ted, and they had lifted her up in tandem.

"Go ahead and take your lunch break, dear," Dotty said as she returned to the front. "And if you see Ted, you don't have to hurry back on our account. It's a slow day so far."

Liz hoped Dotty wasn't trying to play matchmaker. Ted was handsome, but she didn't feel that kind of a spark, not like she did with Josh. Liz chuckled at the thought as she walked to 7-11 and bought her sandwich. It was a miracle that she got out of bed every day, and now she was content enough in life to consider whether there was a spark between her and Ted Barlow. It was laughable on so many levels, and mostly because between the pair of them, Ted Barlow was the town drunk and Liz thought, he was still the catch.

Liz walked the few blocks and turned the corner, and she could see the vintage green car slowly driving by the gas station again. The car stopped, but Liz could still hear the low rumble of the engine. The green paint gleamed in the sunlight, and from a block away, Liz started to appreciate that this was a show car. It was a perfect restoration like the ones at the auto shows that her husband had dragged her to back when she still cared to appease him.

Ted sat on the bench, and the car stopped in front of him so that he could look in the passenger window. Liz slowed her walk and watched Ted as he watched the person in the car. She couldn't hear any words, and as she drew closer, Liz realized that Ted was staring at the blonde woman who was behind the wheel, and she was staring back.

When Liz got to the corner, she turned to go to the gas station so she wouldn't interrupt, but the car started moving again and Ted watched it go down the street. Liz looked at her own car still sitting in the gas station. She wondered when she might give Josh his money back and drive away.

"Josh isn't there," she heard behind her. Liz turned to see Ted addressing her, although he still faced the street watching the green machine driving away.

"I'm not looking for Josh," Liz said, and she approached the bench with the sandwich that she intended to share with Ted. She looked up the street as the car moved away. "That's a nice car."

Ted's head jerked to look at her.

"What? You don't think it's a nice car?" Liz asked amusedly.

"It is," Ted finally agreed. He watched as the green car turned the corner two blocks up and disappeared.

"The license plate is 'John 316'. Isn't that a song by Keith Urban?" Liz's question was sincere, but Ted didn't answer, and she considered his silence. One glance at Ted and she could tell that the memories were never far away.

"Oh," Ted offered, and then he stared across the street at the two-story metal granary for a long time.

Liz peeled open the plastic container and took half of the chicken salad sandwich, leaving the other half on the bench between her and Ted. She ate her half in silence, patient with Ted. She wanted to know who the blonde behind the wheel was, but Liz wasn't going to pry.

She was surprised when Ted finally said, "It's John 3:16, from the Bible."

She looked at Ted, but he kept staring across the street. Liz had been brought up in the church, and she had read scripture before, but she never remembered any specifically by heart. "I don't know that one."

Ted stood up and cleared his throat, looking up at the blue sky. He held his arms wide as though he might catch the sun if it dropped on him, and then he declared, "For God so loved the world that He gave His one and only Son, that whoever believes in Him shall not perish but have eternal life."

LIZ FELT like the schoolgirl who heard the gospel read each week at church without understanding any of it. The words 'eternal life' made Liz think of the loss of her son, and she wouldn't be able to get through the day if she allowed herself to go there. For a moment, she wasn't sure if Ted was being sarcastic or reverent. "Oh," she said. "You know that by heart."

"I should. That's my license plate." Ted looked down the street, but the car was long gone. He didn't see Liz's mouth drop open as she stared at the back of his head. She felt the puzzle of Ted Barlow coming together. It was like she had found all the pieces with straight edges, and she filled out the border and was starting to see a picture forming. Still, she had no center pieces to put in the frame.

"It's a 1968 Chevy Camaro SS."

Liz asked, "And the woman driving your car?" Although, she thought she already knew the answer by the way the lady had covered Ted with a blanket in the middle of the night.

Ted looked at Liz with regret. "That's my wife." He shook his head and grunted out a long breath as though he had just remembered something from the distant past. He sat down and covered his face with his hands, and then he stood up again and turned to Liz.

"I'm married. She's my wife." He swayed with the words, not having slept off all the liquor or exhaustion from the night before.

Liz sat staring at Ted, a thousand questions pressing at her lips, but she didn't speak. Her mother had pressed and nagged, and Liz had run away. She didn't want Ted to feel that pressure. He would tell her if he wanted to and in his own time. Or he wouldn't, and that was okay, too.

"That's my wife," he said again, this time tinged with regret. Ted took three hesitant steps and sat back down next to Liz, and she forgot about returning to work. She turned toward Ted to give him her full attention in case he needed to say more, and although she wanted deeply to hear his story, she would not push.

Ted slumped low, his shoulders sagging and his lips moving like he was talking to himself. He wrung his hands together over and over. It was a whisper at first, a personal conversation, but when he remembered that Liz was there and he wasn't talking to himself, he spoke up.

"It was war, again and again. We were there together. We were brothers. Sometimes people got hurt or killed, but not us. We were on a mission." Ted sat up straight, "And I don't regret it. I served for the future of freedom here and around the world. We all did. We all did."

Liz watched tears stream down Ted's face, and her heart broke for him.

Ted wiped his cheeks. "I like talking to you, Liz. You have a good family. I can talk to you. I never talk to anyone, really."

Liz wondered what her family had to do with anything, but Ted was in a daze, lost in a war that never ended for him, even back in this quiet town. He was the town drunk, outwardly jovial but still alone, even around those who would help him if he would allow it.

"Damnit!" Ted yelled, and his elbow jerked back and cracked one of the wood slats behind him.

Liz jumped and her eyes opened wide. She had been lucky enough to be surrounded by calm men in her life, and the burst of anger startled her. She almost moved away from Ted as he sat with wide eyes and fists clenched tight, but she couldn't leave him now.

"And Gus didn't survive?" she asked cautiously.

"He died. Gus died, and I didn't. Damnit!" Ted stood up and paced, talking to himself. A pickup truck slowly pulled out of the gas station, the white-haired driver looking intently in their direction.

"She's fine. I'm fine!" Ted yelled at the man who took a long look at Liz and then drove away.

"But you aren't fine," Liz said, walking to the payphone to put some distance between her and this towering man. "Gus didn't make it, but you didn't survive either, did you?"

"Like you did?" Ted asked, and Liz was startled. He couldn't have known about her son. She looked at him with her mouth hanging open but had no idea what to say. She saw her dad's car from the corner of her eye and realized that Ted must have recognized another lost soul in her. Although, there was a tiny bit of healing finally happening for Liz, she too was adrift and wandering aimlessly.

Just then, the payphone rang, and it startled Liz. She jumped back a step. She and Ted had been in a trance, staring at each other, and she wondered what it was that he wasn't saying to her.

The phone rang again, and Ted stepped over to answer it. "Thanks for the sandwich, Liz. I think you're going to be late getting back to work."

CHAPTER 10

For the rest of the week, Liz stood behind the register and stared out the front window thinking about Ted and his outburst. Ted was married, and his wife hadn't given up on him. Liz thought that must be real love.

"Is everything all right?" Dotty asked, rolling a box out of the back on a cart.

"Yes, sure," Liz answered, trying to bring her thoughts back into the store. "Do you need me to do anything?"

"Did you see Ted?"

"I saw Ted on Monday, but he wasn't there today." Dotty's voice was friendly, but Liz was cautious. She was still trying to put Ted's life together in her mind. Dotty knew Ted much better than Liz did, but Liz was already weary of small-town gossip, and she didn't want Dotty to get the wrong idea.

"There's no right way or wrong way to grieve," Dotty said with a measure of sorrow in her voice.

Liz's eyes opened wide. She wondered if Dotty had the ear of the priest she had talked to or if Josh had shared her secret. Then Liz realized that Dotty was still talking about Ted.

Dotty shook her head. "I feel bad for that boy."

Liz could see that Dotty was genuinely worried for Ted. She also thought it was a bit funny that she referred to him as a boy, seeing as how he was a grown man who had done two tours in the Middle East.

"There's no wrong way to grieve?" Liz asked, thinking of the last five months of her life and the mess she had made of things.

Dotty shook her head and straightened the items on the shelf closest to the register. "There is no right way to grieve and there is no wrong way. Everyone does it in their own time, and everyone does what they need to get through it." Dotty moved away to rearrange some items on her side of the store as Liz started to unpack the box. "Well, some people don't work through it, I suppose," Dotty continued with regret in her voice. "When the Truman boy's wife died, he drove himself into a tree stone drunk. I felt so bad for them, losing their daughter-in-law, and then losing their own son just months later. But he was grieving in his own way. And those kids lived a fast life with drugs and alcohol." Dotty stopped rearranging the items for a moment. "They were so far gone. They would have needed a miracle to make it through. But others make it through that life-style, so who's to say?"

Dotty moved to the center shelves and began sliding products over to make room for the rest of the items in the box that Liz wheeled over. "It's a fast-paced world, Liz. Everyone is in such a hurry. And with the technology and electronics, it's a wonder that more people don't end up driving into a tree. Comparing their lives and just spouting out with their own opinions without the least thought for the big picture. I bet if they were standing right in front of each other, they'd never say those hateful things."

"It is a fast-paced world," Liz agreed, and Dotty smiled at her.

"You'd know better than me, I'm sure. You must think that I'm just talking out of the side of my mouth over here in this small, Midwestern town."

"Not at all," Liz said. However, she would have thought exactly that before she had experienced small town life for herself. In New York City, there was only New York and the perfected hustle and bustle. No one else in the world knew what it was to lead a real life. High tech sharing was the norm, where everyone considered their opinion the truth over everyone else. It was the new way of life. The rush was a rush, but meeting Josh had changed that for Liz. She could see that life didn't have to be a rush and that anywhere on the planet, people were people.

"Go on home, Liz. I can finish up. You be careful this evening. There are heavy thunderstorms headed our way, and they are supposed to get pretty bad."

LIZ LAID on the bed and thought about what Dotty had said, and then she wondered about Dotty. Dotty's attitude about Liz taking her sister's job had clouded both of their first impressions, but Dotty was very likable.

Liz reflected on many of the first impressions she'd made in her life. She was certain that her first impression on many in this town could be defined by the word *wreck*. Liz was a wreck when she arrived here, but she felt a new beginning for herself creeping up in her thoughts. It wasn't a new beginning for her life in this town per se, but a forward step in her journey. It was an important step that might get her past her grieving long enough to breathe and think about life again.

Liz dozed off, and it wasn't the lightning and crack of thunder that woke her up hours later. It was the rattle of the screen as the wind pounded against the window that pulled Liz from her slumber. She blinked her eyes open and went to the window. It was pitch black outside, and the streetlights seemed to struggle against the heavy air. There was dirt in the air and trash blowing down the street, and in the flashes of lightning, Liz could see the beginning of rain moving sideways.

Her mouth opened as she watched. Liz had seen storms, but she'd never seen the rain come down sideways as though it might angle back up into the sky with the next gust of wind. The direction of the wind turned and then the onslaught of rain was pounding at her window, and she reflexively took a step back. It came down so hard that Liz thought the window might shatter in on her. Liz waited for the next flash of lightning to see if she could recognize Ted on the bench across the street, but the rain was so heavy that she could barely see out. Liz hoped that Ted was safe in the Veterans Club or somewhere else taking shelter from the storm.

Liz heard a long low rumble like the distant sound of a freight train, but there were no trains in the vicinity. The sound of the approaching storm spread over her in impending doom, and she moved to the interior wall of the room. She thought she could hear the long whistle of a distant siren, and then it was the pelting of hail hitting her window, and she instinctively pressed her back to the inner wall of the small apartment.

The storm outside was ominous and the hairs on her body were standing up. She watched sheets of rain stream down the glass mixed in with the hail that pelted the window, and it gave her the creeps. Liz vividly imagined the roof being pried from the building like the lid of a tin can. Liz couldn't remember another storm in her life that had caused this kind of fear. A sudden pounding at her door scared her, and she moved along the wall to see who was there.

Liz opened the door to a petite, young woman with straight black hair who was trying to smile.

"Hi, I'm Kristi, your neighbor."

Liz nodded as thunder rumbled through the building.

"We have to go downstairs for shelter. Those are tornado sirens."

Liz nodded again. "Okay," she said between held breaths. Liz had seen tornado damage on the news before, and she wondered if Sycamore was in tornado alley.

"I've got the key," a tall, lanky man said as he pulled the other apartment door closed. He tried to smile at Liz, too, but she could see the immediacy on his face as he took Kristi's hand and led her down the front stairs.

"Come with us," Kristi said as another round of thunder pounded the building. The dim, orange lightbulbs in the staircase were overpowered by the strobes of lightning that flashed in the window, and it was as though the sun was inside the space.

Liz followed the two down the stairs, and she thought that going outside was a bad idea, but she had no idea what to do in the case of a tornado. At the bottom, Matt turned left toward the mailboxes that were built into the wall and headed down the tight hallway. He handed Kristi a large, square flashlight. Liz watched as he unlocked a door that was built into the side of the wall under the stairs. The light was shone in, and the man went inside and came out with two large boxes. He put them down and wheeled a mop bucket out and then beckoned for the ladies to enter.

Kristi stepped through the door and then motioned to Liz to join them. Liz looked back at the front door.

"You don't want to stay out there. If we get some bad winds from a tornado, it can blow the glass out. Best to be closed in here." Kristi smiled, and Liz went into the small space under the stairs, and the young man pulled the door closed, shutting them into the tiny area.

It was a cramped space, a utility closet, and Liz was glad that he'd taken the boxes out. The couple stood with their backs to the brick wall, and Liz started with another deafening clap of thunder. Sean would have liked this space when he was little. He was always hiding in cabinets and behind beds, anywhere his little body would fit comfortably to wait for his parents to come and find him.

"The storm is on top of us," Kristi said.

The wind and hail had scared Liz. She was conscious of a prayer repeating in her mind begging that they all live through this storm.

"I hope this is the worst of it," the man said, and the couple shared a knowing glance.

"This is my husband, Matt," Kristi said. She put the square flashlight on a stack of small boxes and aimed it at the ceiling to provide some light in the space.

"I'm Liz," she replied, looking at Matt's round face. They were a cute couple, Liz thought.

The thunder rumbled, and Liz and Kristi instinctively looked up at the angled ceiling.

"Nice to meet you," Matt said with a smile, as shadows played up his face from the flashlight.

"Nice to meet you, too."

"You're from New York," Kristi said, and Liz remembered that she was the one with an accent in this town.

"Yes." Liz didn't want to answer many questions about herself, so she spent the next twenty minutes asking Kristi and Matt about their lives. They were from the suburbs of Chicago, and they had met at Northern Illinois University in the next town over. Liz was surprised to hear there was a large university so close to Sycamore because she hadn't noticed college kids around town.

Matt and Kristi had met freshman year. They were seniors now and newlyweds, and they had decided to take the apartment to get away from college life when they weren't at school.

"You don't like the party life that college has to offer?" Liz asked, remembering her time in the dorms and then later at parties off campus. They were very young, and Liz wondered if she'd seemed that young when she was in college. She'd felt so grown up at the time, but she knew now that she'd still had a lot to learn at that age.

"We like to go to some, but we mostly hang out with our friends from work." They were very grown up for their age. As the storm raged on, Liz was glad that they had the presence of mind to knock on her door when they heard tornado sirens. Liz could hear the wind pounding the building even from inside this under-stair closet, and it was worrisome.

In the dim flashlight, Kristi's lips tightened, and Matt reflexively put his arms around her. Kristi's shoulders rose as she pressed her back into Matt's embrace, and for a minute, Liz felt like she was intruding. They were so comfortable together. Matt's intuitive reaction to Kristi made Liz regret that she couldn't remember a time when she felt safe in her husband's embrace. She shook her head and ascribed it to the disgruntled waning years of her marriage which pervaded her memories.

Josh crept into her mind, and Liz wondered what it would feel like in his arms. His hands were strong and precise as he worked, and she thought that there was a comfort in his presence. She found herself daydreaming about his tight physique as the storm passed over.

There was a loud crack of thunder, and they all flinched as the rumble shook the building. Matt tried a tight smile as Kristi turned sideways so that she could hold on to him. In the dim light and with the thunder still rumbling through the space, Liz found herself praying to God that they make it out of that space. She found herself praying for Ted and for the rest of the town. "These are good people," she thought over and over. Her silent chanting made her forget about the storm and stand straight and fearless, and her natural smile seemed to calm Kristi's nerves.

"It's going to be okay," Liz said, and she felt that it was true.

The thunder died down, and Matt went to look out the front

door. "It's clear!" he called back. "I don't hear the sirens and the wind and rain have stopped."

Kristi moved out of the small closet space followed by Liz. They went to look out the window while Matt put the large boxes and the mop bucket back under the stairs.

"The street looks clear," Kristi said. Liz saw that the rain had turned to a drizzle. It surprised her how a storm could rage one moment and then subside to almost nothing in the next.

Kristi pushed the door open, and Liz followed her into the street. The rain had cooled the night air. They looked up and down and saw a little trash around and a garbage can tipped over, but there didn't seem to be any major damage. It was very dark, and Liz realized that all the streetlights were out. She examined the shops that typically had small lights on overnight, but they were all dark.

Matt followed them outside. "Looks like the power is out."

"We were lucky," Kristi said. She stepped onto the curb and kissed Matt. "Do you have any candles, Liz?"

"No," Liz said from the middle of the street. She felt the wind change directions around her and watched the lightning dance in the sky east of town, but there was no thunder, and the storm seemed far off.

"I'll leave you one," Kristi said as Matt took her hand. "Have a good night." They went inside leaving Liz alone in the gulf of darkness left in the storm's wake.

Liz listened to the leaves rustle through the trees. She smelled the fresh air. In the closet under the stairs, she'd been scared. She'd never sat through a tornado warning before, but she'd watched enough of the Weather Channel to have seen footage of the destruction that storms left in their path. She was so thankful that her neighbors had come to find her and bring her to safety and that this small town had been spared. She'd been here for two months, and she'd never run into Kristi or Matt in the stairs or waiting in the hallway for their shared bathroom, and yet they had come to make sure she was all right.

Liz saw a pickup truck turn the corner and she moved over into the parking spaces so it could pass. It slowed as it went by, and Liz realized this was Josh's truck.

CHAPTER 11

*J*osh did a U-turn and pulled into the space next to Liz. He rolled down his window. "Hi," he said shyly.

"Hi." Liz smiled.

"Are you okay?"

"Yes, I'm fine."

They looked at each other and then up and down the street.

"It's after midnight," Josh offered.

"You know the time?" Liz quipped and then bit her lip. "Are you looking for Ted? I haven't seen him in a few days."

"You and everyone else," Josh commented, and then he cleared his throat. "Actually, I came to see how you're doing. They said on the news that a tornado was spotted in the area."

Liz felt herself blush, but she knew he couldn't see because everything was gray in the dim light of darkness. The rain started to sprinkle again.

"Do you want to come inside?" Liz asked and then hesitated. She didn't know why she'd said it. She could have said goodnight and gone inside on her own to get out of the rain, and she was surprised that the question had come so naturally.

Josh nodded and rolled up the window before turning off the

engine. He shined a flashlight in front of Liz as they went inside, and he followed her up the stairs. Liz bent down in front of her door to pick up the large, red candle that Kristi had promised along with a small pack of matches. The door was unlocked, and Liz went inside. She heard the door close behind her and then she heard the click of the light switch on and off.

"I had to try," Josh confessed in the dark.

"Have a seat."

"Thanks." He walked his flashlight around the small apartment as though he was looking for leaks. Liz lit the candle and put it on the small side table. She saw the shadow of her messy bed and threw the blanket over the top. When he was done with his inspection, Josh took the worn armchair, leaving his flashlight next to the candle on the side table to point at the ceiling like a lamp. Liz propped herself in the window.

"I haven't been up here for almost two years," Josh admitted.

Liz looked at him surprised and wondered if he had a girlfriend who once lived here. She thought that she might be feeling jealous and wondered where that emotion might have come from.

"I painted this place and got it ready for Ted when Mr. Thompson said he needed the help."

"Ted was going to live here?" Liz asked.

Josh nodded, and she could tell by his sheepish expression that he thought she already knew. She raised her eyebrows expectantly.

"Well, a few of us were hoping he would take us up on the offer. He didn't go home anymore, and we didn't want him living on the street. So, we fixed it up and we gave it to him."

"That's... wonderful," Liz said, truly in awe. She knew that there were homeless shelters in New York City that took people in, but she couldn't imagine a group of neighbors getting together to do something like this. It made her like the quiet town even more.

"It would have been wonderful if he'd have used it, but he considered it charity and he didn't like the idea. I don't think he ever came in here unless it was very cold outside. And to use the bathroom sometimes."

"Does Ted come up to use this bathroom? I've never seen him in here. I hope that Matt and Kristi don't mind."

"Who?" Josh asked.

Liz smiled. She really was beginning to think that everyone here knew everyone else. "The neighbors that I share the bathroom with. They don't mind?"

Josh shrugged.

"They're college students at Northern Illinois University. They got married last year and moved into the apartment. They plan to stay until they graduate at the end of next year."

Josh nodded and smiled. "Well, you've been socializing."

Liz smiled back. "I just met them. We were locked downstairs in the utility room together during the storm."

"So, you were forced to socialize."

They looked at each other for a long moment, and Liz imagined herself floating in outer space. The rope she had been holding onto became thick and sturdy, and she tied it to her belt to make sure she wouldn't accidentally let it go and float away forever. She liked Josh, and she liked this town.

"Are you hungry?" Josh asked.

"It's a little late. Isn't it?"

"You need to see a clock to know if you're hungry?"

"Okay, ummm," Liz tried to think if she was hungry, and then she was. "Yes, I'm hungry."

"I'm starving. Would you like to go and get a bite to eat?"

Liz wondered where they would find a restaurant open, but she answered by pulling on a cardigan which she had bought at the secondhand store. Josh jumped up from his chair and grabbed the flashlight and blew out the candle.

Liz sat quietly in the passenger seat of Josh's truck as he drove the last few blocks of town. Josh's truck wasn't old enough to be a classic, but by the cassette player mounted in the dash, Liz could see that it was nowhere near new either. The seat was worn but still comfortable, and Liz noticed that he kept the interior very clean. Josh drove by his gas station and then a middle school, and the streets of town were left behind. Liz stared off into the pitch black of the countryside.

Josh clicked on the radio, and a very old country tune was playing. Liz didn't know country music, but she had seen enough Time Life infomercials to know that it was the old recording of the song and not the limited speakers in the truck's cab which gave the music a hollow sound.

"You can choose a station," Josh told Liz.

"This is fine." Liz liked the woman's voice. She liked to look out into the pitch black and to feel that she had somehow gone back in time to a place that she never would have known existed.

The song changed to a male crooner, and Josh tapped his thumb on the steering wheel. "Hank Williams. He's a classic," Josh explained.

"You're a classic," Liz said too quietly for Josh to hear, and she smiled to herself. They moved along the curvy two-lane country road, and Liz marveled at the wood cutout of a German shepherd dog that signified dog training lessons at one house, and the square yellow hand painted sign at another that read "Fresh Honey".

"Those are some large blades of grass," Liz said pointing to the road in front of the truck.

"Hmm." Josh scratched his head. "Looks like leaves from corn stalks. The wind must have really kicked up out here."

Liz thought about her mom. She could hear her mother protesting that one did not go driving off into the dark of night with a complete stranger because who knew what would happen. Liz smiled and enjoyed her mother's words that she had manifested in her own mind. It was the first time Liz had smiled at anything to do with her mother for a long time. There was no judgement in this comment because Liz didn't really care what happened right now. She thought Josh was a good guy, but even if he was a depraved lunatic taking her God knows where, Liz didn't really care. She felt an utter freedom of being in this moment, and she would look back years later and realize that this was another step in her healing.

JOSH TAPPED his thumb on the steering wheel and tried not to look at Liz. He wanted to study her face, and he would wait for the light of the diner to do just that. They passed a wood shaped arrow pointing down a side road that read "Kishwaukee Archers".

"Archers?"

Josh smiled. "Yes, as in archery."

"Do people actually still use bows and arrows?" Liz asked Josh.

He looked at her to make sure she wasn't joking, and then he realized she was more of a city girl than he'd initially thought. "Yes, for hunting and for fun, like a hobby." He had a lot more to say on the subject, but he stopped himself.

He turned north for a few minutes and cut through the one stoplight town of Hampshire before reaching their destination at Starks Corner. Josh pulled into the gravel parking lot and parked.

"How did you find this place?" Liz asked. Josh couldn't tell if she was pleased or teasing him. She walked over to the free-standing farm sign on wheels near the road and shook her head. It had black letters and an arrow on top pointing at the small white building. "Phil's Breakfast and 7up. Really?"

Josh felt defensive as though Liz was picking on him. "Are you kidding? Everyone knows about this place." He said this pointedly, and when he saw her sideways smile, Josh bit his tongue. He didn't want to be defensive. He just wanted breakfast and maybe a little conversation with Liz. And he wanted to look at her in the light of the diner and memorize her face.

"I can tell it's a hot spot," Liz shot back, her arm stretched toward the two other cars in the lot.

"Well, it's probably three in the morning, so the early crowd hasn't arrived yet." Josh noticed his reference to the time of day, and he was surprised at himself.

"Does that make us the late crowd still? I haven't been out for breakfast this late since my clubbing days."

"Baby seal clubbing days?" Josh asked with a smile, and he got a laugh out of Liz. She was unstable but feisty, and Josh liked her. He chuckled to himself and lightened up as he held the door open. Josh quickly surveyed the three-sided counter and walked around the far side, sitting two stools from Ray who was passed out as usual.

"Hi hon, how are you doing tonight?" Betty asked, turning over his coffee cup and pouring the dark liquid in. "Coffee for you?" she asked Liz, who nodded.

The waitress poured Liz a cup and returned the coffee pot to its warmer, and Liz said under her breath to Josh, "Is that your girlfriend?"

"That's Betty," Josh replied.

The middle-aged woman put a menu on the counter in front of Liz, who sized her up. The waitress was fit, wearing black polyester pants and a button up shirt that said "Phil's" on the front. She had an apron tied around her waist, and she moved quickly and effortlessly.

"So how have you been?" she asked politely, her eyes moving to Liz. Josh felt his face redden.

"I'm good. This is Liz. She's new to Sycamore."

"Storm wake you up?" she asked Liz. Then she turned to Josh without waiting for an answer. "It was awful for a while. Chef and I went into the storeroom for about fifteen minutes through the worst of it. Ray stumbled in here soaking wet, but he was already passed out when I got back out here."

"He looks like a drowned rat," Josh said. Then he leaned toward the man. "Ray!" Josh called, but the sleeping man didn't move. Josh shrugged. "The more things change…"

Josh looked at Liz who looked at her menu. "Carte blanche, Liz. Anything you want. My treat."

"Carte blanche," Liz smiled and nodded. "Betty, I will have two eggs over easy with bacon and wheat toast."

"White toast, okay?"

Liz nodded.

"You've got it, honey." Betty took Liz's menu and turned toward the kitchen.

"You're not eating?" Liz asked Josh.

"Betty knows what I like."

"Wow. I don't think anyone has ever known what I would order."

"Welcome to small town living."

Josh liked to watch Liz smile, and this time it made him smile. He had to look down at his arms folded on the counter to keep from feeling like an ogre. He loved looking at Liz in the light, but he forgot that it would also give her the chance to really see him.

"I guess you can feel the love here," Liz countered.

Josh thought that was an odd remark, and he looked at her disbelieving.

"I just mean, it's not all hustle and bustle and you can really get to know people."

"Maybe."

"Maybe?" Liz countered.

Liz stared, and Josh looked around uneasily. He'd been over-looked for decades, and he felt completely self-conscious.

"People really like you, Josh. They have gotten to know the real you over your life. Don't you think?" Liz flashed her eyes at the still sleeping Ray as though he proved her point. Then she looked back at Josh. "Give me your keys."

Josh's eyebrows rose. "Give you, my keys?"

"It's not like I'm going to drive away. I have no idea where we are." Liz turned her hand up and opened and closed her fingers in a grabbing motion, so Josh unclipped his keys from his belt and handed them over.

"Keys like a maintenance man," Liz commented as she weighed the hunk of metal in her hands. Josh knew there were thirty-two keys on the ring.

Liz plucked the key on the end of the keychain next to the Chevy logo. "What's this one?"

Josh liked the way Liz's brown hair dropped across her forehead when she tipped her chin down to interrogate him. He liked the way she crossed her legs on the stool and slowly rubbed her palms together. He thought that Liz seemed happy in a way tonight. She was more alert than he'd ever seen.

She'd always seemed as though she was ready to apologize to anyone who might look in her direction, except when she was sitting on the bench with Ted. Josh noticed a new calm in Liz. She was relaxed. She was like a flower planted and patiently waiting to be noticed but still not caring if she wasn't seen.

"That's the front door to the gas station," Josh said.

Liz flipped the next key around the keyring and looked at him expectantly. "That's the back door to the gas station."

"How organized," she teased. She turned the next key over.

"That's the key to Ted's shed."

"What is Ted's shed?"

Josh shook his head. "Never mind."

"Okay, I'll circle back to that one." Liz turned over another key.

"That's the key to the State Theatre." Another key. "That's the key to Thompson's store." A smile and then another key. Josh paused, looking into Liz's eyes. He wondered if he should tell the truth and how she would feel if he did. He swallowed. "That's the key to Ted's apartment."

Liz looked at Josh surprised to know that someone else would have the key to the apartment. He had told her that he'd painted the place two years ago, not that he still had the key.

He shrugged. "I'm the maintenance man."

Liz nodded and pursed her lips, so Josh reached down to the key ring to move the conversation along. He felt awkward when their fingers touched, like an open nerve ending that had just been struck by lightning. He didn't look up as he flipped to the next key. "St. Mary's Church." He flipped the next one. "The Veterans Club."

"You're a veteran?"

"No," Josh laughed. "You think with my lifestyle the military would've had me?"

Liz shrugged. "I guess not."

"I have that key in case I need to let Ted into the club if it's really cold at night." Josh had only let Ted into the Veterans Club twice at the beginning before they had set up the apartment. It turned out not to be a good idea to lock a drunk into a bar overnight.

"Have you seen Ted lately?"

Josh shook his head. He'd been wondering the very same thing. He had noticed a change in Ted since Liz had come to town. He wasn't sure exactly what that was; maybe Ted was a bit more chatty than usual. Liz had been a catalyst for Josh as well. He'd been at the gas station in the morning and roaming around at night more than ever. And here he was in the diner with Liz, their hands within inches of touching.

"I wonder where he went," Liz said, and then turned her attention back to flipping the keys over. They were halfway through the pile. "And this key?"

"Blain's Farm and Fleet in case I need some extra stuff that

Thompson's doesn't have. And those are for my house and the garage and the barn."

"You have a barn? I never knew anyone who owned a barn." She sounded surprised and also like she was badgering him.

"It's a glorified shed. I just store some old stuff in there. I'm not a veteran, and I'm not a farmer either." Josh shrugged.

"What are you?" Liz asked.

Josh took a moment to consider that. "I'm a gas station owner," he told her, but for the first time in a long time, it didn't feel sufficient.

Liz nodded her head and handed back his keychain, although they weren't done with the game of going through the keys. She whispered, "I was a mom."

"You will always be a mom," Josh said more confidently than he felt. He didn't know the first thing about parenting, and he'd seen her so upset at the church that he didn't want to stir things up.

"I am a mom," Liz whispered with a tight frown. She turned toward the counter and her shoulders hunched forward.

Josh had no idea how to react, and he felt almost panicked that he would lose this moment to her past, but he didn't want to not ask if Liz needed him to listen. "Do you want to talk about it?"

As if on cue, Betty brought their plates out, and that seemed to snap Liz out of her melancholy. Josh handed Liz her fork, and they both dug in without another word.

CHAPTER 12

*L*iz was so grateful that Betty brought the food out when she did. She felt the peace drain out of her at the mention of her past life. The conscious thought of who in the world she used to be and who she might be now took hold again. Liz had enjoyed the drive out in the pitch black, and in the diner even, she felt like she was on a different planet with only three people in the whole world. Well, five if you included the cook and Ray who was still passed out on the corner stool.

Josh squirted ketchup on his scrambled eggs, and Liz looked over to see what his 'usual' was. It was a pile of eggs and five strips of bacon, and Liz thought it would take her three sittings to finish that much food.

The smell of the food woke Ray from his drunken slumber, and he lifted his head up and opened one eye.

"Did you save me some?" he asked.

"Betty, look who's awake," Josh called over the counter. Betty had been hanging back on the other side of her space, and Liz got the feeling she was trying to give them some privacy.

"Welcome back," Betty said to Ray as she placed a fresh cup of coffee in front of him. "I'll put your order in with Cheffy."

Liz ate some of her eggs and let her eyes wander past Josh to see what Ray would do next. He was fumbling with the sugar, and Liz was sure that he would drop the glass jar on the floor.

"I already added the sugar, Ray," Betty called over, and Josh gently removed the glass jar from Ray's hand.

"Thank you, sweetie," Ray said, taking a big gulp of the coffee.

"You must think everyone around here is a drunk," Josh said to Liz.

"Why would you say that?"

"Well, you've been exposed to Ted and now Ray."

"Nothing good happens after dark," Liz said with a smile. "My grandpa used to say that."

"Well, I disagree."

"You would. It seems like you have built your own world after dark."

"I guess I have," Josh said, taking another bite of his eggs.

"I've never seen someone put so much ketchup on their eggs."

"I can put ketchup on anything. It's practically a food group."

Ray sipped his coffee and put his hand on Josh's arm. "But you don't put ketchup on a hot dog, son. It's just not done."

Liz nodded at Ray. "Noted."

"No comment," Josh said.

Liz was back to enjoying herself. She wasn't trying to get by this minute or holding on to the right now so that she wouldn't expose her mind to the past. She was feeling real pleasure in the conversation. Happy was a long dormant emotion that she thought was gone forever. She smiled and smeared jelly on her toast.

Ray leaned forward and stared at Liz, trying to decide if he knew her. "And who is this nice young lady you've brought out to Phil's?" he slurred.

Josh made a face at Liz that said 'sorry', and then he leaned back a bit to introduce her. "Ray, this is Liz. She just recently moved to Sycamore. Liz - Ray."

Ray smiled. "Hello young lady."

"Hi."

Then he turned his attention to Josh. "Where's Ted?"

"You know Ted?" Liz asked.

"As you can see, they frequent some of the same establishments," Josh interjected.

"I do know Ted!" Ray said, leaning dangerously over to get closer. Josh had to push Ray upright onto his stool. "I haven't seen him this week. That's not like Ted to just up and forget about us."

Liz wondered who *us* was, but she was afraid to ask. She looked to Josh and noticed his crinkled forehead. He was also worried about Ted.

"Should we look for him?" Liz asked.

"Not tonight," Josh told her. "He'll come back around when he's ready." He tried to sound certain and even offered a smile with his answer, but Liz could see that he wasn't sure that was true.

They finished eating and Betty brought the check. "Hey, Josh. Chef's wondering if you can give him a ride back to town. It'll save his wife the trouble of driving out."

"Sure, if he doesn't mind riding in back tonight. The road should be dry by now."

"Are we going?" Liz asked.

"If you're ready. Did you want to order something else? They have great pie here."

Liz smiled, thinking of a hot apple pie sitting in the windowsill of an old farmhouse. It was a stereotype, a flashback from an old cartoon, but it was a nice thought. "Not this time."

"Not this time. Noted," Josh said with a self-satisfied smile, and Liz realized she had opened the door to other nights like this. The thought made her giddy, and she smiled back at Josh.

Josh left money on the counter under the handwritten check. "Thanks, Betty," he said, and Liz stood, ready to leave. They both said goodbye to Ray, whose incoherent reply was lost among the bite of hash browns he was chewing.

"Don't be a stranger," Betty said to Josh.

Liz stepped outside and was surprised to see the early signs of dawn in the sky. It was the almost imperceptible change of black sky to gray. A short man wearing a light brown work jacket and jeans tossed a backpack into the back of Josh's truck before climbing in and sitting down with his back to the cab.

"Thanks, man," Chef said to Josh in a thick, Hispanic accent.

"Sure," Josh said, and the man laid down in the bed of the truck, using the backpack as a pillow.

"I didn't realize it was so late," Liz said, and Josh shrugged. She could see that he really didn't care about the time, and it was baffling. Liz sat in the passenger seat of the truck and looked over her shoulder. She was concerned about the man in back. She'd never ridden in the back of a pickup truck. Seatbelts had been the law her whole life.

"He'll be fine," Josh assured her. He pulled a detached key from his large key ring and started the truck, but he could see that Liz was still concerned. "Don't worry. I grew up taking rides in the back of trucks. He'll be okay."

Liz nodded but wasn't convinced.

"Well, if it makes you feel better, you could ride back there, and he could ride up here."

Liz's eyes opened wide, and Josh laughed. "City girl," he said as he pulled out of the gravel lot.

The short drive back to Sycamore was quiet but pleasant. There was a gray haze of light brightening the fields of short corn, and Liz could see more of the road ahead. The drive out had been all stars and nothingness, anything beyond the head-lights out of reach. The ride back was an embraceable black and white reality without enough light yet to show color.

Liz wondered why she had picked through Josh's keys. She had intended to prove that people did care for him, and it had turned into flirting. She'd been talking to Josh more this week since she didn't have that outlet with Ted. Ted was a safe island. He was more ruined than Liz had been, and on top of that, he had a wife. Josh was a question mark to Liz, and she could feel herself wanting to know more and more about him. Still, she hoped to see Ted Barlow back on his bench tomorrow.

The two-lane road twisted and turned past houses in some areas and went straight on for miles in others. They crested a hill and were about to make the curve left toward town when she heard Josh gasp.

"What the...?" he trailed off, and he pulled the truck over. Liz thought there might be something wrong with the truck, but she didn't sense anything apparent.

Liz saw Chef behind them. He sat up and then followed Josh's gaze. The two men stared across the low corn to their left. They had a bird's eye view of the acres just below. Liz's eyes searched in the pink light of dawn until she saw it. There was a huge section of the field torn up. She could see a wide swath of black soil surrounded by the burgeoning green of the fledgling corn stalks.

"What?" she asked, not certain of what she was seeing. She felt the truck move as Chef jumped over the side. Josh got out and followed him across the road for a better look, so Liz followed suit. They stood in silence and surveyed the acres of torn up field and patches of mangled and missing corn.

"The tornado just missed the town," Chef said, pulling his cell phone up to his ear. He walked a few steps away, but he didn't need the privacy. Liz couldn't understand him as he quickly spoke in Spanish.

"Everything okay?" Josh asked when Chef put the phone in his pocket.

He was trying not to panic, and Chef's words came out stilted in his thick accent. "Yes. The kids slept through it, but my wife says it was a bad storm. It must have been worse here than at the diner." He went back to Josh's truck and hopped in the back, ready to go check on his family.

"We should go," Josh told Liz, and they got back into the truck. He was quiet after that, although he was always quiet, but Liz could see concern on his face as he drove the rest of the way.

"Are you okay?"

"I didn't know it touched down," he said. "It was really bad over here. I live west of town. It's good that it just hit dirt, assuming that's the case."

Liz was shaking her head in disbelief. Josh was saying that a tornado had touched down right there where Liz could see the ground torn up. They'd driven past that area on their way to the diner too much in the dark to have noticed anything out of place. "I'm used to watching the bad storms roll in on television like everyone else in the city."

"You don't have a TV anymore," Josh pointed out.

"I don't have power right now either."

Josh turned the radio on and moved the dial to the AM station that broadcast from the next town over, but they were playing music and there was no news to be heard. He drove past the Jewel grocery store that Liz had seen earlier. They should have turned into town at the stoplight.

"I think you missed your turn."

"Chef lives on the other side of town, and Peace Road goes straight there these days."

As dawn got brighter in the sky, Liz looked past the random strip malls and the scattered homes and tried to see if there was any damage from the storm. Josh's head was swiveling from side to side as well. Liz wanted him to keep his eyes on the road, but she didn't say anything. After a minute, they saw a section of downed trees and then another, and then sporadic trees snapped clean off at the base. She remembered the wind and rain pounding her apartment, and she realized just how damaging the storm could have been.

The two-lane highway curved to the left and she saw apartment buildings on her left and a field to the right. They saw the brown trunks of the utility poles snapped in half and miles of thick black power line lying dormant next to the road. Josh turned into the parking lot of the apartment complex, and Liz could hear someone calling to him. It was a woman's voice.

Chef jumped out of the bed of the truck and looked in Josh's window. "Marissa says you should come up. She's kind of freaking out, Josh." Both men looked up to Chef's wife who was standing on the balcony of the second floor and frantically pointing across the street to the field.

"Oh boy," Josh said as he parked and got out of the truck. "Did you see those power lines?"

"Looks pretty bad. Power's probably going to be out for days," Chef said in his thick English.

"Tell Marissa not to let the kids out to play until the power company is onsite."

They looked up at Marissa who was waving her arms frantically.

"Come on up for a minute, Josh."

Josh nodded. He turned back to Liz as an afterthought. "Do you want to come up?"

"Should I?" Liz asked.

"Your call," Josh said.

Liz didn't know if that meant she was invited, but she decided to go. The daylight on her eyes combined with being up half the night was making her tired, and she didn't want to fall asleep alone in the parking lot.

"You guys are friends then?" Liz asked.

"I've driven him home before," Josh admitted. Liz smiled, knowing that was just about as definitive of an answer as Josh could probably give about anything.

"Do you know his real name?" Liz asked, assuming that might answer her first question.

"He's the cook at the diner, but he wants to be a real chef someday," was Josh's explanation. Liz shook her head, and she decided she would ask Josh more questions when she was awake enough to have a conversation.

They followed Chef up the outside stairs that turned back in half flights between the buildings. When they got to the door on the second floor, Marissa was waiting, and she put her finger up to her lips to shush them as they entered. She kissed Chef and then led them across the living room to the small balcony.

"Oh man," Josh said as he stepped outside. Liz saw the cornfield across the street, and her heart dropped. This field had been ripped up by the tornado as well, and they could see acres of black dirt where neatly planted rows of corn had been. The line of the funnel had moved northeast and stopped a hundred yards from the road.

"My God," Chef said, and he squeezed past Josh and Liz to hug Marissa. They exchanged some soft words, and Liz could tell they were both frightened and relieved.

"It's a miracle," Marissa said in her accented English.

Liz understood the reality, that the funnel of the tornado had come so close, but she wasn't sure why Josh seemed shaken.

"I've never seen anything like it," Josh said, and Liz nodded but she didn't reply. She'd never seen a tornado, and in fact, she still hadn't. Here, she saw the best possible scenario for the lingering destruction of a tornado. It was acres of lost corn crop, but she wasn't shaken up about that.

"Is Sycamore prone to getting a lot of tornados?" Liz asked.

"Northern Illinois gets its fair share, but they aren't too often around here. Mostly warning sirens and then just storm damage without actual funnels touching down." Josh scratched his head as he stared at the field. "First the field on the east side of town and then this. It's amazing. The tornado was on track to rip right through downtown, but it looks like it jumped over instead."

"What?" Marissa asked.

Chef talked quickly in Spanish, and when Marissa heard the news, she crossed herself with a blessing, and Liz could see the reflection of tears on the woman's face.

"It was loud, but the kids slept right through it. I heard the siren, but they were sleeping, and we weren't near the windows, so I just sat next to them while the storm passed over." Chef held his wife who was visibly shaken.

Josh shook his head. "It's one for the books." He turned and led Liz outside.

"Get some sleep, you two," he said quietly as he closed the apartment door. They walked slowly to Josh's pickup truck. Liz heard a distant buzzing noise and looked up to see a small airplane fly over the damaged area, circling back to get a better look.

Josh was quiet on the short drive to downtown, giving Liz time to think about the night. Chef's apartment was sparse, but Liz couldn't help and reflect that he had goals. Marissa took care of the kids, and together, they had hope for the future. Liz wondered what her own future might look like. She had been so self-involved in her despair that she hadn't thought of planning a life beyond the one she'd had with Sean. Liz thought she would stay in this town, and she thought that maybe she should find her own place. She could start small like Chef and Marissa in a place of her own instead of staying in Ted's apartment.

Liz felt drained as the sun rose higher and blinded her as they headed east. She saw the Farm and Fleet that Josh had the key to, and the State Theatre and Veterans Club that Josh had the keys to. Then he pulled up in front of her apartment: another place that Josh had the key to. She looked over at Josh and noticed the small lines next to his eyes. He was older, and Liz wondered just how much older he could be. He was still young, but there were the tell-tale signs of both age and experience in his countenance.

"Do you want to come up for some coffee?" Liz asked.

"No," Josh said. "I mean, yes, but I want to go check on any damage around town, and then I'd better get back to check on Mom. I left her right after the worst of the storm had passed, so..."

So, Josh lived with his mom. Maybe he wasn't as old as she had been thinking. Liz got out of the truck and turned back to Josh.

"I had a good time," he said, and then his eyes widened, and he smiled. He seemed surprised that those words had come out of his mouth.

"Me too." She walked slowly toward the apartment and heard Josh pull away as the door to her building closed behind her.

Liz was ready to lay down and sleep when Josh dropped her off, but she had to be at work in two hours, so she made instant coffee and sat in the chair next to the window and put her feet up on the small hassock. Liz cupped the mug in her hand and sipped the hot liquid, and she found that she was grateful for the coffee.

She wondered about Chef and his family and where they might have come from. She had moved back in with her parents when she was struggling financially after the divorce, but Liz didn't feel like she had lived hand to mouth. It was an illusion though. She had both struggled financially and spent what she wanted without a true budget. She saw in Chef and Marissa people who were willing to sacrifice for their goals. Liz sipped her coffee and marveled for a long time about people who were just trying to make it day to day in the world.

This made her think of Darren and when they had first been married. They were both working new jobs and there wasn't a lot of income. They had a small apartment, albeit larger than the one she was in now and larger than Chef's apartment. And Chef had three kids to support, which couldn't have been easy. But for Liz and Darren, it was just the two of them, newlywed and learning about the world, and they had made it work.

This thought made Liz smile, and for the first time in years, she didn't feel angry at Darren. She allowed the nostalgia to take her back all those years. They were young and in love like Matt and Kristi across the hall. Then, when they had Sean, they were scraping by like Chef and his wife. The world was a lot of the same stories playing out in different people, but still each story was unique. Liz wondered how her story would play out, and that thought made her think of Ted Barlow.

Liz wondered where Ted had gone. Although she'd only been here for two months, she felt closer to Ted than she had with many of her friends who she'd had for years. She mostly sat on the bench while Ted slept, but they also had some serious conversations with no judgement. Liz knew that her friendship with Ted was genuine and made with the care that friendships in the world should be. She didn't have any life left in her for the good-timers or the cocktail parties. Liz only had time in her life for truth.

She closed her eyes and wondered about the truth of her life. Her life was a mess. It was a daily prayer to keep moving forward. *Toward what?* She didn't know. It was Thompson's General Store and a green park bench next to a payphone. It was a car in a gas station that didn't know if it was coming or going. It was a rope that held her tethered above the planet. Liz smiled realizing in her mind's eye that the tiny string had grown into a thick rope. She grabbed tighter to it with both hands and pulled gently, slowly moving closer to earth.

CHAPTER 13

$\mathcal{L}$iz listened to Dotty and Mr. Thompson talk about the tornado, but she didn't comment. She couldn't shake the feeling that she had made the tornado skip over the town. The other night, when she was in that small closet with Kristi and Matt, Liz saw how comfortable they were together. She was embarrassed to be packed in so close while so easily recognizing their love for each other. She'd felt like an intruder. Still, in the fear of the unknown, Liz had prayed she would live through the storm. She had seen life again in the couple, and it had scared her more than the possibility of the tornado, but it also caused her to hope again.

So, when Dotty commented on how fortunate they were that they'd been spared the worst of the tornado, and what a miracle it was that the funnel had skipped over town, Liz kept silent. There was a whisper of a voice in her head telling her that she'd been some part of the petition that had saved them all.

The news spread fast once the local paper released an article showing images of the torn-up corn crop and the downed power lines on either side of town. The second day after the tornado had missed the town, a Chicago TV news affiliate flew out in a helicopter to get live footage, sweeping from the west, over the small town, and off to the east where the tornado had touched down again. People watched on the news, and when they came into the store, they would talk to Dotty and Mr. Thompson and excitedly play the footage over and over on their smart phones.

"Have you ever seen a tornado, Mr. Thompson?"

"No, I can't say that I have. I've seen plenty of bad storms and there have been tornados that have touched down not too far from here. We do live in a place where tornados are sometimes a threat, but they're always random. Did you look at the newspaper or see the news report though? This one seems different. It stopped and started, or sort of leapfrogged over the town. They recorded doppler radar that shows the top of the funnel stayed intact, but the bottom dispersed on one side of town and then reformed on the other side. That seems like a miracle to a lot of people around here."

Liz had seen both sides of town with her own eyes, but she didn't want to share that for fear of prodding questions about where she was or who she was with. Liz had spent a large amount of time daydreaming about Josh and his quiet smile and the way his sandy blond hair was neatly combed back when he didn't wear a baseball cap, but she wasn't ready to admit anything out loud.

"Have you seen Ted?" Liz asked to move her thoughts away from Josh.

Mr. Thompson didn't seem too concerned. "Well, if you're worried that he got carried off in the tornado, don't worry about that. I haven't seen Ted for almost a week."

"Is that typical?"

"Nothing about Ted is typical, but I wouldn't worry too much," Mr. Thompson said as he straightened out some items that didn't need straightening.

Liz could tell that for all his calming talk on the matter, he too was concerned for Ted.

"The car show is in a week, so we'll be getting in extra stock. Can you work some extra hours this week to cover the front so Dotty and I can work on inventory?"

"Sure," Liz agreed.

"It's the largest car show in the area," Mr. Thompson told Liz with pride.

She was never into old cars, but Liz was interested to see if she would spot a certain green Chevy among the rest of the entries. Liz looked out the window, straining to see if there were any blankets on the bench across the street and blushed when she saw Josh coming in the front door.

Josh stepped in the store and tried to smile, waiting for the bell to stop ringing as the door closed behind him before he stepped up to the register and looked at Liz.

Mr. Thompson wondered if he had seen a ghost. He didn't move from where he was, standing in the short aisle near the counter.

Josh was tall, but he was hunched over a bit as though he was trying to hide like a turtle that only came out of its shell at night. Liz didn't want Josh to hide. She had liked her time with Josh and felt calm in his presence, but she could see Mr. Thompson staring at him open-mouthed, and she knew that Josh was uncomfortable.

"Hi," Josh said timidly to Liz.

They weren't a couple. They were just two souls stranded in the same boat. She had spent time with him in the dark of night, and still here in the daylight, Liz could feel herself being drawn into him, and she did not resist.

Josh stared down at the counter. "I just wanted to make sure that my account is all right here. You know that my arithmetic is correct."

Liz smiled. She was a teacher, yet she hadn't heard the word arithmetic in a long time. "Everything is fine." Liz glanced at Mr. Thompson expectantly, but he didn't even nod his head.

"Good," Josh said to the countertop. They'd had so much to say the other night, but today in the public eye, they were both quiet. Liz waited for something more, but she was left to stare at a patch of a yellow fish emblem sewn onto his olive-green baseball cap. They all stood like mannequins for a half a minute before another customer came in and broke the spell.

"Are you going to come by the station tomorrow?" Josh asked. Liz noticed that it wasn't only being seen in public that was making Josh nervous. He was anxious, and she was glad that she had that effect on him, because she had thought of little else lately.

Mr. Thompson snapped out of his trance and cleared his throat. "Well, Josh, if you want to see Liz, you'll have to ask her on a proper date," He walked around the counter to stand next to Josh. Josh looked at Liz. Her cheeks were burning as she stared at her boss who had a huge smile on his face. He patted Josh on the shoulder.

"Hmm," Josh grumbled, obviously uncomfortable.

"Come back later when you've got something to say," Mr. Thompson said with a laugh, leading Josh to the door. The door jingled and Josh went out, and Mr. Thompson winked at Liz.

"Bye," Liz said as Josh left the store.

"Was that Josh Davis?" a gray-haired Lilly Weathers asked no one. "Mr. Thompson, I think that was Josh Davis." She was full of surprise as Mr. Thompson had been at first, but he'd come out of his stupor and tried to hide it.

"Yes, that was Josh Davis. He shops here too, you know. Plenty of folks do." Mr. Thompson's defensive tone stopped Mrs. Weathers for about five seconds before she moved toward the small gardening section.

"Well excuse me, Mister Know-it-all. Not everyone in this town gets to see that boy as often as you do. If you ask me, his mother should have put her foot down years ago. The way he slinks around this town without anyone seeing him. And making us pay for gas with a credit card! I have lived eighty-one years without a credit card, and I did fine all by myself. And to carry a credit card just so I can get gas when I should be able to pay cash is ridiculous!"

By the thick-rimmed glasses, Liz wondered if the older woman should still be driving at all.

"Why don't you go to Shell out on Sycamore Road?" Mr. Thompson prodded. He knew she wouldn't go there as he tried to avoid Sycamore Road when he could. For years that road was farmland, then there were some small stores and restaurants and a Kmart. But in the past ten years, DeKalb and Sycamore had sprung cookie-cutter rows of townhouses and stretches of subdivisions that brought every chain store in America to their door. They were over an hour from the heart of the Windy City, yet still affected by the growing population.

Mrs. Weathers scoffed at Mr. Thompson, but she took her time in the store today, constantly glancing at Liz who waited at the counter without a word.

"You know that boy?" Mrs. Weathers finally asked as she placed one roll of fishing line on the counter.

"Not really," Liz answered nonchalantly, although her heart was still racing from his visit and her eyes had been looking for him in the street. "He shops here."

"I've never seen him shop here," Mrs. Weathers remarked as she took in the store to see if anyone else was present.

"I've never seen you shop here," Liz commented matter-of-factly. She meant no disrespect toward the older woman, but Mrs. Weathers grabbed her fishing line and stepped away from the counter aghast at the statement. Mr. Thompson bent over at the waist laughing hysterically.

"I've been coming here for over sixty years, young lady. I'd advise you that if you have nothing pleasant to say, that you just keep your remarks to yourself!" Lilly Weathers would have scrambled for the door if time and gravity hadn't taken their toll.

She moved like a sloth, and her hunched over back allowed her to watch each foot move her closer to the door. "Good day," she jeered.

Mr. Thompson continued to laugh as Mrs. Weathers went out and then peered back in the front window and shook her finger at him before moving on.

"I really made her mad, but I don't remember her shopping here," Liz said innocently. "She walked by a few times outside one day, and Dotty told me that she was a harmless old lady out for a walk. She looked in about seven times though."

"Mrs. Weathers walks around town to hear the latest gossip. Gives her something to do."

"She didn't pay for the fishing line."

"She'll bring it back next week and put it back on the rack." Mr. Thompson said this as if it were a normal occurrence, but Liz knew that in her New York City, people pulled a gun for less. With so many characters in one place, Liz wondered how Mr. Thompson could run this store and still make a profit.

"Come to think of it, Liz, you'd better look out for Lilly Weathers."

"Why? I thought she was harmless."

Mr. Thompson pointed behind Liz where Mrs. Weathers was back in the window, hunched over and staring in. "Because Josh Davis is something of a topic in this town, and he came out here to see you."

"He didn't come to see me," Liz defended innocently.

Mr. Thompson winked and nodded, and Liz felt her face and ears burning as bright as a Macintosh apple. She was cornered, and she didn't dare face Mrs. Weathers.

"What's his story, Mr. Thompson? How did Josh get the keys to the city?"

"So, you know about Josh's keys?" It was a statement framed as a question, and Liz knew that Mr. Thompson was on to her.

Liz bit her lip and looked away, glad to see Mrs. Weathers had moved along.

"Josh is a handsome boy. I should say, he's a handsome man. He must be over forty years old."

Liz nodded, surprised that Josh was much older than she had guessed.

"He has a good business, takes good care of his mother. He's what we would call respectable. I went to school with Josh's mother, and I was friends with his dad," Mr. Thompson said regretfully. He leaned on the counter across from Liz and looked out the window, but Liz could tell that he wasn't seeing the street. He had the same faraway look her dad got when he was reflecting on the past.

"When Josh was eleven, his dad died of a heart attack. It really affected the boy, and for a long time everyone just let him alone to grieve. But his mother told us that it was more than that. She said that something in him changed. She said that he picked up the clock and turned the clock hands back right then and there, and then he sat still like he was waiting for something to happen."

"What was he waiting for?"

Mr. Thompson rubbed his chin. "Well, it took a few months for her to figure that out. She talked to some doctors, and they reckoned that Josh turned the clock back to see if somehow time could turn back, and his dad would be alive again. I know it sounds crazy, but who can say what a parent's death at that age does to a boy? After that, Josh never counted on the time of day again."

Liz was stunned that this adult man she had gotten to know had been living without time since he was eleven years old. She was amazed at the resiliency of the town and the people who knew Josh. They had allowed him to have this lifestyle for decades.

"So, his mom just went on letting him not use a clock to be on

ANITA RENAGHAN

time for anything?" It was unreal, and Liz couldn't imagine that she was right on that count, but Mr. Thompson nodded his head.

"Oh, she tried just about everything short of military school, but there was no getting through to Josh. And family and friends came together and got the gas station setup with one of the first pay at the pump machines. Some of us would look in on the station when she or her brother couldn't be there, and once Josh graduated high school, he took over the station, and he's been doing that ever since."

"How could he have gotten through high school without showing up?" Liz asked.

"He showed up to some of the classes some of the time, and a doctor friend diagnosed him with a disorder that got the school district to assist with his way of life. It takes a village sometimes."

Liz thought of her own trials of being a single mom after divorce, and she knew that it had taken a lot of hands helping her to get through.

"And he's smart as a whip. He's got the key to the library down the street too, and he's probably read every book in there." Mr. Thompson tapped the counter twice. "Over the years, he just started staying away from most places during the day aside from his gas station. He fixes some cars when people have time to wait for the repair. He's talented and charges a fair price, but you must be patient to get your vehicle back sometimes. Maybe that's all going to change now."

Liz looked at him questioningly, and Mr. Thompson winked.

"Looks like there's a reason Josh is willing to be seen around town again."

"I don't know about that," Liz said, but she could feel her face burning in embarrassment for the second time in the past ten minutes.

LIZ GRABBED a sandwich and walked down to Josh's gas station on her lunch break like always, but now the bench next to the payphone sat empty. No one had seen Ted. Liz hadn't talked to him since she had found out that he was married and that the mysterious woman in the green muscle car was his wife.

The store in the gas station was usually closed, but now Liz saw the 'Open' sign flipped over, and she could see the round face of Billy Noodles inside. Liz wondered if Josh was there, too. She didn't see her car next to the roll door, so she walked around back, and it was there, parked next to the shed. When she saw the padlock on the shed, she wondered if that was Ted's shed, and she wondered what might be inside.

Liz thought about mentioning her car to Josh. When she would visit with Ted, she had looked it over for minutes at a time, thinking about her mom and her dad, and especially Sean. She remembered driving him out to the edge of the suburbs to a pumpkin patch that offered hayrides and taking him to a local Easter egg hunt in the spring. There were so many memories in that car, and Liz would stand on the edge of the sidewalk and wonder if she should buy the car back. She had enough money for gas to return home. But she also wondered if she should just let it go and put it behind her along with her old life. Liz reckoned that the memories weren't in the car. They were in her mind and in her heart. And since Josh never brought the subject up, the car still sat dormant.

Liz walked with purpose today. After Josh's visit to the store and Mr. Thompson's explanation of why Josh lived the way that he did, Liz wanted to see him. She thought that knowing his background might better help her to understand what he was all about. She'd never known someone to disregard time the way that society had dictated it since the invention of the clock.

Liz's steps crunched on the gravel, and she saw Billy emerge from the back door of the store and make a beeline for an old brown pickup truck that had seen better days. Although he was a blond, his straight hair and round rimmed glasses made Liz think that he'd been enamored with the early Harry Potter movies and had stuck with the look.

Liz followed him and noticed Josh for the first time. He was working under the hood on the old truck. Billy's eyes opened wide, and he pushed his small notebook under Josh's nose and tapped it with his finger a few times.

"Hi, Josh," Liz said, and Billy's eyes opened even wider.

Josh leaned around the hood smiled at Liz. "Thanks, Billy. Go back inside and watch the store for me."

Billy walked back to the faded metal door, his eyes never leaving Liz. He opened the door and stepped in, his round face leaning out to watch her until he finally pulled the door closed.

"Sorry about that. He seems to be a fan of yours," Josh said.

"Well, that's nice." Liz shrugged, unable to think of the right thing to say. She watched Josh wrench on something under the hood. Liz had never learned about cars. She was content to stand quietly and split her attention between Josh's work and the leaves blowing in the trees that grew along the small trickle of a stream here at the north end of town.

Josh was capable under the hood, and he seemed proficient with tools. Liz wondered how he had made it this far in life with his habit of not watching time in the least. She was grateful for his quirks though, because he might have been the only man on the planet to buy her car and then store it without a word.

Liz drew circles in the gravel beneath her feet and wondered what to say. She'd never had an issue talking to Ted, but Ted was gone, and no one seemed to know where. She had spent a little time with Josh but never seemed to know what to say. "Mr. Thompson doesn't know where Ted is either. Do you think he was carried away in the storm?"

Josh smiled and kept his eyes on his work. "I'm sure the storm had nothing to do with it."

"But don't you think it's strange that he's been on that bench every day until now? That storm was awful."

"The tornado didn't hit the town, and Ted isn't known to go out into the crops. I'm sure he's sleeping it off somewhere safe."

Liz hoped that was true. "I just wish that…" She really preferred to talk to Ted. Josh was safe enough, but Liz sensed within her a need to please him, and she was old enough to recognize that feeling. She had a crush. "Ted told me about his wife the other day. I just hope that I didn't open a wound."

Josh nodded and stepped back from the truck. He wiped his hands on a rag and then wiped the sweat from his forehead with the back of his arm. "There's a lot of history there."

Liz waited for more, but Josh ducked under the hood and continued to work. She looked at him expectantly, and she could tell by the way his eyebrows moved that he noticed her watching him.

"I'm fixing this truck for the car show. Mr. Johnson enters it every year, and he never wins. He parks it in his yard after the show and lets it sit all year, and then two weeks before the car show, he has me tow it in and get it going again."

"I heard the car show is a pretty big deal. The Thompsons have been talking about it for a couple weeks."

"Yep. Everyone in town goes."

Liz rocked up onto her toes and wondered if Josh would be going to the car show during the day when the cars were in full view, or if he would go at night and just see the cars that were parked under the streetlights.

"Do you go?" Liz asked just as Billy stepped out the back door of the store and thrust his notepad in front of Josh again.

"Thanks, Billy. Send him around back. I'm almost finished."

"I'll go."

"You can stay," Josh said, but Liz had already turned.

"I should get back to work," she called over her shoulder.

An elderly gentleman in a button up plaid shirt and tan slacks tipped his hat as Liz walked by, and she smiled at him. She assumed this was Mr. Johnson, and she could see by the hitch in his step why he parked the truck all year round.

She had all but forgotten about her sandwich, and Liz went to Ted's bench and sat down to eat her half of the chicken salad on wheat. She looked across the street at the steel rotundas and she could hear machinery at work, but she still had no idea what machinery made that sound. She looked up and down the street and watched the few cars turning into the gas station. Liz realized that her attention was easily pulled away from her Saturn. She was more focused on Josh and Billy and the way the wind made the top of the trees rock back and forth. She still thought that she had made the tornado hop over the town, and she wondered if this small part of the earth had been saved just for her.

Liz was deciding to stay in Sycamore for now, and she considered getting a better paying job like the one she'd had as a teacher. She would have to find out if her credentials would carry over. She had already decided to get herself an apartment of her own. She didn't mind Ted's apartment, but she didn't want to take advantage of the kindness she'd been shown. She wondered about Ted again, and then Liz felt a pang of guilt. She hadn't called her parents since the day she had arrived. It had been two months since she had borrowed some change from Ted, and Liz couldn't believe how fast that time had gone.

Liz took a deep breath as she approached the payphone. She put her sandwich on top and felt for change in her pockets, but she knew that she didn't have enough. She picked up the receiver and dialed the operator to call collect. She heard three clicks and then ringing, and the phone was answered on the second ring.

"Hello?"

"Ma'am, I have a collect call from Elizabeth Campbell. Do you agree to accept the charges?"

"Well, my yes! That's my daughter."

"Thank you." The operator's voice disappeared with a click.

"Elizabeth, are you there?"

"Yes, Mom. I'm here."

"Oh, thank God that you're all right. You are, right? Okay, I mean?" Liz didn't think that she'd ever heard her mom short for words before.

"Yes, Mom. I'm just fine."

"Where are you?"

Liz cleared her throat. "I'm in the same small town that I was in the last time I called. I just called to tell you that I'm sorry for not checking in like I promised. I just needed to clear my head. You know?"

Liz waited to hear disappointment in her mom's voice. She waited to hear the begging for Liz to just come home. But there was silence, and then Liz heard her mom take a long breath.

"Can you tell me how you are doing? Where are you? You're my baby girl, Elizabeth. I'm worried." Her mom was pleading but not demanding, and Liz felt another pang of guilt.

"I'm okay mom. I'm trying to take a step forward. I'm not just lying in bed all day anymore, so that's something."

Liz could hear her mom crying on the other end of the line, but she didn't try to comfort her.

"I'll keep in touch, I promise. I just need a little more time to do this right now without anything reminding me." Liz looked up and saw Billy Noodles watching her from inside the gas station, and she felt good about the promise of her decision to stay for a while. "I'm worried too, Mom. I'm worried that I'm not out of it enough to not stumble backwards."

"I understand that it must be hard with everyone watching you and expecting you to go on with your life and that's not easy. And I guess New York and especially this house is a reminder of your life with Sean and that must be difficult. I'm sorry if I pushed too hard."

"It's okay, Mom. I probably would have done the same to Sean if I was in your shoes. I was just stuck." Liz grunted and shook her head, remembering what she could of the months that she had spent in bed immersed in grief.

"Well, we are here for you, Elizabeth. You're always welcome here, but if you need to start over, your father and I understand."

Liz thought of her father's faraway stare and grief-ridden silence. Liz and Darren had never coped with Sean's death together. She never had the time that she needed to grieve with Sean's other parent. Her ex-husband was at the wake and the funeral, but he never seemed devastated. Liz wasn't sure if he blamed her for the accident. If he did, he never said it. It was like their marriage, she thought. He was at his own son's funeral, and yet he was keeping his chin up on what must have been the worst day of his life. Darren never let anyone peek into his heart. In Liz's eyes, that was what had caused the end of their marriage.

Liz recognized more fatherly grief for Sean's death in her own father's reaction. Everyone had told her that they were sorry for her loss, but not her father. He had lost as much, and Liz knew he was inconsolable. Where her mother tried to put on a brave face and move on with life, her father hadn't faked a smile even once.

There were more sniffles on the line. "Your father says that you're just trying to move on and get your life in order, but I'm not as strong as him. I need to hear from you. I need to know that my baby's okay."

"Well, that's why I called. I'll try to do better. Mom. I'll talk to you soon. Goodbye."

"We love you, honey."

Liz hung up the phone and grabbed the rest of her sandwich. She let the tears dry on her cheeks as she walked back toward work.

CHAPTER 14

*J*osh watched Liz walk away. She had changed in the time that he had known her. She walked with purpose and her head up, noticing the world around instead of slowly hunched over and defeated. He was glad to know that he might be part of her finding happiness again. He stepped back and wiped his hands before moving to the driver's seat and firing up the old truck for Mr. Johnson.

"She's a real looker," Mr. Johnson said above the muffler's rumble.

"She'll do. I don't know that you'll place this year. You've got some tough competition." Josh said this every year even though Mr. Johnson's old truck hadn't placed in fifteen years. But the retiree loved to enter the car show and to spend three days talking the good 'ole days with the onlookers.

"I was talking about the girl. I don't recognize her."

Josh smiled and shook his head, but he didn't comment. Mr. Johnson wasn't wrong. Liz was pretty. She was more than just pretty, though. She was easy to be around, and he didn't feel pressured to act in front of her. Still, he didn't want to let on.

"You should ask that one on a date," Mr. Johnson prodded.

Josh clenched his teeth. He wanted to ask Liz on a date but being called out by Mr. Thompson in the store had reminded Josh of a heart-to-heart Mr. Thompson had tried to have last year. He told Josh that he was less reliable than Ted Barlow because Josh lived on a whim.

"At least Ted Barlow has some sort of schedule. He's on his bench in the morning minding his payphone, and later in the day, the bartenders at Veterans Club and PJ's Tavern know when he's going to show up for a drink. But you have no schedule in the least, and that makes you completely unreliable, Josh."

Josh knew that Mr. Thompson was trying to help. And he was pretty sure that his mom had put Mr. Thompson up to it, but it still hurt to hear.

Old Mr. Johnson climbed into the truck. "Life's too short, Josh. Make the most of it."

"Well, you are right about that," Josh agreed. He pulled his tools from the edge of the engine compartment and let the hood slam closed as Mr. Johnson climbed into the big, brown beast. The truck hadn't grown over the years, but Mr. Johnson was shrinking with age.

"You're going to need a step stool next year," Josh badgered with a laugh.

"Eh!" Johnson replied with the wave of a hand. "We'll settle up when I collect my winnings."

Josh nodded, knowing that there was no way that this truck would place in the car show. But this was part of their arrangement, and Josh knew that Johnson would be back to pay next week and that he'd have a lot to say about every other truck at the show. Josh closed the heavy door so Mr. Johnson wouldn't fall out. He stepped back, wondering if Johnson still had enough muscle in his leg to push the heavy clutch down.

As soon as the brown truck was around the building, Billy emerged from the back door again. He walked over to Josh and held his notepad out. Josh looked up at Billy who nodded his head, and they both went inside. Josh and Billy looked out the front window. He could see Liz on the payphone, and even though she was too far away to see clearly, he wished that he could read lips.

"I wonder who she's talking to," Josh said.

"Don't know," Billy replied, and Josh glanced back at his typically silent employee. They watched in silence for another minute.

"I wonder what kind of sandwich that is. It's going to bake in the sun if she leaves it up there much longer."

Billy scribbled on his notepad and thrust it in front of Josh.

"Chicken salad? How can you know that?"

Billy wrote for a minute and then handed his notepad over. *Ted says the chicken salad has the blue cellophane lid, and the PBJ is clear, and the tuna salad is yellow. Ted says that he likes to see the blue wrapper on account of him liking chicken salad.*

Josh gave the pad back to Billy. "Have you seen Ted lately?" Billy shook his head, and they both looked back at Liz. She had a sideways smile, but she was also agitated, twisting the hard metal cord around her hand. Josh was jealous. He wanted to know who she was talking to, but Liz would know that he was snooping if he walked outside to look.

Liz was a mom, and she lost her son in an accident, but Josh hadn't been smart enough to ask her about her son's father. Josh hadn't considered Liz being married, and as he watched her body language, he could tell that she was talking to someone that she really cared for. He moved to the front door and opened it, and then decided eavesdropping wasn't the way. He paced, wondering if the Thompsons might know, but he wasn't ready to chat with anyone about his personal feelings. It was all too awkward anyway, especially after his last visit to Thompson's.

Josh wished that Ted was around because Ted had spent more time with Liz than anyone, and he might know or at least have been sitting on the bench when Liz made the call. Josh scratched his head in defeat. If he wanted to know, he would have to ask Liz.

She hung up the phone, and Josh thought that he might take this opportunity to ask Liz to go with him to the car show. They would have to go in the morning before the place filled up, but he assumed she would have to work that day anyway. Josh walked across the station past the pumps to try to catch Liz, but when he heard the low rumble and saw the green 1968 Chevy Camaro SS, he stopped in his tracks. It was Ted's wife, and Josh didn't know what to tell her. He had no idea where Ted had gone off to, but she always worried, and Josh didn't think he could face her today.

He turned to head back into the store when the car rolled by. When it didn't stop in front of the station, Josh turned to see the Chevy parked a half block down next to Liz who was stopped on the sidewalk. She stood there for a minute, and then she opened the passenger door and slipped inside the green machine.

"GET IN," the beautiful blonde woman said to Liz who was bent over with her mouth open. She'd heard the car and had stopped to see if by some miracle Ted was inside. Instead, it was Ted's wife, and Liz felt cornered.

"I don't know where Ted is," Liz said.

"You work at Thompson's. I'll give you a ride back to work."

"It's only a couple of blocks." Liz didn't know why she was resisting. This woman undoubtedly had questions about Ted that no one had answers to, and Liz was embarrassed.

Liz wasn't with Ted, nor did she have any intention of pursuing a romantic relationship with him. The thought was ridiculous, and Liz smiled to herself as she thought of Josh. There was no attraction with Ted, even on the surface. But Liz had spent a lot of time getting to know him, and she was worried.

Still, they'd had serious conversations, and Liz didn't want to share that time with anyone, especially Ted's wife.

The blonde woman's eyes bored into Liz. "Let me give you a ride."

Liz shrugged in defeat and stepped into the car. "Do you want a sandwich?" she asked sheepishly. The woman ignored the question, tapping the gas pedal, and the car lurched away from the curb. Liz admired her outfit of designer blue jeans and elegant powder-blue sleeveless blouse. Her lipstick was dark but not flashy. Liz snuck a second look because the woman's eyes were fixed on the road. She decided that Ted's wife was a knockout.

They turned right onto State Street, and Liz fidgeted with the sandwich container. She wasn't sure what she could say and although Ted's wife hadn't asked her a question, Liz was sure there were questions forthcoming. The blonde turned the wheel to the right and pulled the car into a spot on the street next to Thompson's. She turned the key back and the low rumble ceased. The blonde cranked the window handle and the window slid up, so Liz did the same. The woman sighed and opened the door.

"Thanks for the ride," Liz said.

"Do you have a minute before you go back to work?"

Liz hesitated with one foot out the door. She looked back at the gorgeous blonde and noticed the puffiness under her eyes. The confident stare that had been focused on the road eroded into obvious distress that was palpable to Liz. "Sure."

The woman nodded and got out of the car, letting the door's own weight drop it closed. Liz followed suit, and they were both on the sidewalk looking at each other. Liz eyed the store guiltily because she didn't want the Thompsons to see her out here with Ted's wife. Dotty could live on this topic for a full week.

Liz looked across the street to the bench, but Ted's wife had already turned toward the door that led up to Liz's apartment. It was Liz's turn to sigh, but she nodded, and they both went inside.

Liz followed the woman up the stairs and unlocked her apartment door. They went into the front room, and Liz wished she had made the bed. They stood face to face, and Liz realized just how much taller Ted's reed-like figure was over his wife.

"Listen, uh…"

"Donna. My name is Donna Barlow if you didn't already know that. And you are Liz, and you're new in town." This was said with a matter of fact that Liz had come to appreciate in a small town where it was apparent to everyone that they all knew everything.

"Hi, Donna. Nice to, uh, meet you," Liz said indecisively. She wondered what made her so uncomfortable with Donna. She had no real relationship with Ted, but she somehow felt anxious in this woman's presence. Maybe it was because Liz was staying in the apartment set aside for him by some of the townspeople.

"I haven't been up here in a long time," Donna said, looking around at the same sparse furnishings that came with the place.

"Has everyone been up here before?" Liz said under her breath.

"I wanted to ask you how Ted is doing."

"Fine, I guess." Liz's meager shrug made Donna bite some of her dark lipstick away.

"Oh, good," Donna said, the sting of jealousy laced in her tone. "I mean, I haven't seen him in any of his usual places for a few days, and I'm worried because of the tornado."

Liz realized too late that Donna must have wanted to come up to see if Ted was here staying in the apartment with Liz. "No!" Liz threw her hands out. "I mean, when I've talked to Ted, he's been okay. I mean, a bit drunk and sarcastic a lot of the time, but he's in there, you know?" The women shared a look, and Liz realized that she needed to make it clear. "I haven't seen him since before the tornado. I was just asking Josh too, and he hasn't seen Ted. So…" Liz's face blushed when she'd said Josh's name, and she stood motionless like a deer in the headlights.

"Oh, I see," Donna said directly, and Liz wondered just what she had discerned. Donna wandered to the window.

"We were living in South Carolina where Ted was stationed. I mean, I was living there. Ted was gone overseas to Afghanistan, and after his second tour in the Middle East something happened, and Ted really changed." Donna paused, and Liz knew that the something was Gus' death. "I tried, I really did, but when he got his orders for his third tour, I couldn't stay there alone, so I moved back to Sycamore to be near my family. After his third tour, Ted got out of the Army and returned, too. But he wasn't really Ted. He was so angry and drunk all the time."

Liz nodded with her mouth open, shocked to hear that Ted had done three tours of duty. She'd seen documentaries and movies on the war in the Middle East, but she knew that she would never understand what Ted had endured.

Liz considered Donna and her willingness to stick around and wait it out. She'd been married enough years to know that there are ups and downs. "No judgement here," Liz said. "I'm divorced myself, so I know how tough it can get. But why?"

"Why, what?"

"I mean, I like Ted. I can see that he probably was a great guy, and he's a war hero and all. He even helped me out. But you're so young. Why do you stay married to him when he's living on the street? Why don't you move on?"

Liz was startled by her own words. They had come out so easily, but they echoed in her ears as Liz considered that maybe she had the same option. Maybe she didn't have to live the rest of her days stifled in the memory of her son.

Donna turned her back and looked out the window. "I know that Ted doesn't seem like the greatest husband, but he's all the love I have in the world. We were high school sweethearts, and I couldn't imagine life without him. I know it probably seems like I live life without him anyway, but I have hope for the man that I married."

Donna turned back to Liz with her chin up and a tear in her eye. "After his second tour, he was so angry and there was no getting through to him. So, I broke up with him. And he begged me to keep him. He begged me to stay. Literally, down on his knees hugging my waist and begging, and I stayed. And do you know the one thing I never do? I never wonder what would have happened if I would have walked out that door. Do you know why I never wonder?"

Liz shook her head.

"It's because that's not what I chose to do. I chose to stay with Ted. So, the wondering doesn't matter. I don't know why this is happening to us, and it hurts, but I can't go back there and change my mind. I can only make my choices in the now. And right now, Ted's back." A harsh laugh broke through her lips as she threw her arms up. "Well, he's somewhere."

Liz cleared her throat. She was glad to hear Donna's point of view, but she was uncomfortable hearing this. She felt like she was betraying Ted by hearing the other side of the story. Not that Liz had heard Ted's side of the story.

Donna moved to the door and turned back to look at Liz who had been watching intently. "I know that Ted's running from something, like he's not addressing something that he just can't bear to face. I just wish he'd let me in again, you know?" Liz nodded. "Can you let me know if you see him? Josh knows how to reach me."

Liz watched Donna leave the apartment. She stood still, like she'd been hiding in plain sight and now the game was over, but she couldn't bring herself to being found out. The green muscle car rumbled to life on the street below, snapping Liz out of her trance. She lurched in a panic for the door, realizing that she was probably late returning from her lunch break.

That afternoon at work, Liz tried to busy herself, but she caught herself staring out the window of Thompson's General Store on several occasions. With the arrival of the car show, there was still plenty to do. The shelves were overstocked with water, sunblock, and snacks, and there were baskets of umbrellas set out for sale, along with foldable lawn chairs. There were even some small Igloo coolers for sale, and blue gel ice packs stuffed in the ice cream cooler.

They didn't usually sell these types of items, but Liz understood that these would be hot ticket items during the car show. They would need to be stocked for the visitors who would be window shopping, but also for the hundreds of entrants who would be sitting outside in the humid heat all day on the last weekend of July.

Liz thought about Ted Barlow and where he could have gone, and she thought about Donna Barlow who seemed very wise for her age. Liz wondered if Donna's quiet calm came from years of experience with a husband who was first gone overseas to fight for his country, and then watching out for the same man who had never quite returned. Liz knew that she would be a wreck if she was in that situation. But maybe Donna Barlow was all cried out.

Liz would never forget her son, but maybe she was supposed to find a new life. Donna had said that Ted was running from his past, and Liz understood that all too well. She wondered if Donna's words had been meant for her to hear. So, when Mr. Thompson told her she could leave for the day, Liz found herself heading south, walking through the streets past large historical homes and headed for church.

LIZ SAT in the last pew. She was surprised to see several people here on a weekday afternoon with no formal mass happening. A couple were kneeling with their heads bowed, and a one man was staring up at the large crucifix. The door opened and someone came in and stood next to her, and when they didn't move forward into the church, Liz looked up. It was the priest who had prayed for Sean, and Liz knew that she had come here to see him.

"Hello again," the priest said. Liz couldn't remember his name.

"Hi," she replied, looking back to the cross. No answers came.

"You look well," the priest told her. "I'm Father Brown, and Josh told me that your name is Liz. It's nice to meet you, Liz."

"It's nice to meet you," she said cordially, making eye contact again. Liz wanted to talk to Father Brown, but she felt self-conscious in the quiet of the church with others present.

"Should we take a walk?" Father Brown asked as though he'd read her mind. Liz nodded and followed him outside. They strolled slowly around the block that contained the church and the school and a large parking lot.

"The church is much busier now that there was a tornado that almost hit the town. People have remembered again that this is a short life, like they do around New Year's Eve. I suppose that's something you already figured out." Father Brown held his hands behind his back and walked slowly, turning slightly to meet Liz's eyes.

She glanced over and thought that he might be wondering if she was going to have another melt down.

When she didn't reply, he continued. "I used to think a lot about the circle of life. It's a beautiful thing really. Children are born and raised, and I have found that no matter their station in life, whether rich or poor, everyone seems to have a grievance with their parents. Maybe that's nature's way of making sure that everyone leaves their parent's home eventually. I don't know."

Liz nodded and felt a bit ashamed of the way she had driven away from her parents without a word. She should call her mom again soon and then maybe once a week.

They had walked by a church activity center and then around back to the parking lot where they rounded the last corner of the red brick school. The parking lot dead ended at the back of the school and Father Brown slowly arced their path back toward the front of the church.

"Then as parents grow older and frailer, the children have also grown older and have the opportunity to forgive their parents' transgressions. Their age gives them new insight they never had as children. And so, the circle continues. Anger, understanding, forgiveness."

Liz felt the priest was looking at her now, but she shifted her gaze up to the cross on the church. "And what of my son? There is no circle of life for him." Liz wasn't in despair anymore. She was here today in search of an answer. She had looked everywhere, turned over every stone, and she thought there was an answer in front of her that she just couldn't see.

There was a long silence as they came to the church door, and Father Brown turned toward Liz with a pained expression. "Your son isn't suffering. He won't have the circle of life, but he knows the glory of God. You don't have to stay nailed to your cross for him, Liz. It's okay to move forward."

Liz nodded her head. Father Brown's words were like a cleansing pool to Liz, and she bathed in their healing tones. She now understood why she had come here today. It was Donna Barlow's words about choices and not wondering what could have happened. Donna Barlow was all in, and she didn't second guess any of her choices. Even at a time when her husband lived on the street as a drunk, she didn't wonder 'what if?'

Liz had pondered it all afternoon at work as she stared out the window of the store. It seemed that her whole adult life was running through her mind, trying to find the exact moment that she could change to make the accident not happen. Liz had blamed her ex-husband for years and for everything. She blamed him for wasting her twenties on a failed marriage. She blamed him for leaving her and Sean. She blamed him for her failing finances and for her having to move back into her parent's house. Sean had liked it there, Liz knew. He liked having his own room where he could leave his toys out and pin pictures of race cars and airplanes to the walls. He liked when his grandpa would come in and tell a story about one of the airplanes that they had tacked up together. Sean had liked that life, but Liz had barely noticed at the time. She was too busy looking at the world through the lens of hostility that she held toward Sean's father.

Liz rubbed her cheeks. Donna Barlow had made her choices, and she didn't bother with a different road taken or even with licking her wounds. She plowed forward without apology, and she didn't move on, although she could. And Liz had driven halfway across the country to gain permission to move on, and she had to.

There was an answer in Father Brown's words, and she would try to receive it. Liz would accept this priest's permission to go on living. "I've heard that the tornado missing the town is a miracle," Liz said.

Father Brown smiled. "Sometimes people see miracles where they need to, and sometimes they really are miracles."

Liz liked the way Father Brown talked. It was as though he were a sage seeing answers everywhere that he looked.

"So why do some people find a way to move forward, and others don't?" She was thinking of herself and of Ted Barlow. In these last two months, Liz had made great progress, and yet Ted Barlow had been back from war for a couple of years. "Have you seen Ted Barlow?"

He shook his head. "Seems Ted left with the tornado. I say that figuratively, of course."

"I haven't seen him either," Liz said.

"Let's say a prayer for Ted." And so, as they stood outside the door of the church. Liz reflexively bowed her head and let Father Brown's words about the circle of life pour back over her and mingle with his request to God to keep Ted safe and to help all lost souls find their way forward.

CHAPTER 15

*J*osh was working on an old junker that a college student had brought over. Josh was always leery of college students paying their tab, but this boy gave Josh two-hundred fifty dollars cash for the parts up front, so Josh figured he'd only get stiffed on his time if the kid didn't come back.

He was under the car looking at the transmission and exhaust pipes when Billy's quick footsteps crunched on the gravel. Josh knew that meant Liz was headed here. Josh wiggled his shoulders and pulled himself out from under the car and Billy shoved his notepad at him.

"Easy, Billy. Liz is here?"

His eyes were wide behind his round glasses as Billy nodded enthusiastically.

"Thanks," Josh said, wiping his hands. He busied himself under the hood even though he didn't have any work to do on the engine yet. Josh wanted to make sure he had a good view of Liz when she visited, though he rarely said anything of substance to her. He would putter on a car and Liz would sometimes talk about the people who came into the store or how small-town life was interesting. She talked fast, and Josh liked her accent. He liked that she was coming out of her shell with him. Josh wanted to know everything about Liz.

Billy must have wanted to know about Liz, too. Instead of running back into the store when she came by at lunch time, Billy would sit on the old, rusted stool that was against the brick wall, and he would take notes. Josh read some of those notes, and he could see that Billy had a crush on Liz. Josh couldn't blame him. He was suffering the same crush.

Today, Liz was wearing faded jeans and a green blouse. The front was cut low and the sleeves were cut high for summer, and Josh tried not to stare as she moved toward him.

"Hi, Billy," Liz said in a flirting tone, and Billy hunched down and smiled, frantically writing on his notepad.

"Hi, Liz," Josh said, peeking out from behind the hood.

Liz came over to look. She half smiled and said sarcastically, "Nice car."

Josh shook his head. "Not even when I'm done with her. But she'll run solid for a couple more years if the owner doesn't beat on her." Josh pulled on some hoses and cleaned out the air filter.

Liz put her hand over her eyes to shade them from the sun and looked around at the trees. "This weather is like New York in July."

"Does it remind you of home?" Josh asked.

Liz hesitated. "It's almost exactly the same," she said mockingly as she elbowed Josh's ribs. "Except you have more skyscrapers here." Her arms opened wide, referencing the trees.

He'd served that one up to her and Josh deserved the sarcasm, but he liked it. Josh stepped back from the beater and took a deep breath. He had finally resolved to ask Liz out on a date.

"So, Liz," he said formally, and she jerked her head back to look at him. Josh tried to read her expression. He hoped that he was reading her correctly because he thought she looked hopeful.

"I was just wondering if I could take you out sometime."

Liz bit her lip. "Okay."

Josh smiled at Liz's smile. It had taken him two weeks to get up the courage after Mr. Thompson had walked him to the door of the store, and he was panicked at what else to say so he busied himself under the hood again. Liz walked around the car toward Billy. He flipped to a clean page and scribbled before holding the notepad up to Liz.

"No, Billy. It's just going to be me and Josh."

Josh leaned his head around the hood and gave Billy a death-stare, and Billy shrank back on his stool.

"So, Josh. When should I expect you?" Liz asked.

Josh's eyes opened wide. He wasn't sure what to say. He'd been thinking so much about how to ask Liz out and what she would say in reply, that he hadn't made actual plans. He felt sweat around his neck, and he looked at Billy who scribbled something in his notebook. Josh wanted to walk over and read the words, but he refused to take advice on girls from Billy Noodles.

Josh was frozen, and Liz turned to walk away. When she reached the corner of the building, she turned back to Josh who had stepped around the car to watch her leave. "You can't ask a girl out and then expect her to wait all night to see if you're going to decide to show up," Liz called back. Then she was gone.

Billy hopped off the stool and held the notepad up to Josh, and Josh knocked it to the ground. He regretted it in an instant, and Billy bent down to pick up the notepad and went back inside. Josh threw his wrench in the gravel and sat on the stool and listened to the voice in his head.

It always happened like this when Josh felt cornered. He was a grown man and yet his mom did this to him a few times each year. And some of the other people he knew around town also tried to get Josh to commit to some specific day or time to get together.

Josh covered his face with his hands. He seemed to be the only one who knew that time didn't mean anything.

He pulled his feet up a rung on the stool so his elbows could rest on his legs. He hid his face in the heels of his hands. There it was again. Time. It was trying to catch up to him. Josh grunted. Ted Barlow had been the one person who seemed to understand Josh's feelings on time, at least Josh had thought he did. But over the months, Josh could see a pattern in Ted's behavior, and it was set around the right time to do things throughout his day. Even the lost and drunk Ted Barlow was a slave to time.

Josh's anger suddenly changed to fear, and he hopped off the stool and sat in the front seat of the car that he'd been working on. He tried to hold back the tears, but a couple got away and ran down his cheeks. The memories were back. The day he'd run out on his dad overwhelmed him, and Josh felt a physical ache in his stomach.

He leaned forward and cupped his head in his arms, trying to block out the sunlight. His eyes moved frantically with his thoughts. "The clock doesn't know what I need," Josh whispered over and over.

He remembered how still his dad's body was lying on the bed. "The clock doesn't know what I need," he repeated desperately.

He remembered his mother crying out in utter helplessness. "The clock doesn't know what I need."

He remembered the uselessness of the wake and funeral and how it all flowed together perfectly on schedule and didn't fix anything. *The clock doesn't know what I need,* he thought.

Josh removed the grip on his head and tried to calm himself. Maybe he could forget Liz. He felt confident until he looked up and saw the Saturn station wagon parked on the back of the lot next to Ted's shed. *The clock doesn't know what I need.*

But maybe, just maybe, Liz needed the clock. And if Josh was going to take her out, she needed him to tell her a time. He'd enjoyed all their time together, even the first night when she'd followed him to the theatre. They were strangers then, but a lost and aimless Liz had found Josh that night.

"The clock doesn't know…" Josh tried again. He wanted more than anything to spend time with Liz. He wanted to take her out on a date and find out everything about her past and who she was and who she wanted to be. He couldn't just come in at sunrise every day just in case she was going to happen by the station. "The clock doesn't know. It doesn't know," Josh argued out loud. And in his mind, he watched Liz walking away.

LIZ WAS ARRANGING the lower shelves when she heard the bell ring. "Be right with you," she said, standing up and straightening her smock. Mr. Thompson came out of the back.

"I've got it," Liz said as she rounded the shelf. She stopped in her tracks. She'd seen Josh only an hour ago, and here he was, standing at the door with his baseball cap in his hand. He looked like a child who was trying to get up the courage to admit that he'd broken a family heirloom.

"I think it's for you anyway," Mr. Thompson teased, but he didn't return to the office in back. He hooked his thumbs under the straps of his overalls, and he nodded at Josh who stepped toward the register.

"Hey," Liz said with a smile as she met Josh at the counter.

Josh nodded and swallowed. "Hi," he said. Liz noticed his sharp, green eyes. "I uh…"

Liz wanted to say a hundred things, but a voice in her head was telling her to be quiet. Josh looked like he had a stomachache, and for a moment she thought he might have come here for an antacid. "Are you okay?"

Josh nodded. "Tomorrow night at seven," he said to Liz. Then he turned and walked quickly out of the store. He'd forgotten to wait for an answer, but he was going to assume that Liz's crooked smile meant 'yes'.

~

LIZ HAD BEEN DOING small laps in the apartment for almost an hour, alternately looking at herself in the mirror and looking out the window for Josh who was late. She remembered for the tenth time how he had so casually turned the hands of the clock back on the first day that they had met. She remembered what Mr. Thompson had told her about Josh and his father and the way Josh had never been the same. She knew that he lived a lot of his life late at night, and she wondered if he was going to even show up.

She watched for his truck as several classic cars pulled into town. The big, heavy frames painted in vintage colors reminded her of the few car shows that she had gone to with Darren. He had ogled the cars, but Liz couldn't enjoy the nostalgia in the imposing heat of the day, nor the thought of the money that they didn't have to spend on a luxury item such as a classic car.

She took a deep breath and let it out slowly. She knew that she had to put these thoughts behind her because that life was over, and this older and wiser Liz would not make the same mistakes. And it was Friday night and Liz had a date, at least she hoped that she still did.

The knock at her door startled Liz. She opened the door and looked at Josh who was wearing his trademark blue jeans and a T-shirt with baseball cap. Josh smiled, and Liz felt that tiny flutter in her stomach that told her that she liked Josh, although she was perturbed. She thought that she could smell motor oil, and she noticed a stain on Josh's jeans.

"Sorry," Josh said, as though he'd read her mind. Then Liz realized he was apologizing for his tardiness.

"I'm ready," Liz said, pocketing her key and closing the door behind her. Liz was also wearing jeans, but she had put on the nicest blouse that she owned and had spent some time in the mirror trying to get her hair right. She'd let it grow for five months and hadn't cared about it until today, but at least she had cared. Josh had obviously come straight from the gas station.

They walked down the stairs and out onto the sidewalk, both with their hands stuffed in their pockets. Josh snuck glances in her direction, and Liz could see that he was just as curious about her as she was about him. She decided that she had to accept his apology, or her night would be ruined before they went anywhere.

Outside, they strolled the bustling sidewalk. Liz hadn't seen the downtown area this busy, and she could see why the Thompsons had been preparing so diligently. The car show wasn't for two more days, and there was already a noticeable crowdedness. They turned the corner and Liz saw her Saturn parked next to the old hotel.

"Got to run it. If it sits too long, you could have issues," Josh said a bit sheepishly. "I hope that's okay."

Liz swallowed hard. "It's okay."

Liz was surprised when Josh opened her door. She'd never dated anyone who had held her car door open for her before. When Josh ran around the car and slid in next to her, he noticed Liz's expression.

"My dad used to do that for my mom," he said, and Liz bit her lip.

"I didn't know that we were going to drive anywhere."

"We don't have to."

"No, it's good," Liz said.

"It's Kishwaukee Fest this week."

Liz knew about the festival, although she hadn't really wanted to go. Parades and street fairs seemed like a lifetime ago, and she couldn't imagine Josh around throngs of people either.

"There is something I wanted to ask you, Liz." Josh seemed to flinch with the words. He turned onto the main road between Sycamore and DeKalb and sped up with traffic."

"Yes?"

Josh glanced at Liz. "Are you married?"

Liz smiled. "No. I'm divorced." His shoulders relaxed, and she could see that he was relieved.

"Good," Josh sighed. "I mean, not good. I mean, that must have been rough. It's just that you have a son and the registration on this car is in a man's name. I just wanted to be sure."

"Your honor is intact, sir," Liz jibed. "Actually, it's my dad's car." Liz suddenly felt guilty for taking her dad's car. She wondered what he'd been driving since she'd left town. "So, what goes on at a Kishwaukee Fest?"

"The Kishwaukee River runs through these parts, so that's where the name comes from. It's just your average small-town festival."

Liz didn't know exactly what to expect because she'd never been to a small-town festival. She looked out the window at the many stores and fast-food restaurants and recognized the names of some nationwide chain stores. When they came to a residential area again, Josh stopped next to a wide driveway, but it had cars parked along each side, so he moved on down the street until he came to an open spot where he parked the car. Liz looked around and saw others getting out of their cars with lawn chairs and blankets, but she didn't see or hear any telltale signs of a festival.

Josh parked and they both got out of the car. Liz noticed too late that he was trying to get around the car to open her door, but she had already gotten out, so she waited and let him close the door for her. When Josh looked up at her, they shared a knowing smile that made Liz inhale deeply. She had spent time alone with Josh, but now she was feeling nervous and self-conscious and all the things one feels on a first date.

Josh watched the others who made their way up the sidewalk, and he looked stricken. He moved to the back of the Saturn station wagon and opened the hatch, pulling an old brown and mustard yellow blanket from the back. Liz watched him intently.

"I'm sorry. I wasn't as prepared as I thought I would be."

"It's okay," Liz said as Josh pulled out her father's old blanket. It was another moment of surreal for Liz, but it didn't feel as foreign as she had expected it to.

They followed other couples and families who were carrying lawn chairs, blankets, and coolers. They walked a block and turned up a long driveway to a parking lot. Liz was expecting to see throngs of people and a carnival, but the far-off music was a pleasant jazz. She could see a red, brick building ahead, and as they rounded the large trees, she saw that it was a huge house. Her eyebrows rose and she looked at Josh who seemed pleased with her expression.

"The Elwood Mansion was built for Isaac Elwood in the late 1800's. He didn't invent barbed wire, but he was an entrepreneur, and he tweaked the original patent to make it better."

"Wow. That's kind of random."

"Well, folks around here take pride in our local history, I guess," Josh explained, and Liz thought she heard a bit of a drawl in his voice.

"So, he built a kingdom on barbed wire?"

"You could say that. I mean, look at this mansion." Josh's smile turned serious. "Think about it. All that farmland that needed to be fenced in so the cattle couldn't get out."

Liz had seen a lot of the farmland lately, but she'd never considered it before. "And all the barbed wire around prisons," she offered.

"And all the barbed wire used in the first World War," Josh said, and then grimaced.

"Very romantic," Liz teased as they followed the families onto the large, grass front lawn. There was a band on the front porch of the mansion. It was made up of about twenty performers like the bands she had seen in old movies. "Are the keys to the mansion on your keychain?"

"Wouldn't you like to know?" Josh responded, shaking his head.

"We never did get all the way through those keys."

"There's time," Josh said, and Liz felt her face blush, reminding her again that it had been so many years since she'd last been on a first date.

As they wound their way through the lawn chairs and blankets, Liz could hear different horn instruments playing random notes behind her.

"I'm sorry we missed the Jazz Quartet. But next up is Bill O'Connell's Chicago Skyliners Big Band. They're really good." Josh found a spot of grass behind most of the lawn chairs, and he spread the blanket out. He noticed the oil stain on the blanket. "Sorry, again."

"That's okay," Liz said, sitting down and relaxing. "Feels a bit like home."

～

IT WAS difficult to see the band this far away from the mansion, but Josh could tell that Liz was still enjoying herself. He wondered if he should have taken her somewhere without noise so they could talk, but even at the gas station when Liz stopped by on her break, he didn't talk much. He preferred to listen to what Liz had to say about the town or the trees or the cornfields. She was seeing for the first time the place he'd always lived in, and her fresh eyes brought new life into Josh's world.

Josh liked sitting next to Liz on the blanket. He didn't have the nerve to hold her hand, especially after she'd pulled hers away outside the bakery. But sitting on that old blanket together made him feel like they were alone on an island. They were out of reach of the world, and nothing could touch them.

Josh had always liked big band music. He recognized some of the songs from old movies he had watched with his mom. There was something about the layers of musicians working together that made him feel good about people. Josh watched Liz watching the band, her brown eyes showing specs of gold in the fading light of the sunset. He wanted to see the world through her eyes. He wanted to know everything about her, and he realized that he knew almost nothing. But he knew that she was a good person, and he knew that it was too late for him even if she wasn't and angel. Josh was hooked, and he was never letting go.

They both enjoyed the evening. They were able to talk for a while when the musicians took a short break, and once the concert was over, Josh and Liz remained on the blanket as the families packed up around them. He liked the fact that Liz wasn't in a rush either, and back in downtown Sycamore when Josh parked the car and closed Liz's door, he found that they were holding hands on the short walk back to her building. They climbed the stairs, and Liz unlocked the door, but she stayed in the hallway to linger. They laced their fingers together and looked uneasily around the small hallway making little eye contact.

"Well, goodnight," Josh said, mentally daring himself to lean in and kiss her.

"Goodnight. See you tomorrow?"

"I'm not sure. It's a busy weekend."

"Oh, that's right," Liz said, remembering the car show. "Will you be at the gas station all weekend?"

"No. I'll probably be around the car show," Josh admitted.

"Well, you know where I'll be," Liz said. She was scheduled for two full days at Thompson's.

Josh stared into Liz's brown eyes and tried to lean in for a kiss, but he was nervous. "Tomorrow morning won't be so bad. It gets busy later in the day after the festival winds down and everyone comes to Sycamore in the afternoon. And Sunday will be very busy," Josh told Liz. He didn't want to talk about the car show, but his nerves wanted him to postpone.

He could see that Liz was about to say something more, but he finally summoned up the courage to try. He pulled her hands close to his side and their lips mingled together in a shared secret. He ran his hand through her hair and pulled her closer into a long kiss. He felt the urge to pull Liz up into his arms and carry her into the apartment. He let the moment pass and pulled away. He liked to see the pink on her cheeks and the welcome smile on her face when he bid her goodnight.

Josh drove to the gas station and swapped Liz's car for his truck, spending the whole way home reliving each minute of their date. They had kissed. He had kissed her, and it was the softest sweetest kiss of his life. He felt both elation and panic because he could really fall in love with Liz, but Josh knew he had a bad track record with women.

Josh had hardly dated because girls didn't like when he didn't show up or when he showed up three hours late or at two in the morning. And the few women who didn't mind his random life-style turned out to be too aloof to carry on a relationship. But this was different because Liz was different.

He hated the fact that he had shown up late and smelling like motor oil, but it couldn't be helped. Josh was lucky that he had gone at all. After Liz had stopped by on her lunch break and Mr. Johnson drove away in his truck, Billy had found Josh sitting in the car holding his head in his hands. The memories could still stun Josh into inaction, but with Billy's coaching, Josh had found enough courage to walk down to Thompson's to officially set up a date with Liz. Once the date was official, Josh returned to the station and threw himself into work, trying to ignore the voice that was prodding him to give up on time.

Twenty-four hours later, Josh was a wreck. He'd been arguing with himself about keeping time and why it was important, but he knew it was a farce. Billy had watched Josh work on the small car all day, his lips pursed tight and his pen waving furiously over the pad of paper. When Billy was leaving for the day, he tapped

Josh in the head with his notepad several times to get his attention. Josh admitted that he was afraid he wouldn't show up for his date with Liz, and Billy had scribbled threats on his notepad. Josh had to show up for Liz or apparently, Billy would beat him to a pulp. The thought had made Josh smile, but this was not a laughing matter.

After much pacing and awkward conversation where Billy talked more than he wrote, Billy told Josh not to leave the gas station. Billy wrote down that he would be back to make sure that Josh went on the date. Billy went home by five every day, and he had to go home now to eat dinner.

And God bless the boy, he had come back and argued with Josh in stunted speech and scribbles that it was time. It was past time, and Josh knew that he had to pick Liz up now or never, but just as he'd been doing all day, Josh wrestled in his mind about time itself. He still wondered what it mattered, and at the same time he knew that today it did matter because it meant a future possibility with Liz. Whether or not he believed it, this meant hours that Liz had set aside for him, but the old voices that said *screw time* wouldn't let him go.

It was Billy after an hour of scribbling notes on the notepad and trying to get Josh to read them who finally threw the notepad and the pencil at Josh. Billy very rarely spoke but now he was yelling. "Josh, don't be a fool!" The words came out strangled because Billy's vocal cords couldn't seem to handle the pressure of his anger. "Don't be a fool. I know your dad's death messed you up."

Josh looked sideways at Billy and took a step forward. A rage he kept at bay forced itself to the surface. This was not a subject that anyone ever broached with Josh. His fists clenched but just as quickly released because Josh could never take his frustrations out on Billy.

"Everyone knows it, Josh, so don't look so surprised. You've got to get over it." They stood still, staring at each other until

Billy shook his head. He picked up his pencil and notepad and wrote furiously, holding the notepad out to Josh. *If you're not going to meet Liz, I'm going to go. Liz deserves more than this.*

Billy's face was red, and he was crying behind his glasses. Josh felt ashamed. He never really felt sorry for Billy because they had always been friends. But now with Billy yelling and furiously pointing at the clock, which he had set to the correct time, Josh saw Billy how other people must have seen him. The short round face on the short round body and the glasses that looked good on others looking geeky on him. The oversized clothes trying to hide the oversized body and the notepad and pencil that cut Billy off from the world. In that moment, he did feel sorry for Billy, but only for a second. He owed Billy his respect and the boy had earned it. Heck, Billy hadn't been a boy for a long time. He was a young man.

Billy was right. His dad's death had messed Josh up, but it wasn't for the reason that people thought. Sure, Josh missed his father and had grieved his loss, but Josh realized a few years ago that he was really afraid of his own death. It's why he went to church sometimes alone in the dead of night. He could picture himself lying in his dad's place, dead to the world, and Josh couldn't begin to face his own mortality.

Josh started to see himself clearly for the first time. Mourning a father who was gone had turned into utter defiance of time and the realization of the truth of everyone's life: that it would end in death.

But shouldn't he take a chance? Wasn't it worse to hide out? He shook the morbid thoughts from his head. No matter the real reason, Josh was messed up, and he was about to blow things with the only woman who had looked twice at him in five years. He had to decide right now if he was going to live or let Liz go.

Billy stood on a chair to take the clock off the wall. He looked straight at Josh and tossed the clock, smashing it on the floor, but Josh stopped Billy from storming out.

"I'm going, Billy. I'm going. I'm sorry and thank you. I owe you."

It was Billy who found a clean shirt in the storeroom and convinced Josh to wash up and put the clean shirt on. And it was Billy who patted Josh awkwardly on the shoulder and handed Josh the key to Liz's car and nodded, pushing Josh out the back door of the station. Looking back, Josh had no idea why he had taken her car, aside from the fact that he had been too afraid to question anything more for fear of regressing.

It was pitch black when Josh pulled up to his house. The light on the porch and the garage barely lit the ground around them. Josh turned off the truck and looked at the house for a long time. One date and one kiss had changed his life. Josh wondered if this country farmhouse could be good enough for a big city girl like Liz.

CHAPTER 16

 n Saturday, Liz was starting to feel excited about the car show. She kept hearing the souped-up engines of cars as they rolled into town, and she kept looking out the window to see if it might be Donna Barlow cruising State Street. But there was no sign of the green machine, and there was still no sign of Ted Barlow. As far as Josh and the Thompsons knew, no one had spotted Ted all week. They all remained cavalier on the outside, since Ted was a grown man and in charge of his own activities, but Liz could tell that they all felt as worried as she did.

She listened to the local teenagers who came into the store excited to be going to the carnival in DeKalb. Several families visited the store in late afternoon, and Liz nodded at the parents who'd had long days, and she smiled at the small children who were over-tired and were making the whole family crabby. Liz helped everyone with their questions, and Dotty was especially glad that Liz was there. Dotty told her that most employees, including her own sister, usually ditched work this weekend to enjoy the festivities.

Liz was happy to work, though. The energy in town was palpable, and Liz was starting to feel part of something good. The car show allowed her to interact and observe, and Liz was seeing so many more of the townspeople than usual. She took her lunch break, but she didn't walk to the gas station to see Josh. She knew he might be there today, but she wanted to walk around downtown and see the work taking place. Several of the side streets were already blocked off in anticipation of the cars arriving in town, and tents were in place outside some of the restaurants and bars. It was good to see the downtown come to life. As Liz walked, she started to daydream about her life in Sycamore and what it might become.

After losing her job as a bank teller during the Great Recession, she had finished her last year of college and gained her certification to teach. She wondered what she might need to do to teach in this town. It might be a daunting prospect, but the more she walked the few short blocks that made up downtown Sycamore, and she saw the care going into this car show, Liz embraced the prospect of reinventing her life. She regretted losing Sean and his memory would always be part of her, but she knew in her heart that there still might be more to her story.

After work, Liz continued watching the downtown area liven up from her window as cars and motorcycles swarmed the town in anticipation of Sunday's car show. She fell asleep late that night daydreaming about the possibilities and woke to a knock at her door. It was still dark, and Liz rubbed her eyes as she opened the door, surprised to see Josh standing in the hall.

"What time is it?" Liz asked reflexively, realizing too late that Josh was the last person on the planet who would know the time.

"It's going to be morning. Do you want to go to the car show?"

Liz felt irritated having been woken from the soundest sleep that she'd had in years. "I'm working today, Josh."

Josh tilted his head down and grabbed the rim of his baseball cap before looking back at Liz. "I know you have to work later. I mean right now. The sun is coming up and it's good to go before everything starts. Most of the entrants will be rolling into town really soon."

Liz wanted to turn Josh down if only for showing up unannounced at this hour, but standing in the doorway reminded her of their kiss, and she blushed in the darkness.

"Sure," Liz said sleepily, wondering just how early entrants pulled into town. "I'll meet you downstairs in fifteen minutes." Josh turned and left, and Liz grabbed her kit for the bathroom and took her time brushing her teeth and fixing her hair. She looked at herself in the mirror for a full minute, something she usually avoided. Liz remembered her thoughts from yesterday about staying in town and getting a job as a teacher. She felt a new life unfolding in front of her, and she wondered if it would include Josh.

He was handsome and patient, but he was unorthodox in his lifestyle. She didn't know if she could really invest in someone who didn't use clocks to tell the time. Now that she was awake though, she did have to admit that she was excited to see him again. And the music last night, it was still playing in her mind. Liz had forgotten about music because she had avoided it all these months. She didn't want to hear music in her suffering. It somehow symbolized life. But Josh had brought it back for her, and Liz was grateful.

Liz ran her fingers through her straight brown hair that fell below her shoulders these days. She smiled to make sure her teeth looked good. She hadn't worn makeup since Sean had died, and she didn't have any now, so she rummaged through the drawers and found Kristi's light pink lipstick. Liz rubbed some on her cheeks for color and then returned to her apartment to change clothes. When she opened the door to the street, Josh was leaning against the building with two small coffees in his hand. He offered one to Liz.

"Thank you." Liz took the cup and sipped.

"I'm sorry," Josh said. Liz stared at him, wondering if there was something wrong with the coffee. "I mean, I'm sorry to just show up like this and wake you up. I know it's not right, Liz."

Josh ducked his face under his baseball cap and took a sip of his coffee.

"Okay," Liz said, glad that he seemed to understand without her needing to bring it up. She looked up and down the street and noticed the clear blue sky that was getting brighter by the minute. She saw some cars and motorcycles, but there were a lot less than she had expected. "So, where are these cars?"

Josh took Liz down the street for a pastry at Elleson's Bakery and as soon as they were back on the sidewalk, Liz could hear the rumble of motorcycles and she could see the bright colors of vintage cars rolling into town. The four blocks of the downtown were cordoned off and the only cars allowed through were the ones entering the show. They walked to Ted's bench and sat down as Josh rattled off the year, make and model of everything with a motor that came down the street. Volunteers appeared and began positioning the entrants into their parking spots for the day. A block away at State and Main, Liz watched a crane hoist a huge American flag into the air.

Josh told stories about car shows past, and when he got up the nerve, he placed his hand over Liz's on the bench. Liz felt his hand move over hers as he slipped his fingers into her palm. Liz squeezed Josh's hand and held on tight, but she didn't say anything.

"Am I boring you?" Josh asked.

"No," Liz smiled and slid close to Josh, pulling their interlaced hands onto her leg. Josh rambled on, and it made Liz feel special because he hardly said two words in a typical day. Although unorthodox, he had let her into his world, and it was like noticing a beautiful photograph that had been somehow disregarded. "So, do any of the keys on your keyring fit any of these cars?"

"No," Josh said a bit jealous. He traced circles on the back of

Liz's hand with his thumb and Liz relished his affection. She could feel herself coming back to life, pulling on the rope in space, wanting and needing to arrive in this place on earth.

Mr. Johnson drove by in his truck, and he slowed and smiled at the couple on the bench, pulling Liz from her daydream.

"Thanks for waking me up," Liz said wryly. She squeezed Josh's hand and then let go to stand up. Josh stood, too.

"It's early still," Josh said.

"You're telling me." Liz was enjoying Josh, but she was ready for the quiet and safety of the inside of Thompson's General Store. It was her domain, and she felt secure there. The thought was hilarious to Liz because she was from the largest city in the United States. Still, Elleson's Bakery was drawing a crowd of people who were starting to fill the sidewalk, and she was supposed to be at work an hour earlier today.

They said goodbye, and Liz crossed the street and looked back at Josh who was watching her go. She waved and felt like a fool, and Josh waved back. When she looked up, she saw Mr. Thompson and Dotty watching her closely from inside Thompson's General Store.

The bell rang when Liz entered, and the Thompsons had scrambled away from the window, although they didn't get far. Dotty turned back with a knowing smile.

"Good morning, Liz."

"Good morning." Liz moved behind the register and pulled on her smock, and she watched Dotty watching her. Liz pursed her lips.

"So, you and Josh Davis then," Dotty offered.

Liz knew that there was really no mystery here. Josh had been coming around Thompson's store in person during the day to pick up his items, and each time Dotty and her husband noted out loud that he must be there to see Liz because he hadn't come in the store during the day in over a decade. "He took me to the concert at Elwood House on Friday. It was nice."

"Oh, very romantic," Dotty offered.

Liz tried not to smile. "Although he woke me up this morning unannounced, so that wasn't a date that you were watching." Liz was making a jibe at Dotty because she knew they had been gawking, but the jest went over Dotty's head. Liz felt like a teenage girl who'd been caught staying out too late. She didn't like it, so she vowed to stop this moment.

"That's sweet," Dotty pushed. She watched Liz and waited for more, but Liz took another tac.

"Can I ask you both something?" Liz said loud enough for Mr. Thompson to hear. He immediately appeared which made Liz think that he, too, might be hanging over the back fences about Josh. "Why did you help me when I came to town?" Liz asked sincerely. "Why did Daniel give me that apartment on faith that I would pay him the money eventually? It's very kind, it's just not how the world usually works."

"Well, we told Daniel that we would give you a job, so we were pretty sure that you'd have the money for the apartment," Mr. Thompson said.

"God will provide," Dotty said with a nod.

Mr. Thompson continued, "How it really came to pass was that Ted Barlow came in and told us that you were lost and that you really needed our help."

Liz laughed, able to look back on her condition when she arrived in Sycamore. She felt grace in the path that she had taken since running out of gas. She realized that there was grace in every turn of the wheel she had made since leaving New York that led her to this town.

"Ted Barlow said that I was lost?" she asked incredulously.

"Well, we saw you sitting on that bench, and we wondered who you were. Then Ted came in and told us in no small terms to give you his room. He only stayed there for a couple of weeks one time over a year ago. We decided that if he was wandering around downtown, we would keep the room for him in case he was ever ready to use it. So, when he told us to give the room to you, we just did."

Liz was stunned. She thought that it had been Ted's apartment at one time, not that it was his apartment even now. "Ted Barlow?" Liz asked again. She wondered how, before he even knew her, the town drunk could have understood her situation when no one who had known her all her life had been able to empathize. Liz bit her lip. "I still owe him five dollars and forty cents for the payphone."

"He'll turn up. He always does," Mr. Thompson assured Liz as he returned to the back of the store.

"Can I ask you one more question?" Liz asked Dotty who nodded attentively. Liz hesitated, unsure of how to ask. "Um, I'm a teacher. I teach first grade."

It wasn't a question, but Dotty smiled. "That's wonderful, Liz. We'd hate to lose you, but when you're ready, there are some people we can introduce who might be able to find you work as a teacher."

Liz smiled, wondering how she could have gotten off on the wrong foot with Dotty. The woman was wise and caring, and Liz was ever grateful. "That would be nice," Liz said, trying not to choke up at the thought of restarting her life for real. The bell rang and they turned to see the first customers of the day.

"Here we go," Dotty said, and Liz spent the day inside the store helping more people in one day than she had in the whole time she had worked here. She looked out the front window and spotted Josh a few times. He was admiring the cars and Liz could tell that he was also checking up on her. Liz also kept her eyes peeled for Ted Barlow. She had seen him almost every day for two months, and he had disappeared. She was getting very concerned for his well-being.

In the afternoon, Liz spent her half-hour lunch enjoying the car show. It was called "Turning Back Time Weekend", and Liz finally understood why. The streetlights that lined downtown were decorated alternately with flags in patriotic colors. There were classic cars for blocks, and people mingling and filling the closed off streets. It was a crowd, but nothing like a New York City crowd. It was pleasant, and the sky was blue, and everyone was happy to share their story.

She could hear patriotic music on the loudspeakers, and Liz was surprised when a World War II bomber flew low over town followed by five small vintage aircraft. It was very exciting, and Liz found her hand on her chest and her mouth open looking toward the sky. The rest of the day went by quickly, but Liz didn't see Josh among the crowd again.

Liz spent the next few days strolling around different areas on her lunch break, picturing herself making a life here. Liz was searching for Ted, but she was also looking in different neighborhoods near downtown trying to imagine where she might live and work and who she might become.

Josh came by the store several times that week and bought items that weren't typically on his list. Liz wanted to spend more time with Josh, and she knew that he was coming to see her at work since she hadn't been going to the station on her lunch breaks. He never had much to say, especially under the watchful eyes of the Thompsons. Liz liked the time she spent watching him work on cars, but she was working on her own plans now. She daydreamed about a future with Josh as she put pieces in place to reassemble her broken life.

One evening, he was waiting outside the store when Liz got off work. He asked her if she wanted to grab dinner, but Liz was tired that day. She recommended that if he wanted to take her out, he needed to ask her properly. Two days later when Josh stopped by the store, he asked Liz out to dinner for the next evening. Liz was excited and she happily accepted with a smile.

"Don't be late," she said partially in jest.

"Don't be late," Mr. Thompson repeated like a stern father.

Josh tipped his hat at Mr. Thompson and smiled at Liz, and

the next evening, he didn't show up late. In fact, he didn't show up at all.

Liz was forced to eat some peanut butter and crackers before turning in early. She felt empathy for Josh and his brokenness, but she knew that when she saw him next, she would be upset. It was the payment that came with the embarrassment of being stood-up on a date.

Liz was woken up that night by a knock at the door after eleven, but she ignored it.

"Come on, Liz. I'm sorry that I'm late. Will you at least let me in to explain?" It was Josh, trying to talk loud enough for Liz to hear but not so loud as to wake her neighbors.

Liz pulled the blanket up to her nose to keep herself from answering.

"You know that I have a key, and I could come in anyway."

Liz held her tongue because she knew that Josh would never do that. At least she was pretty sure that he wouldn't. Her breathing felt loud as she tried to stay silent. She was curious and she was mad, and she wanted to torture Josh with her silence as he had tortured her by standing her up. When she heard his footsteps on the stairs, his leaving startled her into action. She jumped out of bed and pulled on some jeans. She forgot to put on shoes as she was preoccupied with giving him a piece of her mind.

"Josh," Liz called on the sidewalk as the front door banged against the doorjamb. Josh was opening the door to his truck when he turned back and smiled, but by the look on Liz's face, he could see that she wasn't amused. It had rained earlier, and the street was wet, but Liz barely noticed. She stepped into the damp street in her bare feet.

"I'm so sorry, Liz. I didn't mean to be late."

Liz thought that Josh was both sincere and simultaneously that the words meant nothing to him. The fury that had pulled her out of bed and down the stairs subsided, and Liz realized that she hadn't daydreamed about being in outer space for over a week. The recognition pulled her back from the tirade that she was about to unleash on Josh.

"Well, I'm sure you didn't mean to, but you were, Josh. It's rude, and it really makes a girl feel like next to nothing."

Josh looked at the ground and then down the street, but Liz wanted to make sure that they understood each other. She walked to Josh's truck and closed the door leaving him standing on the street next to her. She took his hand in hers and waited for him to look into her eyes.

"Listen, Josh. My son died, and there is no going back. But if it was me who died, I hope my family would carry-on and not hide from the world like you are."

His face crumpled, and she knew that she'd hit a nerve. Josh shook his head and took a step back, but Liz held on tight to his hand and waited for him to speak. He didn't say a word.

"My friend said this once, that childbirth is like experiencing a horribly painful death, only you somehow survive. She reasoned that this must be such a painful experience because a part of the mother's soul is being ripped off to help create life for the child."

Liz turned his hand over and put her other hand on top of his. She held on with both hands, but he didn't meet her eye. "Part of me died with my son, Josh, and I will always live with the loss of Sean in my heart. When I first came here, I had been hiding for months. I thought that it was ingenious the way you had set up your life, but now I see that it's not good. You haven't even really given yourself a chance."

Josh gently pulled away until Liz let go and, and he opened his truck door without looking at her.

"Whatever you try to tell yourself, this isn't living, Josh. Get a clock. Get a watch. Tell the time. Hell, it's passing anyway. You can't stop it." Liz was more pleading than angry, and Josh sat in the truck, but Liz slipped her body inside the door. "And I know you think that it doesn't matter, but it does. Anyway, it does if you want to date this girl."

Liz stepped back and let Josh close the truck door. He didn't start the truck, though. He rolled down his window and sighed, finally looking Liz in the eye.

"Do you want to go to the movies?" Josh asked with a half-smile.

"I would have loved to, Josh, but earlier tonight. I have an interview tomorrow that Dotty got me. I'm going to teach again."

Josh nodded. "That's great, Liz. So, you're staying in town?"

"It looks like it."

Josh looked down at his hands and cleared his throat. "Well, if you need a car, I know where you can buy one cheap."

CHAPTER 17

*S*ince the night of the tornado, Josh had stopped leaving lists of items on the counter for Liz to pack up. Instead, he went to Thompson's during the day and purchased things two at a time. He hadn't asked Liz on another date since after the car show when he had stood her up, but she was friendly, and Josh could tell that she did like him by the way she lingered in conversation.

Josh quickly found out that he was bad at small talk, and he was glad that the Thompsons gave them space when no one else was in the store. The request for another date was always lingering in his mind, but Josh didn't want to stand Liz up again, and he never got the guts to ask. He would watch the way she tucked her hair behind her ear, and the way her eyes lit up now when she smiled. He had been struck by her beauty when he had first laid eyes on her, but as she pulled her life together, she had bloomed into the most beautiful woman he'd ever known.

Liz had gone to the movies with him twice when she was new in town. Both times were nights that he had gone by Ted's bench hoping that he'd see Ted sleeping there. Josh had moved on toward the theatre in the dark of night, happily surprised to find

Liz following him into the theatre. Of course, that was before they'd gotten to know each other, and Josh didn't count either movie as a date.

He'd told his mom about Liz. Josh had taken to sitting on the front porch to look out over the fields of corn. He thought about life in a way he'd never considered before. Sometimes his mom left him alone, and sometimes she joined him. Josh told her everything that he knew about Liz. She would listen quietly and nod, and Josh could see her biting her tongue. He never asked his mom for advice, though. He knew that she would say what Ted or Billy would say, only she might put it in a nicer tone. And Josh didn't want to hear it.

His life was simple, and he'd always liked that about himself. He didn't bother anyone. He had taken care of his mother since he was old enough to realize that's what he was supposed to do. He was a business owner, and although he didn't keep regular hours, he took pride in his work. Josh had never considered leaving Sycamore. He knew the seasons here, and the festivals, and the people that he needed to know. He knew the rhythm of life even if he didn't know the time. At least, he thought he had, until Liz came to town.

Josh watched the brown tips of the corn stalks rustle in the breeze, and he saw in them the change of the summer season into fall. Time was passing, and he was wasting it without Liz. He'd let the rest of summer go by as a coward, unable to ask her on another date for fear of letting her down.

Josh thought through his own death. He was obsessed with it in some way, trying to ignore the fact that like everyone else, he had aged over the years. He wasn't vein in that regard but trying to ignore his fear had gotten him nowhere. He rationalized and negotiated and yet there was no way around it. No matter how many times he turned the clock back or ignored it all together, his time would come. And for all his dismissing time, he now acutely noticed it as a slow ticking torture in the back of his mind. It was reminding him that he could not have Liz. Josh needed to figure out a way back to not noticing time. He had no idea where to go from here, but he would focus on that one thought until the answer presented itself.

Josh thanked his mom for the tea and put his glass inside. She nodded and watched him leave. Josh was going to drive all of DeKalb County again if that's what it took to find Ted Barlow. The tornado hadn't hit the town, and it was like a miracle. It worried Josh that like a different kind of magic, it had whisked Ted away.

Josh would have asked Donna if she'd heard anything, but they hadn't talked in over a year. They had argued over the apartment and then they had argued over Ted's shed. Donna was convinced that if he had nowhere to go, Ted would eventually go home. But that was a woman's wish. Josh knew that Ted wasn't ever going home if he couldn't get right in his head.

Josh put the pedal down and the dust on the road spread out over the corn behind him. He was tired of Billy's sideways stare and the taunting words on the notepad. Josh needed Ted's advice about Liz for a change.

THE SUMMER WAS BECOMING fall and daylight withered shorter and shorter. Liz was working her new job as a substitute teacher for the local school district and filling in at Thompson's when she wasn't at school. One of Dotty's old friends got Liz into the elementary school on a trial basis, and Liz was planning to investigate getting her certification to teach in Illinois.

Liz had called her parents and told them that she was doing good and that she had started to teach again. Her mom was relieved, but Liz still didn't tell them where she had ended up. Liz wanted to complete the transition back into normal life before she saw them again because she was making strides, but she was afraid she might slide back into her depression. Her dad didn't say much. He just wanted to know that she was okay. Liz's mother had been adamant and then sorry for pushing and then cryptically interested in the town and the local people that Liz had met.

Liz had a cell phone again. It was a flip phone that she kept in the apartment like a land line. She'd had to get it for the school to contact her when she was applying for the job. She had only given the number to the school and to the Thompsons. She had called her parents from Ted's payphone though, and she was surprised it had taken her change. Ted Barlow had been missing for eight weeks. Everyone was worried because this was the longest amount of time that he'd disappeared for, but they were still hopeful that he'd come back around.

Donna Barlow drove by most days. Some days Liz was at the store, and she would hear the car idle past. Other evenings, Liz would be looking down on State Street from the apartment when the vintage green machine would rumble by. Liz often wondered if she should go out and talk to Donna, but she had no idea what to say. And Liz had plans to clear out of the apartment over the store in two weeks. She had found a small garden apartment on Locust Street just a few blocks from downtown.

Liz prayed that Ted was okay. She was so glad that she was finally trying to move on with her own life, and that alone gave her hope for Ted to do the same. If she saw him again, Liz would do what she could to help. She was starting to understand what the people of this town had done for Ted and why they had tried so hard for him.

Liz was lucky, and she knew it. Before Sean had died, when Liz was going through her divorce, she remembered her mom telling her that she was fortunate.

"Your car has only broken down in the driveway. You have only gotten flat tires in a parking lot or in the garage."

"How can you say that I'm lucky, Mom? I'm getting a divorce."

"I'm sorry about the divorce. But Liz, you are lucky. Every time it feels like life is getting out of control and you have to walk through quicksand, someone puts a rock in front of you, under your feet, and you find stability again. You are going to be okay."

Liz had felt such anger toward her mom when she'd said that. Her life felt like it was over when she had gotten the divorce and had to move in with her parents to find her footing. But she had found it, and she reminded herself again that Sean had been happy there. And she had lost her baby boy, and still some left-over grace was laying rocks in front of each step for stability.

Liz cried in the dark of her apartment in Sycamore, Illinois. She could see each rock that had been put underfoot in the last four months. She had driven blindly, halfway across the United States and ran out of gas here, in this place where there were people ready to help. She had life within her again. She felt the grace that had been given to carry on. Liz didn't know what was to come for her or for Josh or anyone, but she knew she was going to keep moving forward.

THE PAYPHONE HAD BEEN RINGING for weeks. Josh saw Liz use the payphone when she stopped by three days ago. She said that she was calling home and she wasn't sure how it would go, but when she had hung up, she just waved across the lot and walked away. She hadn't sat down on the bench and cried, so Josh was assuming the call went okay.

"I'll get it," he said to no one as he crossed the parking lot. He noticed Ted's empty bench and shook his head in worry. He'd checked in with the Thompsons and the Veterans Club and everywhere else he could think of, but no one had seen Ted for two months.

"Hello?"

"Hello! Ted, what are you doing there?"

"No, this is Josh."

"Josh. Oh."

"Is this Donna?" Josh asked, but he knew it wasn't. He could tell the lady was older and was east coast by the accent. "You know Ted? When is the last time you talked to him?"

There was silence as the caller remembered. "I haven't talked to him in weeks."

Josh's eyebrows perked up as he wondered about this new layer to Ted Barlow's life. "I'm not sure where he is. No one has seen him around town for a couple of months."

There was silence.

"Hello?"

"I've been calling for weeks," she complained. Her polite tone turned perturbed. "Why is it that you never answer the phone? Why even have the phone if you aren't going to answer it?"

Josh considered the question. "I don't know. I guess it was here when my dad died, so I just kept it on the lot. Besides, it's a payphone at the edge of my gas station, so I don't always hear it or walk over here to answer it. I guess that was Ted's job."

The caller cleared her throat. "What town is this I'm calling? Where are you?"

"Sycamore, Illinois," Josh answered, even more puzzled. Ted had some strange friends.

"Sycamore," he heard a long sigh. "Sycamore."

"We're one to three hours west of Chicago, depending on the time of day," Josh told her.

"Thank you," she said, and then he heard the click of the line going dead.

One to three hours west of Chicago - why had he said that? It was the first reference to time he'd made in twenty years.

~

THE NIGHTS WERE TURNING cooler with the approach of fall, but it was a hot and sunny Saturday as Liz grabbed a sandwich and walked down to the gas station at lunch to visit with Josh. Since she had started work at the school, she didn't see him during the week anymore, and the absence had made her grow fonder. Josh was pleasant to be around. He didn't ask questions, and she had found returning to work at a school brought back tough personal questions that Liz had learned to sidestep for now.

Josh was working on a black compact car today, and the heat of the sun in his long sleeve flannel shirt was making him sweat. As Liz's shoes crunched on the gravel around the back of the station, she could see that Billy was already outside with his notebook held out toward Josh.

"Hi, Billy," Liz said before she greeted Josh. Billy frantically wrote in his notebook and then smiled hesitantly at Liz before going back inside.

"Wow, he smiled," Liz said.

"I told you he was a fan of yours," Josh intoned as he put the wrench down and wiped his hands clean. Liz pulled the wrapper from her sandwich and held it out toward Josh.

He shook his head. "You go ahead. I just ate breakfast."

It was convenience store tuna fish on wheat. Although Liz knew she could save money if she stopped grabbing sandwiches from the local 7-Eleven for lunch, there was a comfort in this habit, and she wasn't about to change anything about her small-town life.

Josh watched her chew and so Liz looked away. She liked the way Josh watched her because she could tell that he cared for her, and Liz understood that she was ready for that again in her life. She took another bite as the back door of the station slammed all the way open, and Billy ran to Josh. He pointed and scribbled and stabbed the paper with his fingertip, his eyes wide.

Liz was chewing and she couldn't ask what was wrong, so she stepped closer to Josh and looked over his shoulder at the paper.

It was filled with small, perfect letters, and Liz recognized the handwriting from the lists that Josh left with Mr. Thompson. She had thought that was Josh's perfect writing, but now it made sense to her that Billy would have perfected the alphabet while writing in his notepad each day.

She admired the neat rows of letters at the top and then looked at the bottom of the small page. The writing was still neat, but Liz could tell that it was not Billy's usual scrawl. He'd written it frantically as he had run outside.

Billy poked with the tip of his pencil at the words. *Old Liz is here*.

Josh and Liz looked at each other and wondered what the cryptic words meant, and then Liz understood.

"Hello, Elizabeth." It was her mom, standing here behind Josh's gas station in Sycamore, Illinois.

CHAPTER 18

*L*iz forgot how much she looked like her mother, but Billy reminded her by pointing at her mom and then back at the paper.

"Hi, Mom," Liz said, her eyes filling with tears. She put the sandwich on top of the black car and surprised herself by stepping quickly into her mom's arms. "Mom, I'm so sorry," Liz said. Her mom squeezed her tightly and then stepped back, and her gentle smile let Liz know that everything would be okay.

Josh and Billy watched as Liz wiped her eyes dry.

"What are you doing here?"

"Well, I'm here to see you, of course."

"I mean, how?" Liz trailed off.

"Hello," her mom said to Josh and Billy.

Liz had been shocked to see her mom, and she tried to recover. "Mom, this is my friend Josh. Josh, this is my mom."

Josh smiled and leaned in to shake hands, but then reconsidered, holding his dirty palms up. "Nice to meet you, Mrs. Campbell."

"Hello, Josh."

"And this is Billy," Liz continued, but Billy didn't respond. He scribbled furiously on his notepad and ran back into the gas station.

"Well, okay," Liz's mom said.

Liz stared at her mom. She was dressed in black pants and a long-sleeved blouse with a fall block pattern on it. Her makeup was perfectly applied, and her dangling earrings glimmered in the sun. Liz had forgotten how pretty her mom was, and she looked younger than Liz could remember.

"You look good, Mom."

"Well thank you, honey. I'm just so glad to see you." She took Liz's hands and spread them apart to get a better look at her daughter. Liz was wearing a t-shirt and jeans that had a hole in one knee. Liz was certain that she wasn't up to par with New York City standards, but she was comfortable, and she could tell that her mom was trying to make a compliment.

"I see you still have the car," her mom said, looking at the shiny Saturn that sat in the back of the lot.

"I'm sorry, Mom," was all Liz could bring herself to say in explanation.

Her mom smiled and squeezed Liz's hands. "It's okay, honey. Your father couldn't be happier that you drove off in that old thing. When you didn't come back, you forced his hand. He finally went out and bought that Buick Regal he's been ogling for the last ten years. It's used, but it's very nice."

Liz grinned and nodded. She had forced her dad's hand in a good way, then.

Billy slammed the door open again and looked around before skirting close to the building toward Josh. He thrust his notepad under Josh's nose. It was so close to his face that Josh had to push it away to read it.

"Ted?" Josh asked Billy. The short boy nodded furiously and then went back into the store.

"Oh, yes. I brought Mr. Ted Barlow with me," Liz's mom said decisively.

Liz's mouth fell open as her eyebrows rose in question.

"You know Ted?" Josh asked.

"Oh no, not really," she said as though it had been a silly question. "I just met Ted today. He was up at Rosecrance Rehabilitation Center in Rockford. I flew in yesterday to pick Ted up this morning. I didn't think I would find you by just standing in downtown Sycamore, Elizabeth. I knew it was the only way I could find you for sure."

Liz laughed and a few more tears found their way to freedom. Her mom had no idea how wrong she was. This was not New York City, and if she would have stood in downtown Sycamore, Liz would have surely seen her mom within a couple of hours.

Liz's mom said all of this as though it was perfectly natural, but Liz and Josh were baffled. They had been looking for Ted for two months, and somehow Liz's mom knew where he was the entire time. Liz's mom smiled. "Ted wanted to come here to this place," she said with her hands open and looking around the gas station with a shrug, "and while I was dropping him off, I saw your father's car parked back here."

Liz waited for more of an explanation of how her mom knew Ted, but Josh walked away without another word and disappeared around the side of the building to see for himself. Liz and her mom followed. They walked across the lot to the payphone and in front of the bench where Ted could see them. After missing for two months, here was Ted Barlow. He was decked out in a shirt and tie and sitting on his bench with a small bag and a bunch of flowers.

"Ted!" Liz said, struck by the change. Ted stood up, his slacks and button-down shirt a crisp change from his usual Dickies and t-shirt under the long trench coat. His eyes struck Liz the most. They were clear and free of the heavy bags underneath.

"Hi, Liz." Ted held the flowers to his chest and smiled. "What do you think?"

She stuttered, "I...I think you look great."

Ted nodded at Josh who nodded back. Liz's mom walked up to Ted and adjusted his tie, which looked funny because she was five-foot-two and Ted was six-six. When she was done fidgeting, she pulled his tall frame down by the shoulders to give him a peck on the cheek.

"You have my phone number, and I will expect an occasional phone call. I don't want you hanging around this payphone waiting to hear from me."

"Yes, ma'am," Ted said, trying to smile.

Or trying not to cry, Liz thought.

"That was you on the phone?" Josh asked.

"Depends on who's asking," Liz's mom replied, and Liz started to understand how her mom had ended up here.

"Ted," Josh said nodding his head to the left, and they all immediately looked up the street. Ted's green 1968 Chevy Camaro SS rounded the corner two blocks up, and everyone tensed. Liz's mom patted him on the shoulder and walked back toward the pumps in the gas station, and Liz and Josh followed.

Ted picked up his bag from the bench and pulled the flowers in tighter. He stood stock still as the car idled down the street. He looked like a man waiting for a firing squad, and Liz wanted to go stand with him, but she knew that he had to do this part alone.

"You've got this, Ted," Josh said just loud enough for his friend to hear. Ted looked back at them and tried to grin, but he was terrified that his wife, whom he hadn't spoken to in almost two years, would drive right by him.

The low rumble of the engine slowed as Donna came even with the gas station. Liz tried to see into the car, but the angle was wrong, and she couldn't see Donna's expression. She knew instinctively that Ted's wife would stop and take him home. She knew from the day that his wife had come to visit. Donna was in love with this man. For the first time in her life, Liz truly understood the marriage vow 'in sickness and in health'.

They held their breath for Ted as the car stopped in front of the bench. The windows were open, but no one spoke. Ted's wife looked at him for a long minute.

"Tell her," Liz's mom chirped. Liz put her hand on her mom's wrist to silence her, but it was the encouragement that Ted needed to speak.

"I'm sorry," he said shakily to his wife who sat in the car and looked at him. "I'm so, so sorry."

With that, her door opened, and Donna got out of the car. Liz could see the tears that had run rivers of mascara down her face. Ted took a hesitant step forward, and his wife ran around the front of the car and leapt into Ted's open arms. They stayed there crying together, Ted swaying his wife off the ground in his tight embrace. Eventually, he put her down. She was tiny next to Ted, and he hunched over and looked into her eyes. She put her hands on his cheeks as though she was memorizing his face.

"I didn't know where you were. I was so scared that I'd lost you for good," she said.

"I'm sober fifty-seven days," he answered, and she laughed.

"Come home," she said.

And Ted answered, "Please."

He handed her the flowers and they hugged again. Donna took a long look at Ted, reaching up and touching the dimple in his chin. Ted opened the passenger door and tossed his bag onto the back seat, and when he closed the door, he looked back at his friends and smiled a half-smile of tentative salvation before they drove away.

ALL JOSH COULD THINK about for the next two days was that he wanted the intimacy that Ted and Donna had. He wanted to be with someone he could just look at and know what they were thinking, and he wanted someone to know him in the same way. Josh wanted that with Liz, but he assumed that her mom had come to town to collect Liz and take her home. He wasn't sure that he'd get the chance.

Josh sat on the front porch and thought about his parents, seeing them in a new light. They were two people in love who had built a life together, and although that life had been cut short, it was no less special. Josh didn't know if he could bring himself to change his life. He was forty-three years old, and he didn't know if he could make new habits, but he was determined to try. Liz was right when she'd told him that this wasn't any way to live, and more than anything, Josh needed to push past fearing death if he was going to truly live life.

He went inside and found his mom in the kitchen. Her smile turned serious when she noticed the determination on her son's face.

"Hey, Ma. Do you have Dad's pocket watch?" He knew she did. She'd tried to give it to Josh when he was sixteen, and she had offered it to him once a year since. It was her way of nudging him into his future.

She nodded and quickly put her coffee cup on the counter, and Josh could see by her tight smile that she was holding back a comment, or maybe it was tears.

THEY DROVE the rental car the few blocks to the town center, and Liz introduced her mother to Mr. Thompson and Dotty. They promptly gave her the rest of the weekend off so that Liz could spend it with her mom. Liz watched her mom's interactions closely, knowing she would catch glimpses of disapproval in her daughter's choices, but aside from her mom's typical big-city air about her, she was pleasant and accepting of everything she saw.

Liz had so many questions for her mom, but she wanted to wait until they were alone. They ran into Kristi and Matt in the hall upstairs, and Liz made introductions.

"I'm moving," Liz told them. "I found a garden apartment over on Locust Street." Kristi and Matt were happy for Liz. They had rarely seen each other over the months, and Kristi lamented that she would miss sharing the bathroom with such a tidy woman. Liz had reacted to that by looking at her mom whose face was uncharacteristically blank at the comment of a shared bathroom.

Liz opened the door and led her mom in, straightening up the few clothes she had left on the chair and tossing the blanket across the bed. She held her hands out and smiled, and her mom looked around and then went to look out the window over State Street.

"Here, take a seat, Mom," Liz said, offering her mom the chair. Liz's mom sat, and then Liz sat on the bed and waited for the tirade, but none came. They looked at each other several times before Liz realized that her mother was purposefully holding her tongue, and Liz knew she had her father to thank for that.

"You put Ted in rehab?"

"Well, he mentioned that facility in Rockford a couple of times, and I was so glad to know your general location." Her mom's lips pursed, and Liz could see that she was making a great effort to say the right things. "And well, Ted is your friend. I could tell when he said that you kept bringing him sandwiches that you cared for him. And I couldn't help my daughter, but Ted is someone's son, so I did what I could to help him."

Liz walked over and bent down to hug her mom who was startled at the gesture because they had never been the hugging type. "That's truly amazing, Mom. Thank you so much." Liz squeezed her mom who squeezed her back, and Liz returned to sit on the bed.

"Oh, it was nothing. I made a bunch of phone calls on Ted's behalf and ended up getting him into a veteran's extended rehab program. I gave them his phone number, and the facility picked him up and took him there. I told them I would pick him up when he was done to bring him home."

Her mom blushed at the ulterior motive of finding Liz's whereabouts. Liz didn't care though. Her mom had done for Ted what no one who knew him personally could do.

"You'd be proud of Ted. I asked him time and time again to tell me where you were, but he wouldn't say a word about it. He kept saying that you were safe and okay and that you just needed time."

"So, you talked to Ted a lot?"

Her mom nodded. "I did. He's been through a lot, you know. The war and the loss took their toll." Her mom looked at the floor, and Liz knew that they were both thinking of Sean now. "Maybe I understand a little better why you ran away."

"I didn't run away," Liz snapped and then sighed. "Okay, maybe I did run away, but you don't understand."

"Help me understand, Elizabeth." Her mom leaned forward and waited as Liz rubbed her eyes. When she looked up, her mom was still waiting, and Liz knew that she had to try to explain.

"When Darren left, I thought that was the worst time in my life. I lost my family, Mom. You and Dad have been married a long time and I'm sure you've had your ups and downs, but you've never lost your family in the bargain." Liz rubbed her knees and crossed the room to look out the window. "And you loved Sean, but you didn't know him like I did and Darren did. No one knew that secret smile he'd share while bumping heads with us, or the way he'd..." Liz choked and had to concentrate to keep herself from breaking down. She had to stay strong if she was going to be able to continue to take her next step forward in life.

"And I didn't want to talk to anyone about him. I didn't want to spoil those private moments we had because they were all that I had left. I think the only person I could have talked to really was Darren, but he's moved on, and so I shut down."

Liz looked at her mom who was wringing her hands and trying not to cry, so Liz looked back out the window.

"I know he was your grandson and you loved him, but he was my son. No one knew him like I knew him, and no one is going to love him like I love him."

"I see," her mom said as she wiped her cheeks. "I suppose I understand. You're my baby, Elizabeth, and although I thought I lost you, at least I knew that you were living somewhere in the world still."

Neither spoke for a long time and then her mom stood and asked to use the restroom. Liz showed her the door in the hallway and then returned to the apartment. She wiped her eyes with a tissue and looked out the window, wondering about the lives of the people who drove by. That was Liz's favorite way to spend time. She watched the town from this window and invented stories about their lives, but it was time to put those stories to bed and live her own life again.

"Well, show me this apartment that you're moving into, and then I'll take you out for a proper lunch. I can't imagine that your tuna salad sandwich is any good now that you left it on that man's car." Liz smiled. She had forgotten about the sandwich, but her mother never missed a thing.

IT WAS slow for a Saturday at Thompson's, and Liz stocked some of the shelves and cleaned the counter. She stared at the covers of the magazines for a while remembering that there was a whole wide world that had gone on without her. She ogled some of the movie stars and swept the floor. She cleaned the window on the front door and then sat on the stool behind the counter. She was surprised to see Ted sitting on the bench across the street. She hadn't seen him since her mom had come to town three weeks ago. Liz leaned forward and stared at Ted. She didn't know if he could really see her through the front window, but he was looking right at her.

She asked Mr. Thompson if she could take an early break, and then she walked slowly across the street toward Ted. He was in Dickies and a flannel shirt, but his trench coat was nowhere in sight. Liz worried that he'd been drinking again until she came close enough to see his eyes. They were different than she remembered. The glaze of the past was gone, and Ted was looking out at the present.

"Hey, Ted." She took a long look at him and noticed that he looked about five years younger.

"Hi, Liz."

She sat down next to him, and they both watched the minimal traffic for a minute. "Everything okay?"

"Yes. Everything is great." Ted smiled. "Donna's at the bakery, and I was hoping you'd see me out here."

There were so many things that Liz wanted to ask, but she only managed, "What's up?"

"Well," Ted let his cheeks puff up with a slow exhale, and he scratched his chin. Liz could see that whatever he had to say wasn't easy. "You still owe me five dollars and forty cents."

Liz smiled and reached for her pocket, but Ted placed his hand on her arm.

"No, that's not it. I was joking. Really, Liz, I want to thank you."

"Me?" she asked surprised.

"Yes, you." Ted leaned forward and placed his elbows on his knees, looking at the street. "I knew something was wrong when you came to town. The way you showed up and left your car in the gas station. Just something about you... I could see that you were broken, too. It kind of woke me up."

Liz bit her lip. It was just over five months ago, but looking back, it felt like years had gone by.

"Thank you for taking the job and the apartment. It made me

feel good about myself that I could do something for someone. Seeing you take the help, and seeing that it did help, somehow let me know that it was okay to try." Ted rubbed his knees and sat back. "And your mother is pretty pushy, too."

They both chuckled.

"Talking to your mom every day helped."

"I'll let her know."

"I still talk to her sometimes," Ted said sheepishly.

"She called every day?" Liz asked. Her mother had told her the general overview of how she had ended up in town, but it seemed that Liz didn't know the half of it.

"She was calling for you, Elizabeth," he mocked, "but she got me by default."

Liz knew by the way her mom had spoken about Ted, that in the long run, she must have been calling for him.

"I never told her where you were, Liz. I just told her that you were doing okay."

"It's okay, Ted. You're off the hook. Josh said the phone rang for days and he finally answered it. He didn't know who was calling."

"Well, your mom is nothing if not persistent."

"That's one word for it." Liz shook her head, but she was so glad for her mom. She would always be her mom's little girl. Liz could finally appreciate what her mom was trying to do for her all those months when she'd finally pushed too hard and had driven Liz away.

"Thanks for the sandwiches," Ted said in a way that let Liz know he was thankful for much more than that.

"Thank you for the company, Ted. I was a bit lost."

"I'm sorry about your son," Ted's voice cracked. "I can't imagine."

Liz closed her eyes and nodded slowly, but she didn't allow herself to go there. There was plenty of time to mourn: in the dark of night, or in the small breaths she took when she saw a mother pushing a stroller, or how she stared at kids' faces when she walked down the hallway in school or by a park, her mind trying to resolve Sean in any of their places. "Thanks."

Ted took a deep breath and then stood as Donna came out of Ellison's Bakery. Liz stood, and the two women nodded at each other.

"Donna, I want you to meet Liz. And Liz, this is my wife, Donna."

"Nice to meet you," they both said, but they didn't shake hands, and neither would ever tell Ted that they had met before.

"See you around," Ted said, and he opened the driver's side door for his wife. She slipped her feet into the car before he closed the door. Ted went around to the passenger side and got in, but Liz wasn't watching him. Liz met Donna's eyes, and they shared a knowing look before Donna pulled away. Liz thought that she and Donna were like two clouds in the sky, floating through each other and sharing perspective before silently parting in the breeze.

Liz sat on the bench and looked up to her window and saw that she'd left her light on. But it wasn't her light in her apartment anymore. It was someone else's space now, and Liz had her apartment a few blocks away. The Liz that lived here had grown up and moved on.

Liz existed and she would keep existing. She had a place in the world beyond the person she had been with her son. She was still Elizabeth - not better, just a different version of herself.

EPILOGUE

*L*iz didn't want to wake baby Ashley, but it was time to go down to the courthouse for the judging of the pumpkins. She carefully pulled on the tiny winter coat and buckled her little six-month-old pumpkin into the carrier. Then she rounded up Matthew and John to put on shoes and coats. Josh and Cody were finishing up at the gas station, and they would meet Liz on the lawn of the courthouse.

Cody was only seven years old, but he followed Josh around like a proud little man. Josh had spoiled his first son, and he had also brought him to the station to "work" since he was old enough to talk. They were two peas in a pod. Reserved but confident, stable, and steady.

His father's pocket watch hadn't completely fixed Josh's timing and dating Josh had been anything but steady. But Cody was born ten months after they were married, and he had reset time in Josh's life.

"Mom, we're going!" Liz called upstairs.

"I'm ready," her mom called back. Liz's parents came to town for a long visit each summer, and Liz's mom came to town for Easter in the spring and for the Pumpkin Festival in the fall. Liz and Josh traded off Thanksgiving and Christmas each year between their parents.

Josh's mom didn't get out much. She still lived in the same farmhouse that Josh grew up in, and Josh drove out there most days for lunch. She was a very proud grandma, and Liz enjoyed their time together. She didn't have a judgmental bone in her body and seemed to take in each moment as it arrived.

Liz clipped the baby carrier on the top of the double stroller and lifted John in the front seat.

"My turn," Matthew protested, but Liz's mom swooped in with a cookie and took Matthew's hand.

"We're going to start down," she said over her shoulder, and Matthew was more than happy to take the cookie in one hand and his grandma's hand in the other.

"I'm right behind you."

Liz locked the back door to their Italianate style home that stood two blocks from downtown Sycamore. Its wood siding was painted red with white trim, and when Liz took a moment to notice, she couldn't believe that it was her house. It had been built in the late 1800's, and it had a historical placard mounted on a brick stand near the street. Liz would never have been able to afford a home like this on her teacher's salary, but it turned out that in the thirty-two years since his dad had died, Josh had never so much as taken a vacation. They were able to buy the house outright, and Josh was still able to help his mom with the rent on the old farmhouse.

Liz caught up with her mom and Matthew, and they rounded the corner to State and Main. There were hundreds of people already gathered on the sidewalk looking over the pumpkin displays. Liz saw pumpkins of every size and shape that were painted and decorated as everything under the sun. A slatted fence had been installed all around the courthouse grass to keep the people away from the displays.

"Mom! Mine is right there!" Liz heard Cody call to her,

pointing at the pumpkin rocket ship that Cody had made. She pushed the stroller toward Josh and Cody as Matthew ran ahead of his grandma. Josh lifted Matthew over his head and the boy laughed until Josh put him down.

"Hey babe," Liz said as Josh gave her a peck on the cheek. Josh looked in on his sleeping baby-girl, Ashley, and then pulled John out of the stroller.

"Lenore," he said to Liz's mom.

"How was work?" Lenore asked.

"Grandma, I got to help dad with a transmission slip differential!" Cody said proudly. Liz was always amazed at Cody's aptitude, but Billy Noodles had taught Cody to read at four years old, and Cody had been reading two classes up since the first day of school.

"Oh!" Lenore answered back, handing Cody a cookie that she had brought for him.

Josh held Liz's hand for a moment, but then he had to go and lift Matthew off the fence. Life was busy and downright hectic at times with four kids, but as Liz looked around at the small downtown and people around her, she couldn't imagine her life any other way.

"It's Ted and Donna!" her mom chirped.

Liz turned and saw Ted and Donna walking over, his very tall frame towering over his wife's petiteness. They had three-year-old twin girls, and when they stopped the stroller next to Liz's, her mom hugged Ted and Donna and gave the twins another cookie that she had wrapped in her pocket. Liz's lips curled into a half smile as she remembered the way her mom would lean down close to Sean when she gave him a cookie in the kitchen back in New York. It was a lifetime ago, but the memory warmed Liz's heart.

They had all come so far. Liz had a second chance at life, and although Josh didn't completely bow down to the clock, he was at the dinner table on time every night. Ted had a good job in

DeKalb, and Donna stayed at home with the twins. They lived in a small house on Peace Road near where the tornado had risen up and skipped over the town. People still talked about that night and what a miracle it was.

"Hello Barlow's," Liz said, sharing a smile with Ted and Donna.

Liz and Donna enjoyed each other's company, especially sharing motherly advice about their growing families. Having recognized each other's past tribulations, and having endured their hardships, they enjoyed a quiet understanding of contentedness in daily life. They were best friends, but they never talked about the summer when Liz first arrived.

Liz said goodbye to follow her boys as they ran off, weaving through the pumpkin displays. Josh had Matthew on his shoulders, and he followed Cody and John as they ran ahead.

Her mom caught up and threaded her arm through Liz's. "I'm going to babysit for Donna on Monday morning so she can meet Ted for lunch. I hope that's okay."

"Of course, Mom. The boys will be exhausted from the Pumpkin Fest Parade anyway, so Monday everyone will be tired and cranky." Liz smiled, and they followed Josh onto State Street.

"Oh, the Confectionary will be open!" her mom said excitedly. She picked up her pace to catch up to the boys who already had their hands and faces pressed up to the front window of the candy store.

"Not too much!" Liz called ahead. "You've already given them two cookies each, Mom."

When Lenore passed him, Josh put Matthew down and dropped back to walk with Liz. "I promised the boys hot chocolate," he told her, taking the stroller.

"They're going to get stomach aches," Liz complained.

"I won't bring it up again unless they do," Josh agreed. "We can stop in at Thompson's to buy some time."

"We can stop in, but you know Dotty will just let them choose a candy to take home."

Josh laughed.

Liz looked two blocks down and saw the sign for the State Theatre lit up. Josh followed her eyes, and Liz took his arm. They were both remembering that first day they had met and the night that Liz had followed Josh to the movie theatre. The lost people that they had been almost ten years ago seemed like strangers to them now, and yet the distant memory felt like it could have been only yesterday.

Liz was glad that she had kept her father's Saturn. It had turned out to be a good family car, and Josh had managed to keep it running. Liz liked to imagine Sean as a teenager riding up in front with her or maybe even asking her if he could drive this time. Liz knew that Sean would have loved his brothers and sister.

Liz looked at Josh and smiled. Though he'd kept them, he didn't need to use the keys to the town anymore. She and Josh had built a wonderful life together, and he had the only key that mattered. He held the key to Liz's heart. She was two months pregnant, and their family was about to outgrow that car. She would tell Josh tonight.

ABOUT THE AUTHOR

Anita Renaghan is the author of six books including literary fiction and a young adult trilogy. She loves a good character study and has been many characters herself including: an aircraft mechanic in the Air Force, a college graduate, a second degree blackbelt, lost, a waitress and bartender, a wife and mother, an account executive, found, and a constantly inventive singer-songwriter. Walter Mitty has nothing on Anita.

Growing up in the Chicago suburbs with her five siblings was a loud and adventurous time, and Anita was often found at the library reading her new favorite author or writing a poem or short story. Her high school English teacher presented the challenge of writing a novel, and that opened a door that would never close. Anita has written many novels in the past thirty years and she loves a good character study.

Anita can often be found zoning-out in a daydream in the Chicago suburbs where she lives with her husband and daughter. In the dark hours of the night, while her family sleeps, she is often perched in front of her laptop writing her next adventure.

Please go to www.anitarenaghan.com where you can find more titles and join the email list to receive a free ebook.

www.ingramcontent.com/pod-product-compliance
Lightning Source LLC
Chambersburg PA
CBHW030819210726
48290CB00002B/671